A Homicide in Hooker's Point

GLORIA TAYLOR WEINBERG

FOREWORD

"Hooker's Point" is a fascinating tale of innocence and pathos colliding in a small community in rural South Florida. The story develops inexorably, building momentum as it evolves, all the while tempting the reader to linger over passages of lush, evocative imagery. I was struck by the author's insightful portrayal of people and places, which brought back fond memories of the simple, authentic life experiences that I had growing up in Clewiston near Hooker's Point.

Eight-year-old Vicki Bayle is a superb unifying character who learns a great deal about life in a very short period of time through interactions with her family and others in this tight-knit community. The beautiful writing style flows seamlessly as it follows Vicki from moments of tenderness and poignancy to the final confrontation of Eric and Frank. The conclusion is first-rate, leaving unanswered questions about the involvement of Vicki and her father in the events of that extraordinary day.—Erik C. Larsen, Attorney, Winter Park, Florida

******

"Hooker's Point is riveting. Weinberg captures a time and a unique place-the culture and life around Lake Okeechobee in the early 50s. It was the deep South, still raw, with the wild not far gone. Through the eyes of a little girl with a big heart and a sensitive nature, we see a chilling facet of the human condition."—Camille S. Yates, author of "Treasured Waters—the Indian River Lagoon," Fort Pierce, Florida

Introduction

Clewiston, Florida, my hometown, hugs the southern rim of Lake Okeechobee, in an area dependent upon agriculture—mostly sugar cane. It is billed as America's Sweetest Town for its sugar production, and each year, it attracts thousands of recreational boaters and fishermen to the second-largest freshwater lake in the United States.

Many of the descriptions of places and events in this novel are based on my childhood memories and those of family members. Some depictions of events, such as the 1928 hurricane that devastated the area, were researched from old newspapers and other written accounts of such events.

This is a work of fiction. The names of characters and the story are products of my imagination or are used fictitiously.

Any similarity between the characters and events depicted in this novel and actual events or people, living or dead, is unintentional.

—Gloria Taylor Weinberg

This book is dedicated to my mother, Ruby Rich Taylor.

CHAPTER ONE

The Kittens

Saturday, September 9, 1950, 1 p.m.

The kitten lay curled on his side in a cardboard box lined with rags, one eye swollen shut, the other dull and sightless. Crimson bubbles formed on his nose with each shallow breath.

"Is he dyin', Mama?" Vicki asked her mother.

Rena May Bayle knelt beside her eight-year-old daughter and kissed her head.

"I think so, baby, but I don't think he's hurtin', you know? I think he just wants you to pet him a little before he goes."

Vicki gently wiped away the bloody mucus with a tissue she tucked in a corner of the box. She had run, sobbing, to Hooker's General Store to get the box.

Reed Hooker stopped loading empty bottles into wooden crates at the back of his store when he heard Vicki coming. He watched her run up a narrow path through the empty lot between his small store and the row of rental houses he owned, just south of Clewiston, Florida.

He opened the dirt-smudged screen door and held it for Vicki, who scaled the back steps two at a time.

Of all the children who came into his store for bubble gum or soda pop, Vicki was his favorite. She had hair like pulled taffy, amber and honey, the top layers bleached pale by the Florida sun. Freckles spattered

1

her nose and spread out beneath large, cola-colored eyes. The dark eyes were unexpected beneath the blonde hair.

Eyes like a spotted fawn, he thought, as he knelt in front of the child to blot one eye and then the other with a clean corner of his butcher's apron. Vicki's eyes quickly overflowed again, and he cupped her chin in his beefy hand and lifted her face to his.

"What's the matter, sugar?" he asked, softly.

"He threw Boots…through the…screen door," she said, sobbing between words. "Mama thinks…his back is broke." Vicki wrapped her arms around the storekeeper's neck, and he stood, lifting the child with him. He carried her past the stockroom and into the store, where he sat down in a wooden rocker next to the cash register.

"Well, if that don't beat all," he said, patting her back and wiping a damp strand of hair from the corner of her mouth. Reed had always wanted children, but his wife was barren. He savored the little-girl scent of the one he held—like fresh bread, warm and pungent. Vicki immediately wriggled down, pleading, "I gotta go back to Boots, Mr. Hooker. You got a box I can have?"

"I sure do, sugar," Reed said, reaching behind the counter for the empty box that once held his new alligator boots. "But who hurt your kitty?"

"Eric Magruder." She spat out his name like something rotten, then wiped her eyes, first with the back of her hands, then with her palms. When she looked up, the tears had ceased, and the doe eyes turned hard. "I hate him," she said. "I hope he dies. I hope my daddy kills him."

The big floor fan in the corner wrenched its face, owl-like, spinning a serpentine strip of used-up flypaper and freeing its prey. Dazed and tacky flies peppered the Coleman lanterns, galvanized washtubs and other items on high shelves, where they were easy prey for the platoon of diligent spiders deployed in the rafters. The spiders regularly rappelled to imprison the flies in silk and lift them away.

Reed Hooker rubbed the back of his neck as Vicki ran out the back door with the shoebox. The cowbell that announced the comings and goings of patrons tolled needlessly from its spring above the doorframe. Where the path took a turn through a head-high patch of dog fennel,

Reed lost sight of the bouncing yellow curls. A few seconds later, Vicki emerged beneath the poinciana tree at the far edge of the lot.

The sun hung high and hot above the widespread tree that neighborhood children called "the play tree." Its low, thick branches served as jungle gym and monkey bars; its two-foot-long seedpods, when they dried black and hard, became bats or swords or paddles, depending on the game the children played.

There was no coolness now in the lacy petticoat of shade spread beneath the poinciana.

Vicki stopped short in front of the bag swing that dangled from a higher branch. Reed could not see the tears that welled anew in the child's eyes as she grabbed the rope and leaned her head against the rough burlap bag, pinched like an hourglass by the legs of children who took turns swinging and pushing. It smelled of pine straw and sawdust, sweat, and faintly of urine.

Suddenly, Vicki drew back the rope and flung the bag as hard and as high as she could. She had crossed the two back yards between the play tree and home long before the bag ceased its solitary swing.

"Vicki's right," Reed said to his wife as he stood looking out the screen door. "Somebody needs to put that sorry so-and-so out of his misery."

The storekeeper's wife sat in the middle aisle on a low stool too small in circumference to accommodate her ample backside. She shifted positions frequently, taking care to tuck the hem of her housedress modestly behind her knees, where too-tight garters held her opaque nylons in place.

"Eric ain't nearly as miserable as them that has to put up with him," Ethel Hooker said. "He tries to drown his misery in whiskey, but I expect it's still there when he sobers up."

She spoke without looking up from the task at hand: marking the price on cans of evaporated milk. She made large, childlike numbers with a red china marker—carefully, solemnly. It was not a task she enjoyed; 10 cents a can was a lot for poor people to pay to feed their babies, but it was a fair price.

Ethel was a plain, uneducated woman, but she was a good cook and a steady worker who knew her Bible.

And she gave her husband a great deal of pleasure in bed.

Saturday, 2 p.m.

Rena did all she could for the injured cat. There was no veterinarian in Clewiston, but even if there had been, there was no money to pay for the services of a vet. Her heart ached, both for the hapless kitten and for her daughter.

She sat at the table next to the window in her tiny kitchen, making circles against a whetstone with the side of a paring knife. It had been her father's whetstone, and one side was concave from years of such stroking. Her mother used to say, "I don't know which Papa finds more rewardin', the whittlin' or the honin'."

An image of her father—in his customary overalls, propped against the wall of the front porch in a ladder-backed chair, pocketknife in one hand and whetstone in the other—flickered in her memory like an old newsreel. Her fingers closed lovingly around the stone.

The kitchen table's red-checkered oilcloth was scrubbed white in spots and darkly branded in circles where hot dishes carelessly had been placed. When it was time for a new oilcloth, Rena would put new over old as she had with the previous cloth. Lifting the bottom cloth just pulled the thin veneer from the tabletop, so she didn't often bother.

She thought about taking the pot of vegetables out on the back porch to peel them, but decided against it. *It wouldn't be any cooler out there*, she thought, looking out the window. Here it was September and it still felt like July.

Rena reached behind the gabardine panels she had hung from a wire stretched across one corner of the kitchen and took a red bandanna from a basket of clean clothes. She folded it into a bandeau and tied it around her head to lift her thick brown hair from her neck. She was an attractive woman, even without makeup, but her husband teased her about being too thin.

"I like my women with meat on their bones," Frank would say, grabbing her behind.

Rena hated that, and she knew he did it just to annoy her.

The slips of orange and yellow zinnias she planted along the side of the house at each end of the plumbago were about spent. The few remaining blooms drooped weary heads against the muck-dusted asbestos shingles she only recently rinsed down.

Where the sun stooped beneath the eaves and sliced the air, dust motes sparkled as they settled. She blew across them and sent them swirling.

"Why do I bother?" she said, aloud. "Lord a mercy, I'm gettin' bad as Mama, talkin' to myself."

She knew once the sugar cane harvest began, attempts to keep things clean would become even more futile.

Rena dreaded the burning of the cane fields. The flash fires seemed to suck up all the oxygen, every breath of air. Ash veiled the sun and floated down on clotheslines and gardens. White chickens turned gray, and cattle gathered in the farthest corners of pastures, shaking their heads from side to side and snorting mucus streaked with filth. The ash sifted through window screens, frosted homes and automobiles, and nothing moved through it without leaving track or trail.

The fires gave her nightmares that tossed her about in bed and sent her gasping to the back porch in the middle of the night, where the smell of smoke drove her back inside again.

Jamaican laborers made a ritual of the first harvest fire. They lit it with great ceremony, chanting and beating their long machetes against their metal shin guards like drums while the flames began a slow waltz from the dry outer leaves of one cane stalk to another. The fire leapt and swirled and raced downwind across the field, burning away the chafe without damaging the cane. Foxes and cottontails, rats and raccoons, opossums and feral cats ran squealing and howling from the burning fields, some of them aflame. Their carcasses littered the roadside and floated in ditches beside the burned fields.

Many locals, mostly young black men armed with long-handled gigs or machetes, lined the roads close by burning fields to dispatch those rabbits they could catch. Rabbit stewed in brown gravy with onions and potatoes was a fall staple in many Harlem households; it was a pleasant change from pan-fried fish and grits, or fatback, pigeon peas and rice.

Rena pushed the image of screaming rabbits from her mind as she peeled the vegetables absentmindedly, but her thoughts drifted unbidden to the events of the morning. The image of the two Magruder boys at her door, their eyes glazed with fear and confusion, each of them cradling a limp kitten, drew fresh tears. She choked them back.

A moment before Patrick and Sean appeared on her back steps, Rena had heard their father's truck leave, gears grinding and tires screeching. When she looked out her kitchen window, she saw Maureen Magruder sitting in the yard, her head bent over her knees. She was gulping air, as if she had just come up from a long dive, and there were angry red marks on both sides of her neck. The splintered, broken remains of her treasured radio lay scattered on the grass around her. Maureen had saved for weeks to buy the radio, taking in ironing at a dime apiece.

Rena had run to help her next-door neighbor. When she was able to talk, Maureen told her what had happened. Eric had come home about dawn, reeking of whiskey, and passed out on the bed. Later that morning, Maureen listened to music on the radio while she ironed in the kitchen and the children played with the cats on the back porch. When Patrick came inside to get some milk for the kittens, Cooter slipped in with him, ran through the kitchen and into the front room where Eric was sleeping.

"Next thing I knew, Cooter went sailing by my head and right through the screen door," she said. "Poor little kitty.

"Vicki had run home to get her crayons just before that, thank goodness. I tried to stop Eric from hurting Vicki's cat, Rena. I begged him, but he wouldn't listen. Sean had run in the house with Boots in his arms, and I knew right away what was going to happen. Eric warned the boys about bringing the cats inside. He told them if he ever caught one in the house he'd kill it.

"I tried to tell Eric that Boots was Vicki's kitten, but it was too late. Then—I don't know why—he turned around and jerked the radio off the shelf and threw it, too. I wasn't playing it loud or nothin'. Anyways, I was standing there with that hot iron in my hand and I just swung around and slapped it right in the middle of his chest."

Maureen stopped and swallowed hard, her hand at her throat.

"He made the weirdest sound, Rena. Not a scream, exactly, but this loud moan, like some kind of wounded animal. Then he put his hands around my throat, and started squeezing. I remember Patrick poundin' on him to let me go, and then I must have passed out. How did I get out here?"

"Oh God, Maureen, I don't know," Rena had said. "Are you gonna to be alright? Do you want me to go to the store and call your daddy?"

"No, I need time to get myself together first," Maureen said.

Rena helped Maureen into her house, and then tried to comfort the children. Cooter was dead, his neck broken. She was sure Boots would not live out the day.

As soon as Maureen regained her composure, she gathered her boys from the field where they had buried their kitten, and walked to the store to use the pay phone. She called Dyer's Feed and Supply and told her father, Randolph Dyer, what had happened.

"Have you had enough of that bastard now?" the old man asked, quietly.

"Yes sir, I have," Maureen answered.

"If I come to get you this time, you're not going back. You understand, that?"

Her father was resolute. He knew this fight was a postscript to others, knew if she stayed with Eric it would be prelude to another. There was a rage in Eric Magruder that frightened his father-in-law, and always had.

"You leave him this time, it's for good."

"Yes sir, this time it's for good," she said.

******

The newly sharpened knife slipped in Rena's hand and nicked her thumb.

"Dammit!" she exclaimed, sticking the thumb in her mouth before checking the damage. She grabbed a dishcloth and sat back down to hold pressure on the cut until it stopped bleeding.

Through the front screen door, Rena watched the Wilsons' tomcat tiptoe along the far side of the marl road in front of the house. She wondered if he would make it past Papa's old hound, Bullet, who lay belly-down under the disabled Kaiser in her driveway. The cat's gray form undulated in the shimmer of heat rising from the road. He stopped and hissed, his back bowed and tail held straight and high. Bullet lifted his head and growled, but did not move from the shade.

"It's too hot to chase cats, ain't it, Bullet?" Rena said, more to herself than to the dog.

She rose and stepped to the chipped porcelain sink and ran water over the bowl of diced potatoes, onions and carrots, wrinkling her nose at the rotten-egg smell of sulfur water. After nearly three years in Hooker's Point, she had grown accustomed to the strange taste of the water, but not its stench.

From the back porch, Rena could hear Vicki talking soothingly to her crippled kitten. She swallowed hard against the bitter acid that rose like fire in the back of her throat and burned in her chest. She swirled a spoonful of bicarbonate of soda in a little sweet tea, and chugged it. Wiping her hands and mouth with the dishcloth, she decided to put the events of the morning out of her mind, along with the suffering of animals. She turned on the RCA console just in time to hear the Mills Brothers' latest hit:

"You're the end of the rainbow, my pot of gold/ You're Daddy's little girl, to have and to hold/ A precious gem is what you are/ You're Mommy's bright and shining star…"[1]

Rena leaned over the sink with her knuckle in her mouth and sobbed.

CHAPTER TWO

The Burial

Saturday, 3 p.m.

Rena turned the knob to lower the heat beneath the stew meat she was browning, and as usual, the flame sputtered, spit and died.

"Dammit," she said, and reached for a match to light the stove again. Instead, she put a lid on the pot, laid the matches on the counter and walked out the back door. She crossed the yard to where Vicki knelt in the grass, a shoebox by her side.

"Vicki, if you wait until I get the stew on, I'll help you dig the hole," Rena said softly.

"I can do it myself, Mama," Vicki said through clenched teeth. She stabbed her way through the thick Bermuda grass with a small trowel, ripping away the long, tough runners with her hands.

"It needs to be deep, Victoria, to keep the dogs from digging it up."

Vicki looked up, her face streaked with tears and dirt, her eyes wide with horror.

"I'm sorry, baby," Rena said, as she turned and walked back to the house.

Vicki sat back on the broken cinder block she'd found to top the grave and picked up the shoebox that held her dead kitten. She had padded it with rags and tucked a note inside saying, "I love you, Boots."

Then she wrapped the box three times in each direction with cord from her kite.

"I won't let nothin' get you, Boots," she whispered, her face pressed against the box.

"'Scuze me, little one, but maybe I could be of help to ya now?"

Vicki looked up, shielding her eyes from the sun, which flared behind the man's head like the tinfoil crown of Liberty she wore in last year's Fourth of July pageant.

"Sir?"

"Ooooh. Sir, she say. Well now, ain't that polite?"

Vicki stood up and stared at Reed Hooker's yardman, who leaned with his elbows resting on a grip-handled shovel. Except for Lester Spivey, who pumped gas and cleaned windshields at the truck stop in Clewiston, Vicki had never been that close to a black man.

"Ah, but it ain't polite to stare, is it now?"

"No sir, I mean, n..no," Vicki stammered.

"Well now, seem to me like ya be needin' a hole dug, ain't that so?"

"Yes sir, but…,"

"And here I am with this big shovel, and nothin' to do till the man come back with the mowin' machine."

Vicki watched as the man stepped up to the spot where she'd been chopping, planted his heavy boot on top of the shovel blade and pushed it deep into the black muck.

"Did Mr. Hooker send you over here to help me, mister?" Vicki said.

"Well, not really, Missy," the man said. "He did tell me about ya little kitty, though."

"His name is… I mean, his name was Boots," Vicki said, solemnly. "My name's Victoria Leigh Bayle, but most people call me Vicki."

"Oh? Now why's that, you suppose, with such a pretty name as Victoria?"

Vicki grinned, and the man grinned back. His teeth were large and white as Chicklets, and his face folded around his eyes when he smiled. He was a small man but solidly built, with broad shoulders and slender hips. His shirt hung by its sleeves from his waist, and his bare skin beaded with perspiration as he dug the grave.

"How come you talk so funny?" Vicki asked.

The man chuckled and stopped digging.

"Where I come from, Missy, you'd be the one that talk funny."

"Where you from?"

"Well now," the man said, returning to his chore, "I was born in Haiti, ya know, but I come here from the beautiful isle of Jamaica."

"Where's that?"

"Long ways from here, Missy, in the Caribbean Sea."

"What's it like there?"

"Ah, Jamaica. Jamaica lie like a jeweled dragon in the ocean, Missy. Jamaica got mountains seven thousand foot high, and beaches like table sugar. And they grow coffee there, and banana—and sugar cane, just like here."

"So, what'd you come here for?"

"Well now…"

"And how come you always say, 'Well now'?"

The man stopped digging, threw back his head and laughed. It was a deep, joyous, musical sound, and it made Vicki laugh, too.

"What's so funny?" Vicki asked.

"Well now…" the man said, and then they both laughed again.

"What's your name?" Vicki asked.

"Mon Dieu! I'm several questions behind, Missy. Let's see…my name is Pierre St. Clair, and I come here to chop the cane."

"To shop the can?"

"No, no, Missy. To chop the sugar cane."

"Oh," Vicki said, still puzzled. "Oh, the sugar cane! You're a cane cutter."

"Well, that's mostly right, Missy, although I don't actually sling the machete much no more. I'm the crew boss now, ya know."

"Why do you keep callin' me Missy?" Vicki said. "I told you my name."

"Ohhh, I do beg your pardon, Miss…what was it now? Oh yes, Miss Victoria."

"Vicki."

"Ahh yes, Miss Vicki."

"Vicki, I said. Just plain Vicki."

"Well now, just plain Vicki, I think this here hole is ready."

Vicki grew somber as she looked down at the deep black hole. Once again, tears washed streaks down her muck-smudged cheeks and Pierre reached into his back pocket for his handkerchief, then checked himself and thrust it back again.

"Here, here, child, this won't do, ya know," he said, dropping to one knee and wiping his hands on his shirttail. Look here what ya done now."

With one swift motion, Pierre brushed two fingers under Vicki's chin, then held them down in front of her face. The teardrops hung from the tips of his fingers and caught the sunlight, refracting it into two tiny prisms.

"See here, Miss Vicki?" Pierre said, softly. "Ya gone and put rainbows at my fingertips."

Vicki stared for a moment at the glistening teardrops, then bent down and picked up the kitten's makeshift coffin and handed it to Pierre, being careful to keep the box level. Just as carefully, Pierre placed the box at the bottom of the hole he had dug, then stood, pulled the shovel from the mound and filled the blade with dirt. Gently, he sprinkled each shovelful until the hole was covered. He placed the cinder-block slab on top of the mound, then drove the cross-shaped spines of Vicki's kite firmly into the ground at the head of the tiny grave. Pierre wiped his hands again and reached to catch a tear that ran down the child's face with his thumb, then quickly withdrew his hand.

"Ya know, Vicki, in Jamaica, the old folk say that in heaven, all the animals be able to talk, just like the mynah bird."

"You think that's true, Mr. St. Clair?" Vicki asked, tears rolling down her cheeks again.

"It might be so, little one," he said. "It might be so."

******

"Vicki?" Rena called from the porch. "Come on back to the house now, and get cleaned up for dinner. And thank the colored man for diggin' the hole for you."

"I do thank you, Mr...."

"Pierre," the man said with a little bow. "It was my pleasure, for certain."

Vicki stuck her hands deep into the pockets of her shorts as she walked back toward the house. Suddenly, she spun around and ran back to catch Pierre, who strode through a field of tall parah grass to avoid walking through the two back yards between the kitten's grave and the store.

"Pierre! Wait a minute," she called.

Pierre stopped and turned as Vicki caught up with him.

"Here," she said, holding out her hand. Cupped in her palm was a large blue and white marble.

"Well now," Pierre said, looking at the marble she pressed into his hand. "Ain't that a pretty thing?"

"It's my lucky shooter. I want you to have it, for burying Boots for me."

"Then what you do for a lucky shooter?"

"Oh, I got other ones. That's just my favorite, so I want you to have it."

"Well then, from now on, it will be my favorite shooter, an I'll carry it with me everywhere to remind me of a pretty yellow-haired girl named Victoria."

Vicki smiled and turned to run back home, and Pierre watched until she disappeared through the screen door. He put the marble in his pocket and walked on through the field toward the store.

Funnels of gnats rose and swirled ahead of him in the field, then melted back into the cover of weeds in his wake.

******

Saturday, 4:30 p.m.

Vicki sat on her bed, coloring, until she heard her Uncle Regis' Nash pull up in front of the house to drop off her father. She overturned her new box of crayons in her haste to run and greet him and tell him all the news of the day.

Rena was getting ready to make biscuits when she heard the front door slam. Frank walked grim-faced into the kitchen, with Vicki in his arms, her legs locked around his waist.

"...And then this nice colored man helped me bury Boots out in the back yard," Vicki said, out of breath at last.

"What colored man?" Frank asked Rena.

"It was Reed's new yardman," she answered. "I was cooking dinner, and I looked out and there he was, digging the hole."

"He was a nice man, Daddy," Vicki said, quickly. "He told me that when we get to heaven, all the good little animals that go there will be able to talk, just like the…just like some kinda bird that can talk, but it wasn't a parrot or a parakeet. I didn't know there were other birds that could talk, did you Daddy? Anyway, he was a real nice man."

"Well, I guess there are some good niggers in this world," Frank said, sourly.

"Was that necessary?" Rena said.

Frank set Vicki down in one of the kitchen chairs and turned to Rena, his face dark.

"I didn't see Eric's truck outside. He still gone?"

Rena was glad the Kaiser was up on blocks, waiting for a new clutch.

"He left hours ago, thank God, and so did Maureen and the boys. She called her daddy to come get her, and she said she's not coming back this time."

"I'm gonna to walk over and ask Regis if I can use his car."

Rena's throat tightened and she grabbed Frank's arm.

"I've been cooking all afternoon and you're not going anywhere," she said. "What's done is done, and going after Eric is not going to bring dead cats back to life. And it sure ain't going to help any of us if you two get into a fight. It'll just make things worse. Please, just get cleaned up for dinner. I know it's a little early, but I just want to get it over and done with so I can finish my Bible study for Sunday school. It's been a long day."

Frank walked to the aged Frigidaire, took out a bottle of beer and popped the cap off against the edge of the sink. He stomped out the back door, sat on the porch steps and lit a cigarette. In the stagnant air the smoke curled around his face like a mask.

"Frank? The biscuits are almost ready." Rena said a few minutes later. "Are you ready for dinner?"

Frank looked out at the kite-stay cross and took a long pull on the beer. "I'll eat when I'm damn good and ready," he said.

******

Rena fixed a plate for Vicki and told her to put away her crayons and come to dinner. She took plates for Frank and herself out the back door and set them down on the porch, then went back to the kitchen to pour two glasses of tea. When she returned to the porch, Frank was gone.

Rena returned with both plates and scraped the stew back into the pot. "Ain't you and Daddy going to eat, Mama?" Vicki said. "It sure is good."

"I'll have some later, baby, when Daddy gets back."

"Where'd he go?"

"I'm not sure, but I bet he'll be right back."

"Mama, why does everybody around here hate colored people?"

"Oh, Vicki, honey, we don't really hate them, we just believe the races ought to keep to their own. The white races are superior to the darker ones. It says that in the Bible."

"Show me where it says that."

"You just eat your dinner and let me read my Sunday school lesson."

"Well, it says an eye for an eye in the Bible, too, and a lot of other stuff that don't make no sense, if you ask me. I don't think white skin makes you no better nor worse than nobody else. I've seen a passel of nasty folks, and ever dad-gummed one of 'em was white. Some of *them* call us 'white trash,' just cause we ain't got a lot of money. It ain't fair."

"Vicki, that's enough."

"Good grief," Vicki said, softly.

"Victoria Leigh?"

"Well, Lord sakes, Mama, can't I even have my own opinion?"

"You can scrape your plate, brush your teeth and get your butt in bed if you don't hush."

CHAPTER THREE

Hooker's Point

Averill Malachi Lee first saw the rich muckland surrounding Lake Okeechobee in 1932, on his way to Miami to meet with officials of Cuba's Blanco Grande sugar company.

He pulled off U.S. 27 near Clewiston, stood at the edge of a wide drainage canal and saw an endless field as black as coal. Huge tractor-pulled disc plows traversed the length of the field, their metal, tank-like tracks turning the impressionable muck to corduroy. Averill Lee knew at that moment he soon would be a wealthier man.

As a board member of Confederate Sugar Corporation, Lee had enjoyed a long, profitable association with Blanco Grande, which exported much of its raw sugar to CSC's New Orleans refinery for processing. Confederate Sugar had recently purchased more than 200,000 acres of reclaimed Everglades wetlands—source of the muck farmers called "black gold"—on which it planned to plant sugar cane and build a mill. Averill Lee, as a representative of CSC, had personally advanced the state of Florida $2 million toward construction of a massive levee to hold Lake Okeechobee in check and make farming the land less risky after the devastating hurricane of 1928.

The Cubans provided some of the expertise and initial manpower for the project.

"Reclamation" of the flood plain, with its yards-thick layer of muck, accelerated at fever pitch once the southern part of the dike was completed.

In 1933, when the Clewiston mill opened, Lee, who claimed to be a descendent of Gen. Robert E. Lee, flew flags of Cuba and the Confederate States of America beside Old Glory, both at the plant and in front of the CSC administration building in downtown Clewiston.

The sugar company built two housing projects for its workers; Harlem was for blacks only and was directly adjacent to the mill. The other project was built on a spur of land south of Clewiston known as Hooker's Point, and it served as temporary housing for crews of white laborers who came to help get the mill up and running.

By1945, CSC had built a modern development for whites closer to the mill, complete with landscaped parks and an auditorium, and put the Hooker's Point project up for sale.

Reed Hooker Jr. bought six of the houses and the company commissary located on land his rancher father once owned. Hooker was a Miami banker who had tired of city life and planned to supplement his retirement with income from the rental property. A few of the houses were bought by individuals, and the remaining 10 were sold to Clarence Hall, a realtor who owned most of the rental housing in the migrant ghettos of the town of Belle Glade. Hall prospered from the poverty of his tenants.

Both Hall and Hooker made minor improvements to the houses, then rented them to those who came to Clewiston looking for work, mainly at the sugar mill.

The houses nearest the store in Hooker's Point were shot-gun shacks with a screened front porch, a living-sleeping room, a small eat-in kitchen, and an open back porch. The larger model was a square box divided into four equal rooms, with a screened porch in front and an open one at the rear. There were no halls. Access to one room was through another.

In each of the models a toilet and an unfinished-concrete shower closed off one side of the back porch. A pipe ran from the shower across the ceiling and down to a shelf on the open side of the porch, ending in a spigot. An enameled pan served as a lavatory.

At the Bayle house, a mirror Rena found at the city dump was mounted on the beam that supported the shelf and the roof. Beneath the mirror, three toothbrushes hung from headless nails—each brush a different color and one smaller than the other two. Flies routinely fed on bits of toothpaste and food left on the brushes.

Across the railroad tracks from Clewiston, State Road 832, which ran through Hooker's Point, was paved peculiarly. Coarse rock had been steamrolled into its surface as if to provide traction for a steep incline. Why, no one knew, since the nearest hill was several hundred miles from the iron-flat Florida Everglades. Horses and tender-footed adults avoided walking across the road's jagged surface without shoes. Neighborhood children ran barefoot across it without notice.

At Hooker's General Store, the road turned in a sharp S-curve, first right, and then left past the Holy Ghost Assembly of God Church. It straightened out by Hall's Court, ran past Experimental Pond, where picnics and baptisms were held, and came out on State Road 80 northwest of Lake Harbor. Hooker's Point Road intersected the paved road at an angle in front of the store and ran past the 10 houses on the anvil of land between the two roads. It curved back to the right at the South Clewiston Baptist Church, dividing the two rows of houses that comprised Hall's Court before intersecting again with the hard road.

Except for the towering Australian pines on either side near the homes by the store, Hooker's Point Road lay unshaded until it reached the church. There, rows of live oaks stretched limbs across from either side to form a block-long canopy.

Between the store and the Baptist church, a scrawny stand of cypress trees stood knee-deep in a mile-wide wetland of razor-edged sawgrass and cattails, which bordered the road on the north. The wetlands were home to blue-eyed ibis, herons and other native birds.

At the edge of the marsh, beyond State Road 80, the Herbert Hoover Dike rose 30 feet from the banks of Lake Okeechobee.

******

Frank and Rena May Bayle moved to Hooker's Point in 1947 from Camp Blanding, a huge Army training camp near Starke, Florida. When construction work ended and dismantling began at the military base,

Rena's father, Cleveland Talloway, found a job as a blacksmith with the sugar mill in Clewiston and Frank Bayle was hired on there as a welder and machinist, skills he learned during his stint in the Navy.

One by one, three of Talloway's four remaining daughters, his two sons, and their families, followed and settled near him. They had followed him to Camp Blanding in 1944 for the same reasons—the promise of jobs, and their reluctance to be separated from their patriarch and from each other.

Victoria Bayle was not yet five years old when the family moved to Hooker's Point. She was awestruck by the greenness of the place. Thick Bermuda grass carpeted the yards. She could roll and tumble and play in it without getting grimy.

There was no grass at Camp Blanding. Yards there were raked, not mowed. When it rained, which was seldom, the water beaded up on the talcum-fine dirt and ran quickly to the nearest ditch. In low spots, it formed puddles of gelatinous gray mud. Children risked whippings to slip and slide and skate barefoot in the mud.

Camp Blanding was a monochrome in gray. Buildings, trucks, and tents were gray. The huge live oaks, draped in Spanish moss and shrouded in dust, were gray. Days were gray.

In Hooker's Point, this new place, days were yellow and blue and warm. Here, there were children other than Vicki's cousins for playmates— strange and exciting new kids who told her things too shocking to repeat.

Before her sixth birthday, one of them, a shy 12-year-old boy, small for his age, taught her new things about her body.

Lavonne Dawson often volunteered to keep an eye on Vicki Saturdays at the kiddie matinee while Rena did her weekly grocery shopping. He was always eager to hold the pretty little girl in his lap in a corner of the front row of Dixie Crystal Theatre. He targeted Vicki for the simple reason that her mother usually dressed her in a skirt to go to town.

He bought her popcorn and Sugar Babies and R.C. Cola.

"Let me show you something you'll like," he whispered in her ear. "It's a special place I can tickle you that feels real good, but you have to promise not to tell anybody, and I mean nobody."

At first, Vicki pushed his hand away and refused to let him touch her there. Her mother had told her that was her private place.

"Just let me show you," Lavonne whispered. "I'll stop if you don't like it."

Vicki's legs soon relaxed, and she leaned her head back against Lavonne's shoulder.

By the time Porky Pig stuttered "Th-that's all folks," Vicki was squirming to get down, but Lavonne held her legs together and rubbed himself between the smoothness of her thighs, whispering, "Shhh, shhhh."

"Remember, this is our secret," Lavonne said, spilling a little cola in her lap to cover the small semen stain. "Nobody else can know about this but you and me."

******

"We spilled a little drink on us Mrs. Bayle; sorry about that," Lavonne said as Rena pulled up in front of the theater. "I bought Vicki a cold drink, but this little wiggle worm, she just can't be still, and first thing you know…"

Lavonne opened the car door for Vicki, then knelt and gave her a hug.

"You're my little wiggle worm, ain't you, cutie?"

Vicki was uncharacteristically quiet on the ride home.

"Well, how was the Superman serial today?"

"It was OK," Vicki said, looking out the window.

"And the Tarzan movie, how did you like that?"

"It was OK."

"Just OK?" Rena said, reaching over to sweep Vicki's hair from her eyes. "Well, guess who I saw at the grocery store? My new Sunday school teacher, Mr. Clarence Hall. He owns all them houses down from the church there, where Granny lives. He's supposed to have lots of money so I can't imagine why he's shopping at the B & B Grocery…"

Chapter Four

The Hurricane

Before the mill opened, most of the people who lived around Lake Okeechobee were fishermen or farmers, like Calvin Magruder and his wife, Ruth, who eked out a living from 20 acres of muckland between Clewiston and Bare Beach. Magruder's tobacco-baron older brother, who lived in Bacon County, Georgia, leased the land to him. Life was hard with seven mouths to feed, but with a couple of milk cows, pigs and chickens, and two strapping teenagers to help with the chores, they got by.

Calvin couldn't have picked a worse time to travel to Georgia for seed and tobacco than mid-September, 1928.

******

Ruth Magruder was kneeling in her kitchen garden when a savage wind came out of a clear sky to the east, quickly followed by blinding rain slanted to the west. She dropped the basket of tomatoes and pole beans she had picked and searched the fields for her 13-year-old son, Eric, who was tilling a section of cornfield harvested early that year.

"Eric!" she yelled over the growing wind. "Bring Molly into the barn and help me coop up the chickens. Look's like a storm is coming, for sure."

By the time Eric had unhitched the mule, his 14-year-old sister, Sarah, was leading the cows from the pasture to shelter, and the younger boys, Evan, 10, Robert, 8, and Jacob, 6, were making great sport of chasing chickens and pigs.

"Alright, now, boys, just leave them be and get on in the house," Ruth said, scanning the darkening sky. "If the chickens fly off, they'll come back, for certain. They know which side their toast is buttered on."

Evan and Robert looked at each other and giggled. Their young Irish mother was always saying stuff that made no sense.

"Alright, alright," Ruth said. "Quit your fooling around and get inside. Have any of you seen Patches?"

By dark, the missing cat was the least of Ruth's worries. She gathered her family beneath a mattress with her Catholic missallette and a rosary, while her home was ripped apart by one of the worst hurricanes in Florida history.

And then, a wall of water hit the house and began to flood the floor where they were huddled.

"Hold on to me, Ma," Eric said, as the house was torn from its foundation and began to drift and spin until it lodged against a tree.

Neither Ruth nor the younger boys could swim, and once the roof separated from the walls, there was little for them to hold to but each other.

******

The storm roared across the Florida coast at West Palm Beach at dusk on September 16, bringing with it a tidal wave that dumped a foot of sand on Ocean Boulevard. Along the coast as far away as Fort Pierce, the hurricane stripped the waterfront of bridges, piers and other structures, then turned west and churned slowly and undaunted over the flatlands toward Lake Okeechobee.

Most residents of the fertile rim of the lake lived without electricity or radios, and were caught unawares by the 150-mph winds of the storm's leading edge.

At 9 p.m., the hurricane stalled and gathered strength over the 760-square-mile lake. The lowered barometric pressure at the storm's core drew up a surge—like water sucked into a straw—that was released in a torrent when the eye passed over, inundating the southern shore from Pahokee to Bare Beach.

"It was like you tipped a saucer of water to one side, then straightened her out again," a survivor later told reporters from the New York Times and the Atlanta Journal.

In the eye, an eerie calm fell over the water. Stars twinkled above a crescent moon that scathed treetops already stripped of needles or leaves or fruit. Shallow-rooted palms and pines swooned together at the direction of the wind. Many people who survived the onslaught of the storm mistakenly thought it had passed and ventured from safe quarters to search for loved ones, neighbors or livestock.

"I hear Patches crying," Ruth Magruder said. "I think he's right next to us here in the tree."

She chanted the prayer of St. Patrick as she pulled herself free of Eric's grasp and crawled across a section of the roof to reach the cat.

"Christ be with me, Christ within me, Christ behind me, Christ before me, Christ beside me, Christ to win me, Christ to comfort and restore me, Christ beneath me, Christ above me, Christ in quiet, Christ in danger, Christ in the hearts of all that love me…

"Oh, sweet Jesus," she said as she looked up and saw a piece of sheet metal spinning toward her, glistening in the starlight, and then her prayers ceased.

******

Many others died when they were caught in the lash of the hurricane's vicious tail; it came in fury from the opposite direction at 200 mph.

As winds began to wane about midnight, dazed survivors clung to rooftops, tree limbs, and to each other. Throughout the night, the rain pummeled them until, exhausted and in shock, mother and child, friends and neighbors by the hundreds released their hold on life and sank into the murky water.

The three younger Magruder boys were among those who slipped away in the dark.

Morning broke with a hush that rippled over a liquid landscape where the great shallow lake knew no boundary. Soon, the screams of mothers searching for children and children crying for their mothers echoed from the glassy water, which stretched as far as the eye could see.

National Guardsmen from all over the state were called in to deal with the survivors, the injured and the dead. Airboats used to crisscross the area repeatedly were silenced to listen for calls of help.

By noon of the third day, bodies began to float to the surface of the slowly receding floodwaters.

Jonathan Stone, a West Palm Beach photographer hired to cover the disaster for a national magazine, watched in horror, his camera idle in his lap, as marksmen with rifles cleared paths through waters that churned with alligators and water moccasins.

"They're not paying me enough to witness this," Stone told a guide after his first day on the scene.

At first, the floating bodies were roped together like felled timber and dragged by boat to barges, where they were loaded in heaps, covered with lime and huge tarpaulins and hauled to other, drier parts of the state for burial in mass graves.

By the fifth day, the stench of death was so strong that few rescue workers could bear it. With bandannas soaked in lemon oil tied over their faces, the work crews began burning the bodies in great heaps on any available high ground. Horses, cattle, dogs and pigs shared funeral pyres with human beings of undetermined color, age or gender.

Officials said nearly 2,000 Floridians died in the 1928 hurricane, and 15,000 residents were left homeless. The death toll could have been twice that. The storm dumped 19 inches of water in the Lake Okeechobee area, and scores of bodies were buried beneath mud and silt that lay four to five feet deep in some areas. Farmers or developers turning the soil years later discovered the skeletons.

******

Calvin Magruder heard about the hurricane on October 3, during a trip into the Bacon County seat of Alma. Townsfolk there gathered around a radio at the feed store to listen to the first game of the World Series between the Yankees and the Cardinals, but news breaks revealed the extent of the devastation in Florida. By the time the Yankees won the series in a four-game sweep, Magruder had learned that only his two eldest children had survived the storm. His home, or what was left of it, was wedged on its side between two uprooted laurel oaks.

It was the second day after the storm when rescue teams in johnboats found Sarah and Eric clinging to a section of tattered roof near the Magruder homestead.

The boy still clutched the bloated, lifeless body of his mother.

"Oh sweet Jesus," said one of the men when he saw Ruth Magruder's body, using the same words she had uttered just before she was decapitated.

The bodies of the three younger boys were never found.

To feed his children, Calvin took to the lake. He bought a boat and fish traps with his meager savings, and built a pier and lean-to shack in a cove on the backside of one of the more remote spoil islands that dot Lake Okeechobee. Eric and Sarah spent the next 18 months on that island, without contact with another human being except their father.

******

The 1929 school year was well underway before Francis DeView, the Hendry County Schools truant officer, was able to track down the Magruder children. Local fishermen had reported seeing them on the island or running fish traps with their father.

Calvin Magruder's shotgun abbreviated a visit from DeView, a Canadian native who spoke with a slight French accent. DeView was a cautious, effeminate man who wore both a belt and suspenders that kept his pants hiked high above his waist. He had a nervous tic that caused his head to jerk forward and to one side, as if his collar were too tight, even when he wore none.

"Mr. Magruder?" DeView called, as he cut his outboard motor and coasted toward the man standing on the pier.

"Yep."

"I've come about your children, Mr. Magruder, to see why they haven't returned to school."

"They ain't coming back, mister. They're needed at home."

"But sir, the law requires…" DeView stopped short as Calvin lifted the double-barrel level with the officer's eyes.

"The law ain't got nothin' to do with my children," Calvin said. "The law don't feed 'em nor put a roof over their heads, I do, and you ain't taking my children nowhere, mister. Was God took the rest of 'em from me, and if he wants these here he'll have to come outta hell again and get 'em. Now, you turn that boat around and get your dandy ass back to town, and leave my children to me."

Francis DeView reported to Hendry County Schools Superintendent Bradley Steele that his attempts to contact the Magruder family had proved futile.

"Did Calvin aim that shotgun of his at you, Francis?" Steele said, smiling. "It's right intimidatin', isn't it?"

DeView shifted his weight from one foot to the other and studied the headline of *The Clewiston News*, which lay across Steele's desk: "Memorial Dedicated to Storm Victims." The subhead read, "Hoover Pledges to Build Dike to Prevent Future Floods."

"I did my best, sir," DeView said, defensively.

The Magruder children were listed in school ledgers as "relocated."

******

Eric took to life on the island just fine. He preferred running trotlines to going to school any day. Sarah hated it. She missed her classmates and going to town on Saturdays. Most of all, she missed her mother. She hated having to cook and wash clothes by hand, and she hated that she didn't even have Kotex when she needed them. She had to use strips of cloth from flour sacks and wash them out in the lake. And she hated the way her father was always staring at her.

One moonlit night, not long after Sarah's 15th birthday, Calvin sat in a dark corner of the shack sipping moonshine from a Mason jar, his left hand shoved deep inside the pocket of his overalls. He watched Sarah's backside wiggle as she scrubbed the skillet, and Eric could see the slow, stroking movement of his father's fingers through the front of his pants.

"What say we take the johnboat and go gig us a few croakers, Sarah?" Eric said.

Sarah turned and read the look on Eric's face, and on her father's, and eagerly agreed.

"You go on by yourself, boy," Calvin said. "I want Sarah to stay here and give me a haircut."

"I'll cut your hair tomorrow, Pa, when the light's better," Sarah said. "I want to go froggin' with Eric."

Calvin stood and backhanded his daughter, knocking her against a shelf at the back of the shanty. The little bit of sugar they had left spilled when the shelf crashed with her to the floor.

Eric moved to help his sister to her feet, but his father stepped between them. He reeked of moonshine.

"I reckon the girl'll be a cleanin' up that mess, now, so you just go on by yourself," Calvin said.

Sarah's eyes begged Eric to stay.

"I guess I'll wait till tomorrow night, now that I think about it," he said. "We got a mess of catfish on ice, and if we don't eat 'em, they'll spoil."

"I said go on, boy," Calvin said, coldly. "I'm right sick of eatin' catfish, ain't you?"

"Yes sir, but…"

"But nothin'. Get goin'."

"I won't go far, Sarah," Eric said, under his breath, "and I won't be long."

Eric loaded a homemade frog gig and a headlamp into the johnboat and paddled across the channel to hunt the shoreline for frogs so numerous their mating calls were deafening.

A full moon and lights along the broken levee made navigating easy, and he had a sack full of heavy-thighed croakers in no time. He had stopped on a small island a short distance away from the camp to skin the frogs when he heard a scream in the distance. He thought at first it was the cry of a limpkin, but then he heard Sarah scream his name and knew immediately what was happening. He had seen the way his father watched from behind the sawgrass when Sarah went to the other side of the island to bathe. He had seen his father standing over his sister while she slept, and he had seen the swelling in the front of his pants.

Eric rowed as fast as he could, but by the time he reached the shack, Sarah was crouched wild-eyed in a corner, with a butcher knife in her hand. Her thin cotton dress was ripped at the waist, and her underpants hung around one ankle. A trickle of blood ran from the corner of her mouth.

His lust satiated, Calvin had passed out on his cot.

"I'd rather be dead than have him do that to me again," Sarah said, without looking up at her brother. "I'll kill him if he tries, and he ain't never gonna stop now."

"Yes he is, sis," Eric said.

At 14, Eric was already nearly six feet tall and hard-muscled from hauling in miles of sodden gill nets. He wrapped his sister in a blanket, gathered her in his arms, and helped her to his father's big commercial fishing boat.

"Stay here," he told her, and then he walked back to the shack.

He filled one pillowcase with clothes and another with pots and pans and utensils, making as little noise as possible. He stripped the cupboard of what little food was there—some coffee, a bag of rice, some dried beans, a can of lard and a little corn meal and flour—and piled it all in the center of a blanket, tying the opposite corners in knots over the loot. He dragged the provisions back to the big boat, hitched the johnboat with its sack of frog legs to the back, and dropped the blanket down beside his sister.

"You alright, Sarah?" he asked.

Sarah watched the moon shiver across the water and said nothing. She still gripped the knife.

"There's some stuff in that pillowcase. Change clothes. I'll be right back."

Eric stopped just outside the shack. Pale yellow light from the kerosene lantern filtered through the mosquito netting that served as a door. He could hear his father's drunken snoring above the din of crickets and frogs and the buzz-saw clamor of cicadas. To the west, a fish jumped with a splash that left black circles on the mirrored face of the water. The frogs hushed for a moment, as if startled by the sound.

Eric pushed aside the netting with the back of his hand and stepped inside.

His father lay in the same position as before—on his back, mouth open, fully dressed. The flap of his pants hung open in front, and a thread of viscid fluid trailed from the dark opening to a small damp stain on his trousers.

From the wall above the door, Eric took down the double-barreled shotgun. He opened the breach to make sure it was loaded. When he snapped it closed, his father stirred in his sleep. Somewhere in the pines above a screech owl called a warning. Eric braced himself, aimed the gun at his father's chest and pulled both triggers. A cloud of blood and brain matter splattered the wall behind the cot. Outside, the night creatures hushed once more, then resumed their raucous chorus.

Eric picked up a box of double-ought shells, then turned and tipped the kerosene lantern against the dry plywood table with the barrel of the shotgun. He watched until the cot was engulfed in flames, then walked back to the boat.

Overhead, the tall Australian pines swayed, drunk with the wind, while the lake reached up the bank after the moon and lapped at the pier.

Eric and Sarah were a hundred yards away when the small tank of propane gas they had used for cooking exploded.

******

"Did you hear that, Mama?"

"I ain't deaf, child.

"They's a fire out there."

"Sho' looks that way."

"Look, Mama, they's a boat comin' this way!"

The fire had caught the dark pines by then, turning sky and water gaudy. Pillars of blue-gray smoke spiraled from the treetops and shrouded the moon. The pair fishing on the bank could see the silhouettes of two people in the boat, a man and a woman.

"Grab up them worms, an let's get ourselves out of here."

"But Mama, the fish is just startin' to bite, now the moon's high," the boy whined. "Besides, maybe them folks be needin' some help. Maybe they hurt, Mama."

"You shut your mouth and do as I say, boy. We ain't gettin' mixed up in no white folks' trouble."

"How you know they white, Mama?" the boy said. "Maybe they colored."

The woman hefted herself from the bank of the rim canal with a grunt, dropped her chin and looked at the boy.

"How many coloreds you know with a boat that big?" she said, and gave the boy a poke with the end of her fishing pole.

******

"What are we gonna tell folks, Eric?" Sarah asked her brother as he tied the boat to a piling on the mainland. "Do I have to tell what he done to me?"

"No!"

He hadn't meant to shout, and Sarah jumped as if he'd hit her.

"No, Sarah," he repeated, softly, prying the knife gently from her grip. "You ain't never tellin' nobody about that. You're gonna say the propane tank blew up and our Pa got burned to death while we was out giggin' frogs. That's what you're gonna say."

Eric held out his hand to help his sister out of the boat.

"And that's all anybody's ever gonna know."

Chapter Five

Sloan's Bar &
Billiards

September 8, 1950, 9 p.m.

The trouble started Friday night as it usually did. During the week, Eric Magruder fished traps and trotlines with his uncle and two cousins out of Okeechobee City—a 35-mile boat trip northeast across the lake from Clewiston. He customarily spent Friday night drinking and playing poker in a back room at Sloan's Bar and Billiards in Clewiston before going home for the weekend.

Typically, Eric won more than he lost, which earned him a reputation and an occasional invitation from the moneyed gamblers who played high-stakes games at the Clewiston Elks Lodge. This night, however, Eric drank heavily and lost heavily. When the poker game broke up just before midnight, he was ill-tempered and spoiling for a fight. He stopped at the bar and bought a half-pint of Jack Daniel's, and as he turned to leave, he bumped into a newly hired sugar company foreman named Carlos Arias who was seated at the bar. Arias spilled his drink.

"Cuidado, que pendejo," Arias said, using a napkin to wipe the front of his shirt.

"What did you say, runt?" Eric asked, spinning Arias around, pulling him from his stool and pinning him against the bar.

"Hey, man, I say nothing. Just 'watch out.' That's all I say."

"Oh yeah? You know, I spent a little time down in Panama after I got out of the Marines. Picked me up some Spanish down there, and what you just said didn't sound like 'watch out,' to me. Sounded to me like you called me an asshole, you sawed-off little spic."

"Hey, man, I don't want no trouble, OK? No trouble."

"Let him go, Eric." Albert Sloan stepped cautiously from behind the bar, a yard of lead-filled pipe held out of sight behind his right leg. He was a head taller and 60 pounds heavier than Eric, but he was a man who avoided trouble if he could. He took a step forward, but kept an eye on the fisherman's gaffe that hung from a loop on the side of Eric's trousers. The two men stared at each other for a minute, then Eric grinned and lifted Carlos back onto his stool. He straightened the man's collar and patted his cheek—hard.

"Hell, Albert, what you so touchy about?" Eric said. "I ain't gonna gaffe this little Cuban prick."

As Eric sauntered out of the bar, Albert poured Carlos a free whiskey.

"Jesus, Joseph and Mary!" Carlos exclaimed. "Who the hell is that?"

"Nobody you'd ever want to mix it up with, friend," Albert answered, as he twisted soapy water from a dingy cloth and wiped the polished mahogany bar free of the spilled drink and rings left by beer bottles and highballs. "He's just one more mean redneck."

Tom Spooner, owner of the Clewiston Funeral Chapel and Crematorium, and its adjacent Floral Arcade, poked the man on the stool next to him in the ribs with his elbow and chuckled.

"You're a lucky sum-bitch, Carlos," he said, and clapped Arias on the back. "Thought for a minute there, ol' Eric was going to throw me a little business."

"Yeah? Well, up yours, Spooner," Carlos said. "I notice that big mouth didn't hang around to tangle with Albert, here, so I doubt he's quite as tough as he thinks he is."

"Think again, son," Tom said. "You know Lonzo Tate who runs the movie projector down at the Dixie Crystal?"

"That guy with the bum arm?"

"Yeah. Well, Lonzo got that bum arm from Eric Magruder. Story is it was over Eric's sister, Sarah. You know that bleached blonde job that lives down by the bait shop in that houseboat? That's his sister. Ain't never been nothing but trash. Too bad, too, 'cause she's a real looker. Got pregnant when she was about 15. Some said it was Eric knocked her up, some said her uncle. People just said that because they lived with their uncle in that houseboat after their old man burned to death out there on one of the spoil islands. Eric wasn't nothing but a kid himself though, so I never put much stock in that.

"Anyway, the baby didn't live but a few weeks. They said it was born with a cleft palate and couldn't nurse, but some folks said she just let the little thing starve to death. She's a piece a work, that one, but Eric acts like she's the Blessed Virgin.

"Anywho, ol' Lonzo, see, he lives in Moore Haven, and he didn't know Eric and Sarah was kin. We were sitting here drinking one Saturday night—I think it was the last call, wasn't it Albert? Anyway, Lonzo, he leans over to Eric and says he thinks he'll amble on down to the marina and get him a little snatch from that whore that lives in the houseboat.

"Eric didn't say a word. He just turned around and buried that gaffe of his in Lonzo's shoulder and ripped the muscle clean out his arm. They took him to Belle Glade for surgery, but that arm still ain't much use to him."

"Did Eric go to jail?"

"Hell no. He wasn't even arrested. Lonzo said he'd rather be a live one-armed man than a dead one, so he never would press charges."

Carlos looked at Albert Sloan and smirked.

"He's putting me on, right?"

"Nope," Albert said, twisting a towel inside a highball glass and then setting it in line with others under the bar. "That's just the way it happened. Took me till three o'clock in the morning to clean up all the blood. Place was a mess."

"Jesus, Mary and Joseph," Carlos said again, crossing himself at the same time.

His hand trembled as he picked up the shot glass and tossed back the whiskey.

******

Friday, 11:30 p.m.

Eric drove to the marina, but when he saw no lights in Sarah's houseboat, he turned around in Wayside Park at the bottom of the dike. He was headed back down Francisco Street toward Main when he passed Tyler Long's white Cadillac. Eric got a glimpse of his sister, snuggled close to Long in the front seat. As the car passed, Eric pulled to the shoulder, cracked the seal on the whiskey bottle and took a long drink. He stuck the bottle between his legs, made a U-turn and headed back toward the marina, jamming the accelerator to the floor. He screeched to a stop in the parking lot just as Sarah leaned in the window to kiss Long goodnight.

Eric threw his truck in reverse and backed around to come broadside of the rear of Long's car, blocking his exit. He tipped the half-pint to his lips again.

Sarah stood, straightened the front of her skirt and looked at her brother. She walked carefully over the pimpled parking lot in spike-heeled spaghetti-strapped sandals, steadying herself on the car. When she reached the driver's side of Eric's truck, she hiked her skin-tight skirt enough to prop one foot on the running board, admired her scarlet pedicure for a moment, then took a cigarette from her purse.

"Got a light, Bubba?" she said, waving a king-sized Pall Mall in front of her face.

Eric took another pull from the bottle, replaced the cap, and reached for a book of matches on the dashboard. He took a Camel from the pack in his shirt pocket, lit it, blew out the match, and tossed the remaining matches out the open window. They landed at Sarah's feet.

Sarah stepped back, a bit unsteady from the effect of several shots of tequila earlier in the evening. She leaned on the truck with one hand, then reached down and picked up the matches and lit her cigarette.

"What's your problem, Eric?" Sarah said.

"Why are you running around with that old fart?" Eric said, softly. "The man has kids older than you for God's sake, and he wouldn't even be seen talking to you in public."

"You don't tell me how to live my life," Sarah said. "I'm entitled to have a little fun just like anybody else, and Tyler is nice to me. He buys me things, nice things, and he treats me like a lady. Now you go on home and leave us be, you hear?"

"He treats you like a whore, Sarah, which is what people call women who run around with married men."

"Like you keep it in your pants all week in Okeechobee, Eric? Well, you can kiss my ass and move this goddamned truck, before I call the sheriff."

"Go ahead. Call him," Eric said, reaching for the bottle again. "I'd be interested to hear what Mr. Long here has to say to the sheriff about what he's doing down here at your place this hour of the evening. Mrs. Long would probably be interested too, don't you think?"

Tyler Long's hands were sweating on the red leather cover of his steering wheel. He wiped them on the seat cover, then reached into the glove compartment for the snub-nosed Colt he kept there. He tucked it in his belt before he stepped out of the car, standing with his back to Eric while he loosened his tie and buttoned one gold button on his navy blazer.

"I gave Sarah a ride home from the VFW hall, Eric," Tyler said, as he faced the pair. "That's all there was to it. Now, why don't you just move your truck so I can go home."

"Why don't you make me, Tyler?" Eric said, grinning.

Long unbuttoned his sport coat and stuck his left hand in his pants pocket, so Eric could see the butt of the pistol tucked in his belt. Eric threw back his head and laughed.

"Ooou-whee, look what we got here!" Eric said. "This old fart thinks he's going to scare me with that little pea shooter. Tell me, Sis, 'cause I know you seen 'em, has ol' Tyler here got the balls to shoot me?"

As he talked, Eric opened the truck door and stepped out behind it. He motioned for Sarah to back up, and when she started to protest, he lifted his shotgun from its carrier across the rear window of the truck and rested the barrel on the open window.

"Eric!" Sarah shouted. "What the hell do you think you're doing? Why do you have to always be such a, such a son-of-a..."

Eric raised his left hand and cut her off in mid sentence. But he never took his eyes off Long, whose pearl-handled pistol looked blue in the light of the mercury vapor streetlights.

"How 'bout it Tyler? Think you could put a slug or two in me before I blow your head off with these double-oughts?"

Tyler Long quickly raised his hands and fell to his knees.

"Good Lord, Eric, be reasonable. Just let me out of here. I won't come near Sarah ever again. I swear it."

"Well, your word is good enough for me, Tyler, you being such a fine, upstanding member of the community and all. So, maybe I won't blow your head off. Maybe I'll just aim for your knees. 'Course, this old shotgun don't group 'em like it used to. Kinda scatters buckshot every which way, you know? I probably ought to buy myself a new Remington, but I got a kind of sentimental attachment to this old gun. Belonged to my Pa, you see. And, it still does a pretty good job up close."

"Come on, man, please just let me go home to my family."

By then, Tyler Long, president of Sugarland Savings and Loan and a First Degree Freemason, had begun to weep. A deep yellow stain spread from the crotch of his white linen pants and circled his right knee.

"You're disgusting, you know that?" Eric said. "You're a sniveling, yellow-bellied candy-ass, and if you ever touch my sister again, I'm going to cut your tiny little nuts off and feed them to you. You got that?"

Sarah started towards Long, but he quickly stood, got back in his car, rolled up the window and started the engine. When she started pounding on the glass, he leaned forward and put his head against his hands on the steering wheel. He didn't lift it until Eric had moved his truck. When he backed the Caddy up, he looked over his right shoulder to avoid meeting Sarah's eyes.

"You son of a bitch!" Sarah shouted after him. "You lying sack of shit!"

A haloed moon ascended from behind the swaying pines, and a thunderstorm that gathered over the lake broke and raced across the marina. Sarah and Eric stood facing each other in steamy silence.

"Let's go inside and get out of the weather," Eric said, as lightening cracked the dark and pea-sized hail danced on the pier and boats at dock.

Sarah took a long drag from her cigarette and flicked the stub in Eric's face.

"I'm not going anywhere with you," she said, her voice rising against the onslaught of the storm. "Men are bastards! You're all bastards!"

Eric stood in the rain and watched until his sister was in the houseboat, then walked over to the pier. He sat down beneath a small shelter where fishermen cleaned their catch and leaned back against a piling. He ignored the bird droppings and fish scales on the worn planks, pulled the half-pint from his back pocket and drained it.

From his makeshift doghouse beneath the pier, Ol' Stogie braved the rain to run and greet him. "Well, hey there, Stogie," Eric said to the dog, "I was wondering where you were. If you come out here to get something to eat you're gonna to be disappointed, though. All I got is chewing gum."

Stogie stood and thumped his tail against the dock, then shook his long floppy ears and blinked at the rain.

"You lazy old mutt," Eric said, as he scratched the aging dog affectionately behind the ears. "If you didn't wag your tail so much, you wouldn't get no exercise at all."

Stogie had been a fixture at the Clewiston Marina for years. No one knew where he came from, but everyone who used the boat ramp gave him a pat on the back and whatever food they had to spare.

He was of questionable parentage—long-bodied, short-legged and slew-footed, sort of cigar-shaped and colored—features that inspired his name. He had learned to subsist on spoiled bologna, Spam, stale peanut-butter-and-jelly sandwiches, an occasional hard-boiled egg, half-eaten candy bars, left-over potato salad and, if necessary, discarded trash fish.

Although he sometimes greeted friends or the moon with a sound somewhere between a howl and a whine, no one ever recalled hearing Ol' Stogie bark.

Even after Sarah Magruder adopted Stogie and fattened him up on a regular diet of dog food and table scraps, he still greeted each fisherman at the ramp. He ate their handouts "just to be polite," Sarah said.

"I know I ain't one to talk," Eric said, as Stogie licked his face expectantly, "but you got a serious breath problem there, my man. I think we could both use us some Dentyne."

When he was satisfied no food was in the offing, Stogie turned and padded back to the shelter of his doghouse.

The rain fell surly and incessant, and the wet wind suffered through the pines and died out against the dike.

"Reckon I ought to get out of the weather, too," Eric said, then walked back to his pickup truck. He was nauseous from the whiskey and extremely uncomfortable in his wet clothes. He rolled up the windows to keep from being devoured by mosquitoes, and the heat was oppressive. He stank of fish and sweat and whiskey and tobacco.

He wanted to go to Sarah and tell her he was sorry. He needed to hear her say she forgave him. But the houseboat was dark and he was weary. He leaned his head against the breath-fogged window and closed his eyes.

Sleep came as it always did, restive and nightmarish:

The rain and wind work in tandem to cage the winged night creatures; vermin revel while owlets beg for them with open mouths. Something monstrous is chasing him through a thick wood. He can hear its heavy footsteps crash through the brush and draw close. He hears it sucking air, feels its foul-smelling breath on the back of his neck. He tries to run and hide but cannot move. He tries to call for help but cannot make a sound. His father breaks through the claws of palmettos and then explodes.

*****

Saturday, 2:30 a.m.

Eric wakened with a start and choked back a dry heave. The pounding he thought at first came from inside his head was someone tapping on the window. As he opened his eyes, the red light of Deputy Oscar Lloyd's patrol car throbbed inside the cab.

"Uh, Eric?" Oscar shouted through the window. "You alright, Eric?"

"Fuck off, Oscar," Eric mumbled.

"I noticed your truck has a flat tire," Oscar said, backing up as Eric opened the door, "and I just wanted to make sure you was alright."

"That so?" said Eric, swinging his legs to the running board.

"Just wanted to see if you was OK," Oscar repeated.

"Well, you're a damn fine civil servant, Oscar," Eric said, falling back on the seat. "Now leave me the fuck alone."

"Ya'll go on home, Eric, and sleep it off," Oscar said, as he returned to his patrol car. "Go on home, now," he said, just before he pulled away, tossing gravel from his spinning wheels.

Eric pulled himself upright, and holding onto the steering wheel with one hand, leaned out the open door and vomited. He was in not any shape to change a flat tire, and he needed a bathroom, bad. He drove the five blocks to the truck stop on the flat tire and paid the attendant $2 to put on the spare, asked him to put a new tire on the rim, and told him he'd come back later to pick it up.

The Budweiser clock in back of the counter read 4:10 a.m. when he got back on the road. The sun was already paling the horizon when Eric crawled in bed beside Maureen.

It was just before noon, Saturday, when he stormed out of the house again.

By the next afternoon, Eric Magruder would be dead.

CHAPTER SIX

Music & Mayhem

Saturday, 5 p.m.

Frank stopped at Phillip's Gas station across from Hooker's General Store, bought another Miller High Life, and told Phillip Townsend to put it on his bill.

Townsend looked over his reading glasses and gave Frank an artificial smile.

"You haven't paid last month's bill, yet," he said, pleasantly.

"Fine," Frank said, digging into his pants pocket. "Here's a five dollar bill. Keep the friggin' change."

Townsend's smile faded as Frank slammed the door behind him and walked to the edge of the road with his thumb in the air.

Clarence Hall speeded up as he drove by in his big black air-conditioned Packard.

Frank gave him the finger and started walking toward town.

Before he reached the railroad tracks, Mary Catherine Fischer passed by in her pickup truck and pulled to the side of the road ahead of him. He jogged to the passenger's side, tossing the empty beer bottle into the cane field beside the road, then realized, as he reached for the handle, that there was a small black child seated next to Fischer.

"I'll just hop in the back," Frank said to Fischer.

"Where are you headed?" Cat Fischer asked out her window.

"Just drop me off at the truck stop on Main Street, if you will."

When Fischer pulled in next to the gas pumps, Frank spotted Eric talking to an attendant putting air into a new tire. The attendant rolled the tire to Eric and he caught it, then he caught a right cross from behind in the temple.

The tire rolled to the curb, circled a few times and fell flat.

Frank stood over Eric with his fists clenched and kicked him in the side.

"What the hell?" said the attendant.

Eric stirred and lifted his face from the pavement, and Frank kicked him again, then walked around him and kicked him in the other side.

"Get up, you son-of-a-bitch," he said.

"That's enough, Frank," Fischer said, climbing down from her truck. "Whatever this is about, that's enough. I've got my housekeeper's child in my truck, and she doesn't need to see this."

"Then take her the hell back to Harlem where she belongs, Cat," Frank said.

Lester Spivey lifted the gas nozzle from Fischer's tank, replaced the cap, and mopped his brow with a bandanna he took from his coveralls.

"Would you like me to clean your windshield, Miss Catherine?" Lester asked, avoiding eye contact with Frank Bayle. Fischer could see the muscle in Lester's jaw clinching with contempt for the white man.

"It's fine, Lester," she replied, "but I'd appreciate it if you'd check the oil for me."

Eric moaned and lifted himself to his hands and knees, rocked back and forth for a moment, then slid back to the pavement.

"I guess I had that one coming," he said, rolling to his back and holding his right hand toward Frank, clutching his ribcage with his left. "Help me up, ol' Buddy."

"I ain't your buddy, Eric, not anymore," Frank said. "I don't care if I never see you again. And don't you ever come near my family again, or I'll kill you."

"Jesus, Frank," Eric said, when he was finally able to sit up. "You know I wouldn't ever hurt Rena or Vicki. I was drunk, and it was a fuckin' cat for chrissakes."

Two bearded young men in short-sleeved white shirts and ties emerged from the station and walked toward Eric, each of them clutching a Bible and wearing a wide-brimmed black hat.

"Do you need help, friend?" one of them asked, offering Eric a hand.

Eric looked up, squinting at the men whose heads seemed to swim in gas fumes and black kettles.

"Who the hell are you?" Eric said, ignoring the hand. "Or better yet, what the hell are you?"

"We are but travelers of God's design, friend, passing through this land according to His will, as thou art also," the man said.

"Well, first of all, thou art not my fuckin' friends, and as far as I can tell, that God of yours ain't done a damn thing for me lately."

"Thou hast already offended thy God on the Sabbath, sir, why seeketh thou to alienate thy neighbor as well?"

Eric tried to laugh but it hurt too much.

"Listen here, you Bible-thumping sons-a-bitches, it was my neighbor here who just whooped my ass, in case you didn't see. But either one or both of ya'll can still give it a smooch before you get the hell out of my face."

"We are more concerned with heaven than hell, pilgrim, and thou wouldst do well to give both consideration."

The two men walked back to their bicycles, placed their Bibles in the wire baskets along with some pamphlets, then rode away.

"How the hell you reckon they knew you was my neighbor, Frank?" Eric said.

Frank spat on the pavement and tried hard not to smile. He stood looking down at his neighbor, the man he had fished and hunted with for the past three years. They and their wives played Rook in the evenings, went to square dances together, helped fix each other's cars and got drunk together. Their kids played together.

He grabbed Eric's outstretched hand and hauled him to his feet.

"This don't change a thing I said, Eric."

"Well, thou art just a little more tight-assed than usual this afternoon, Frank, but I'm willing to call it even if you are."

"It ain't even."

"So, you're saying you'd shoot me, Frank, over a stupid cat?"

The two men stood looking at each other, the heat between them ratcheting higher.

"It ain't just the cat and you know it."

Eric took a step toward Frank, his smile waning with each pain-racked breath.

"How many men did you ever kill up close, Frank? With all them stars penned to your lily-white sailor suit, how many? How many times you ever have brains splash in your face, or pick up what's left of a buddy and drag him back to some shit hole and use him for cover, with his eyes still staring at you? It's a little different than firing those big guns from a battleship offshore.

"You ever really kill a man, Frank?"

Frank took a step back.

"I thought not," Eric said. "You talk pretty tough after you blindside somebody, but killin' is a whole other ballgame, ol' buddy. There's tolerable risk involved. You might want to think about that some before you go around threatenin' people.

"Concern thyself with heaven and hell, Frank, as the pilgrims say."

Eric made his way back to his truck, leaning on the gas pumps. When he hove himself to the driver's seat, he leaned and spat a mouthful of blood onto the pavement.

******

Saturday, 6 p.m.

Vicki lay on her stomach, her chin propped on one fist, watching an army of ants march across the cinderblock top of her kitten's grave.

A large black ant at the front of the line carried a red hibiscus flag while other ants followed with drums of crumbs, silver horns of cellophane, and reeds of straw.

"They're throwin' a parade for you, Boots," she whispered. "Can you hear 'em?"

Mama Kitty high-stepped through the brambles nearby, staggered by a pernicious encounter with a poisonous Bufo toad years earlier. She weaved around the piles of discarded asbestos shingles, termite-eaten wood and tarpaper where she lived, and approached Vicki cautiously.

"Come on, Mama Kitty," Vicki said. "I'll pet you, if you let me."

The wary feral cat dipped her head when Vicki reached for her, and ran back to the security of her lair.

Vicki felt bad for the raggedy cat with no one to love her but roving toms who gave her nothing but a new batch of kittens two or three times a year. Boots and Cooter were from her last litter; neighborhood dogs killed their two littermates before their eyes were even open.

"I'm sad about Boots, too," she said to the yellow eyes that peered at her from beneath a pyramid of tarpaper.

Vicki missed her playmates, but she was glad Patrick and Sean weren't next door today. She wouldn't know what to say to them about their what their daddy did to their kittens. Emotion swirled in her chest and knotted her stomach. Images gathered like a storm in her mind.

She saw Eric climbing the play tree to hang the bag swing for her and the other kids, and remembered how he pushed her so high in the swing she could grab a bouquet of crimson blossoms to bring back to him. She remembered how handsome he was, too, and how he sounded just like Hank Williams when he played his guitar and sang, "Why Don't You Love Me?"

"How could he turn out to be so mean?" she asked her dead cat. "I thought he was nice, didn't you?"

From across the road, Vicki could hear Rachel Padgett at her piano, practicing hymns for Sunday services at South Clewiston Baptist Church, where she played for both morning communion and evening prayer meetings. Vicki rose and crossed the road to sit on the Padgetts' front steps.

She was seated only a moment before five-year-old Buster Padgett started throwing pine burrs at her from behind the cover of the Australian pines that lined the road.

"Will you please stop that?" Vicki yelled at the giggling boy. "I'm tryin' to listen."

Rachel called for Vicki to "Come on in," and for Buster to cease his mischief.

"He's a pistol, ain't he?" Rachel said, as Vicki closed the screen door behind her.

"That's one thing you could call him, I guess," she said, thinking that "brat" might be a better description.

Vicki stood for a moment, letting her eyes adjust to the dark, smoky interior of the room before moving past mounds of hymnals, stacks of sheet music, scattered toys and soiled clothes, to sit beside Rachel on the piano bench.

A cup of coffee steamed atop a stained coaster of last week's church bulletin on top of the piano, and an inch-long ash clung to the tip of the Viceroy burning in an ashtray nearby.

"I need to get up from here and clean up this house, but I'd rather play," Rachel said, stopping in the middle of "Victory in Jesus" to take a long drag on her cigarette. The ash fell on her wide-legged shorts and between her flattened thighs onto the leatherette-covered piano bench.

Rachel stood and swiped it onto the floor, then picked up a towel from a nearby pile to spread over the bench.

"That leather makes me sweat," she said, grinning at Vicki.

"Well, drinkin' hot coffee when it's a hundred and leventy degrees can't help much," Vicki said.

Rachel laughed, and blew smoke in Vicki's face.

Rachel Padgett was one of Vicki's favorite people, even though she couldn't stand the Padgett children, whom she regarded as nasty.

Vicki blamed that on the influence of Rachel's husband, Elton "Slim" Padgett, a tall, lazy, slew-footed man who breathed like a horse with heaves and ate like a pig. Her father said he must have a tapeworm, because he never gained an ounce.

Rachel came from "dark Irish Protestant" stock, she said. She was pleasantly plump and wide-framed, with fair, freckled skin, pale gray eyes, and dark, naturally curly hair.

Slim liked to say, "She's broad in the beam, but she can slide from the side." He accompanied the remark with a jive hand motion, but he made sure he was out of Rachel's reach when he did so. Otherwise, she would respond with a slap up side his bony head.

Rachel's good humor outweighed her lightning temper, however, and she made the best pineapple upside-down cake and peanut butter pie in Hendry County. She had four blue ribbons from the county fair to prove it.

"I like hearin' you play the piano," Vicki said, fanning the smoke away from her face. "I wisht I could learn, but mama said we can't afford piano lessons."

"Well, honey, I never had no lessons, neither," Rachel said, leaning her forehead against Vicki's and running her long, graceful fingers up the keyboard with an exaggerated flourish. "I just sat down behind the piano at the church house when I was about your age and kept plunkin' around till the next thing I knew, I was playin' "The Old Rugged Cross." Haven't stopped playin' since, but you know, I never could teach myself to read music. Didn't have the patience for it, and didn't really see the need."

"So, why do you have all these books, then?" Vicki asked, picking up a dog-eared copy of *World Wide Church Songs*.

"I learned to chord," Rachel explained, pointing to the handwritten Cs and Ds and F-sharp letters above the musical scale on familiar hymns in the book. "I play the notes in the chord with my left hand, like this, play the melody by ear with my right hand, like this, and just throw in whatever else I have a mind to.

"The only bad thing is I have to know how the song goes to be able to play it. Mostly, the books just teach me the words."

Rachel sang along to a stanza of "On the Jericho Road." Her voice was tobacco-weakened and husky, but appealing. Vicki harmonized—a talent, Rachel noted, that doesn't come naturally to most people.

"Do you ever play anythin' besides church music?" Vicki said afterward.

"Well, let's see," Rachel said, tapping ash from the tip of her cigarette and jamming the filter in the corner of her mouth.

Suddenly, the sound of Louis Jordon's "Bovine Boogie" filled the room. Rachel stomped the foot pedal so vigorously that the coffee cup danced towards the edge of its perch, and Rachel reached up and moved it back without ever losing the bass beat. She squinted against the ribbon of smoke that curled up in her eyes and flashed a one-sided grin at Vicki, who bounced and clapped with delight.

"That was the best boogie I ever heard," Vicki said, with absolute sincerity, when the tune ended.

"Well thank you, sugar," Rachel said. "I enjoyed playing it, but don't you tell Brother Spires, OK? He says it's the devil's influence, that colored music."

"Well, I think that's just hateful," Vicki said, soberly. "How could music have a color?"

******

When Elton Padgett returned from town with his daughters in tow, Vicki thanked Rachel for the concert and got up to leave. As she reached the door, the two girls, Cassandra and Nellie, blocked her exit.

"What's your hurry, Miss Priss?" said Nellie, softly enough that her mother couldn't hear from the kitchen, where she stood talking to her husband. At age 11, Nellie still sucked her thumb, a habit that had flattened and elongated her right thumb and left wide spaces between her protruding teeth. She spoke with a pronounced lisp.

"She thinks she's too good to play with us," said Cassandra, a 10-year-old with a pretty face like her mother's.

All three of the Padgett children were blonde like their father, and vulgar, as well.

"Maybe she just wants me to play with her again, Sandy," Nellie said, running her hand in and out of her crotch.

Vicki could feel the blood rush to her face at the memory of the two bigger girls holding her down while Nellie pulled Vicki's pants down and rammed her finger between her legs.

"You ain't so high and mighty now, are you, Miss Priss?" Nellie said in a whisper, her mouth close to Vicki's ear. "'Cause I got your cherry."

The girls laughed as they pushed through the door, bumping Vicki against the doorframe.

Nellie looked back over her shoulder and mouthed, "I got Vicki's cherry. I got Vicki's cherry."

Vicki ran down the steps, across the road, and down to the store.

When she reached the big drum that held kerosene, Vicki stood with her back against the sign that said 18 cents per gallon and slammed the sides of her fists against the board. The big red numbers flapped on their hangers.

The day after that fight with the Padgett girls, long blonde strands of hair had filled the brush when Rena tried to brush her daughter's hair.

She had to tell her mother about the fight, but she did not tell the other stuff. She didn't say that the argument began over something the Padgett girls told her about how babies are made.

"You're lying," Vicki had told them. "I ain't go no hole like that and neither does my Mama!"

Vicki told her mother the truth, but not the whole truth.

"Cassandra pulled my hair and held my face on the ground while Nellie sat on my back and hit me," Vicki said. "You can't say nothin' to Rachel, Mama, 'cause then they'd call me a crybaby and a tattletale.

"And don't tell Daddy, neither, 'cause he'd be mad that I let them beat me up."

"Oh, Vicki, he would not," Rena had said, hugging her daughter. "He'd be mad at those nasty girls."

"He'd be mad at me too, Mama. He'd call me a sissy."

When Rena told Frank about the fight later, that's exactly what he did. Then he taught his daughter how to throw a left hook and follow it with a right jab.

CHAPTER SEVEN

World of Sorrow

Saturday, 7 p.m.

Reed Hooker walked from behind the meat counter to the front of the store when he noticed storm clouds blotting out the spewing smokestacks of the sugar mill and heard the distant rumble of thunder. A menacing funnel dropped briefly from the edge of the bruised band of clouds, withdrew and dropped again, as if considering havoc.

Hooker opened the screen door and propped it with a can of motor oil, then carried the remaining display of cans inside the store. He went back for the sandwich board chalked with the price of fryers, eggs, milk and bread, and looked up to see Vicki coming around the corner.

"Hey, Vicki," he said. "I got something special for you inside."

"For me?" Vicki said. "What is it, Mr. Hooker?"

As she passed him by, Hooker saw that Vicki's thick lashes were wet with tears, her eyes rimmed red.

"Well, before my yard man left here this afternoon, he asked me if I'd give you a present."

"Pierre left something for me?"

"None other. He said he had made your acquaintance today and he thought you might really like to have this."

Hooker reached beneath the counter and pulled out a globe the size of a basketball.

"One of his other lawn customers had thrown it in the trash," he said, "but it looks practically brand new to me."

Vicki squealed with delight.

"Now, the stand it was on was broken, but I glued it back together and clamped it. It'll be dry by tonight, and then I'll sand it down and paint it so it'll be good as new."

Vicki turned the world in her hands, with all its pimply purple mountains and vast brown deserts, its green jungles and blue oceans with tiny islands floating there like jewels, and a cloud crossed her face.

"I don't think my daddy will let me keep this, Mr. Hooker, since it came from a colored man."

Reed Hooker, a deacon and music director of the South Clewiston Baptist Church, was by nature and Christian discipline opposed to deception. He also knew Frank Bayle.

"How about you just tell him Mr. Hooker gave it to you, which is a true statement, is it not?"

"It certainly is a fine gift," Vicki said, grinning again. "I got in trouble at school onced for daydreaming about all them faraway places on the globe in our classroom. Now, I can study it at home, Mr. Hooker. I can't think how to thank you and Pierre."

"How about we celebrate God's creation of this Earth with a little ice cream?"

Hooker walked to the freezer and brought back the confection he knew Vicki favored.

"I ain't got but a nickel, Mr. Hooker," she said, as he peeled the paper from two Creamsicles.

"This one's on me, sugar," he said, taking a big bite out of one and handing her the other. "Was there something else you wanted?"

"No sir, not really," she said. "And I sure do thank you for everything. You're just about the nicest man I know, Mr. Hooker, since my Grannypoppy died."

As Vicki walked out the back door with the globe under one arm, rivulets of vanilla ice cream and orange sherbet ran down the stick and puddled between her fingers. She sat down on the back steps, put the globe in her lap and licked her hand and the Creamsicle while she looked for an island named Jamaica.

"You need a napkin, little girl?" Eric asked quietly, one foot on the bottom step.

Vicki looked up with alarm. For a moment, a look of concern crossed her face. A fist-sized lump on Eric's jaw had begun to purple, his shirt was open down the front, and there was a large, V-shaped brand with ugly blisters on his chest.

The moment of pity passed quickly.

"You get away from me," she said. "I don't need nothin' from you. You killed my kitty and he never did a dadburned thing to you!"

"Vicki, come on, let me say I'm…"

"Don't you say nothin' to me, Eric Magruder. Don't you never say nothin' to me again. How could you do something so mean to a helpless little kitty? How could you be so hateful?"

Vicki threw what was left of her Creamsicle at Eric's feet, picked up her globe and ran down the path toward home.

As she passed her mother's clothesline, she stopped and wiped her hands and her eyes on the corner of a still-damp towel, then sat down on the back porch. The shirts on the line hugged themselves as the sheets applauded a breeze.

Wisps of cloud swirled over the oceans Vicki held in her hands, and her heart felt as cold as the ice that covered the polar caps.

******

Eric looked up to meet Reed Hooker's glare, then crossed the street to where he'd left his pickup. As soon as all the people left, Mama Kitty crept cautiously from beneath the steps of the store and started licking the discarded ice cream furtively, her eyes closed but her ears switching direction, constantly monitoring danger.

Eric ground the ignition several times before the engine started, then sped off, tires spitting gravel against the gas pumps. He was over the railroad tracks before he shifted to third.

As he neared the turn toward Clewiston, Eric pounded the steering wheel and wiped his wet cheeks on his shoulders.

He turned onto Francisco Street and pressed the accelerator to the floor. By the time he hit town, the speedometer needle was out of sight on the right.

The traffic light turned fortuitously green as he flew across Main Street and screeched to a halt, one wheel on the curb in front of Sloan's Bar & Billiards.

******

Saturday, 7:30 p.m.

"Mama, can I ride down to the church with Mr. Hooker for a little bit?" Vicki said, watching her mother fold towels as she removed them from the clothesline, placing them in an old wicker basket atop an orange crate. "He said he won't be long. He's just gonna straighten up the hymnals and stuff, and I could help him."

"You could help me right here and you wouldn't have to go anywhere," Rena said, looking over her shoulder.

Vicki's shoulder's slumped, and she turned to walk back to the road.

"Alright then. I'll go tell him not to wait for me."

"Oh, for heavens sakes, go ahead and go. I don't care. But you put Patsy in her box. You can't take a dog in the church, and she just pulled a pair of clean socks out of the hamper and dragged 'em through the dirt, the little scamp."

Rena didn't mention that she'd used that as an excuse to take a break from her chores, chase the pup around the yard and play tug-of-war with the socks. She tried to maintain a maternal sternness about such things, but she loved the puppy as much as Vicki did. She often held Patsy in her lap on the back steps when no one else was around, picking fleas off the puppy's fat little belly and pinching them between her thumbnails.

"Yea!" Vicki said as she scooped up her puppy and ran through the house, kissed her nose and put her in her bed. "Now you be a good girl and don't give Mama no trouble or I'll catch it when I get back. You just take a nice little nap, and I'll sneak you in my bed with me tonight, OK?"

Reed Hooker sat in his flat-paneled pickup and waited in front of the Bayle house until Vicki came bouncing down the steps and climbed in beside him.

"You mighty eager to be doing such a boring job, sugar," he said as they pulled down the road.

"Wellsir, I was hopin' that maybe I could play on the piano a little bit when we got done spreadin' out the hymnals and stuff," Vicki said.

"Ah-ha, now I get it," Reed said, smiling conspiratorially at the child. "I'll tell you what, why don't you just practice your Mozart while I do all the other stuff?"

"Mozart?"

"You don't know Mozart? Mozart is one of the world's most famous composers, and he wrote his first symphony when he was just about your age. I'll bring my record player to the store and play you some Mozart, OK? Or maybe you'd prefer Beethoven or one of the other composers, like Tchaikovsky?"

"I ain't never heard none of them people play, but I sure would like to," Vicki said. "Do they ever come on TV? My cousin Penny has a TV, and sometimes she lets me come over and watch the shows."

"Well, Mozart and the other classical musicians have been dead now for more than 100 years, but their music is still revered by millions of people," Reed said.

Vicki blushed and looked out the window.

"You must think I'm a complete ignoramus, Mr. Hooker," Vicki said.

"I don't think any such thing. How could you know things you've never been taught? Children need to be exposed to classical music early in life to really appreciate it. It's not your fault that you haven't been, but we'll work on that, OK?"

At the church, Vicki was stunned when Reed Hooker sat at the piano and played Beethoven's "Fur Elise."

"Oh, Mr. Hooker, I didn't even know you could play," she said. "I thought Rachel could play the piano better than anybody, but that was… that was just the most beautiful tune I ever heard."

"Well I don't play very well any more, but I still enjoy trying," he said. "Once music becomes a part of you, you know, you're never truly happy without it. The same is true for any of the arts—painting, writing—but you'll find that out. Just give yourself time, Vicki. Just give yourself time."

By the time Reed Hooker had finished posting the numbers for Sunday's hymns on the board, arranged the music on his stand and straightened all the hymnals on the back of the pews, Vicki could play the melody of the first few bars of "Fur Elise" with her right hand.

He had to correct her only once, and the tempo faltered in spots, but she played it.

Vicki beamed at Hooker when he told her, "You're a remarkable little girl."

CHAPTER EIGHT

Harlem

Saturday, 8 p.m.

The cane cutters lined up for showers as soon as the cattle trucks that hauled them to and from the fields rolled to a stop at the migrant camp on the outskirts of Harlem. The rule was that everyone had to wait until the last laborer was off the truck before the race began for one of the 10 shower heads that jutted through the back wall of the long bathhouse. The competition included much good-natured yelling, shoving, tackling and blocking along the way. Once the line formed, though, the men waited patiently for their turn to wash away the muck that burned and stung like fire ants in every crease and crevice of their bodies.

With the week's wage in their pockets—or the part of it left after money was sent home to their families or paid back to the sugar company for room and board—the men looked forward to a night on the town. Most of them would go to Brown Sugar's Bar and Grill, an easy walk away, for a few beers or a bottle of wine and a chance to dance with the local women. Mack Brown's menu featured curried goat, jerked chicken, hot meat pies and breadfruit pudding to attract the Jamaicans, who were not welcome at some of the other juke joints. The local men resented their easy ways with the women.

******

The Confederate Sugar Company hired Pierre St. Clair as a crew boss largely because he spoke three languages in addition to "proper" English: Creole, his father's native tongue; Spanish, which he learned from his Trinidad-born mother, and the melodious Patois he learned growing up in Jamaica, where the family moved when he was 10. Although Haitian and Mexican workers made up only a small percentage of those hired to plant and cut cane, it was helpful to have someone in charge who spoke their native tongues. Many of them spoke no English.

Pierre chose not to live in the cramped and primitive housing provided by the sugar company. The homes in Harlem were reserved for families, and the small rooms of the three-story barracks had no running water, no bathrooms, and sometimes were shared by four or more men. Occupants often slept on bare thin mattresses hauled to the flat roof to escape the heat. On nights without a breeze, they retreated back to their airless rooms to escape swarms of mosquitoes.

Pierre rented a small studio apartment above the garage of Dr. Abram Moore, the town's only black physician. Dr. Moore's modest home, which also contained his office, was at the northeastern corner of Harlem, closer to town and farther from the sugar mill than the rest of the black community, which was perpetually blanketed by the sickly sweet smell of boiling cane juice. The pulpy remains of the crushed sugar cane, called bagasse, hilled the far side of the mill, souring in wait for the train cars that would carry it north to be turned into cellulose and paper products.

Locals dismissed the stench of the mill as "the smell of money."

Dr. Moore enjoyed long conversations with Pierre on his front porch of an evening because Pierre was an intelligent, respectful young man who did not drink or use vulgar language. Although he was not yet 30, the resourceful Jamaican ran a successful lawn service in addition to his sugar company job, and stayed in Florida nearly year-round.

But there was no doubt Pierre was still an island man at heart. His conversation was laced with longing for the beauty of the Caribbean, and with harsh comparisons to the flatlands of the Everglades. Still, Pierre could make more money in Florida in a season than he could eke from a year's labor in Jamaica. The money he earned supported his widowed mother and seven younger siblings, not all of whom had the same father.

Usually, Pierre avoided the rowdy weekend crowds at the local juke joints, where men often carried hunting knives in their boots, and many of the women had a single-edged razor blade tucked in their cleavage. Few weekends passed without a fight between jealous men or women, or both. Friday and Saturday evenings were seldom quiet for Dr. Moore, who was called upon to stitch up the wounds, most of which were superficial but bloody.

Pierre preferred to sit in Lincoln Square across from the African Methodist Episcopal Church in downtown Harlem and play dominos or whist with a few of the locals. That's where Callie Washington found him just before dark that evening. Callie was Dr. Moore's housekeeper, and although she lived with a local man, she had been flirting shamelessly with Pierre for weeks.

"Why, hey there, baby," Callie said as she sauntered towards Pierre, her full hips swaying beneath a red taffeta dress cut low in front. "Why don't you come on down to Brown Sugar's with me and buy me a drink? They's a band tonight, and my feet's a itchin' to dance with some sweet thing like you."

"Tiny Tim" Tucker, the 375-pound owner of Tucker's Repair Shop, and Rascal Ryan, a rail-thin mechanic who worked for him, chuckled as Pierre squirmed uncomfortably on his backless stool.

"I thought ya already had yourself a man to dance with, gal," Pierre said, without looking up from the domino board. "Don't be distractin' me now. Ya liable to make me lose this game."

"Baby, I could make you lose your mind, if you give me half a chance," Callie said, smiling to show the gold star in her front tooth.

Tiny Tim slapped his legs and hooted, and Rascal grabbed his crotch and gave a long catcall, his shoulders bouncing with glee. Tiny Tim spat between his widespread feet and spoke to Pierre, his voice rising an octave.

"What the matter with you, nigger? You oughta get yourself up from here and go get you some of that while the gettin's good."

"Um, um, um," said Rascal, low and lewd. "My balls is turning blue just thinkin' about it."

Pierre looked up from the game and leaned back against a tree, stretching one leg out in front of him.

"Ya got more than dancin' on ya mind, gal?" he asked.

"Well, we'll see about that after you buy me some dinner and a few drinks," Callie said.

As she walked away toward the bar, she looked back over her shoulder and said, "C'mon now, you black booger. I got stuff to show you."

Pierre caught up with Callie in three strides, and reached to close a catch on the back of her dress. His hand lingered at her caramel neck, already moist with the heat of the night and her own passion. It came away smelling of Blue Waltz perfume and lust.

Callie glanced knowingly at him, ran the back of her hand down the side of his face and kept walking.

The air outside of Brown Sugar's was heady with the scent of marijuana, roasting goat, and the ever-present stench of the sugar mill.

As he approached the bar, Pierre already could feel tension growing among the men milling about outside, where a Jamaican band called The Machetes played steel drums and guitars and cheap island flutes at ear-splitting volume. Their hit of the moment, by lead singer Jamal Higgins, was a crowd pleaser at Brown Sugar's:

"De nigga swing de blade fo 50 cent a hour/ while de crew boss watches from the truck-top tower/ He sit up dere a grinnin', 'cause he got de power/ And even if it rain or shine, don't matter what de hour/ De cane field burn and de bagasse sour, while de nigga swing de blade for 50 cent a hour/ De athey wagon loadin' up and headin' fo de sugar mill, and all we want's to get on back and tussle fo de shower/ Get ourselves a pretty thang as tender as a flower/ Forget about dat burnin' cane and slinging dat machete/ Smoke a little weed till de wee, small hour/ Just smoke ourself some herb till de wee, small hour."

A group of locals outside the bar hurled insults at a trio of men in dreadlocks, who stared back with heavy-lidded eyes and passed a pipe around.

"Good evenin', fellas," Callie said as she sashayed by, followed by catcalls and murmured propositions. She turned again as she entered the bar to make sure Pierre followed.

"Let us have a couple of drafts and two of those rib plates, Mack," she said to the bartender. "This fine black gentleman here is payin', ain't you, baby?"

Mack cut his eyes and nodded toward the jukebox, where Travis Boyd was punching keys with one hand, holding a highball in the other.

"You know he's here," Mack said.

"What the hell, Mack," Callie said. "You don't see no ring on my finger, do ya? He ain't got no claim on me, unless I say he do."

Mack pulled back the tap and filled two beer glasses, then turned to call the dinner order in to the kitchen.

"Hold on, man," Pierre said. "I don't eat pork, and I don't drink alcohol, but I'll pay for the beer and the lady's food."

"Well, I'll be," Callie said, running her hand over the tight black curlicues of hair that appeared in the triangle of Pierre's chest just beneath his throat. "You one of them Jew-maicans, then?"

"Well now, I follow the teachin' of Elijah Muhammad, for the most part, but I got some weakness when it come to the ladies and the weed, ya know," Pierre said, refusing to take offense.

"Gotta bit of Catholic in me still, too, from mon mere and pere," he added, when Callie started fingering the black-beaded rosary he wore around his neck.

"Well, honey," Callie said, "I sing in the choir on Sunday, but that don't make me no nun on a Saturday night."

"I'd be pleased to have a bowl of them collards, Mack, with some a that fine cornbread ya make," Pierre said. "I'll just have a orange Nehi with that, if ya'd be so kind."

"Honey, you got yourself a sweet way a talkin', you know that?" Callie said, and leaned forward to kiss Pierre on the mouth.

It was a long, wet kiss that ended when Travis Boyd plunged an ice pick in Pierre's back.

******

Deputy Oscar Lloyd placed his straw hat on the corner of his desk at the jail, propped his steel-toed cowboy boots on the desktop, leaned back against the wall and closed his eyes. It had been quiet for a Saturday night, and he planned to catch a few winks before the last picture show let out and the kids started drinking beer and drag racing west of town on Airport Road.

He'd already made an early sweep of the dike, shining his spotlight in the car windows of the kids who went to the early show then parked down next to the lake to make out. He didn't harass them further—unless it was a smart-mouth kid he didn't like, or unless he couldn't see their heads.

He had just taken off his gun belt to make himself more comfortable when the phone rang.

"Sheriff's Office, Deputy Lloyd," he said.

"Hey Deputy, it's Mack out at Brown Sugar's. You need to get out here quick, and send us a ambulance, 'cause we got some people hurt real bad."

"Knives or guns, Mack?" Oscar asked, sarcastically.

"Well sir, we got one man cut real bad, and there's a woman who's beat up pretty good. I ain't heard no gunshots."

"Who did the cutting?"

"I think it was one of the Jamaicans, boss, but I was back of the bar, so I ain't seen what happened. Travis Boyd and that gal of his got into it in the bar and I told 'em to take it outside. Next thing I knowed, people started running in from the parkin' lot and I heard a woman screamin' like a banshee."

"Where are they now?"

"I don't know where they is, boss. I just ran to the door and saw a lot of blood and came back in to call you."

"OK, Mack, I'm on my way.

"Son of a bitch," Oscar said, as he dialed Tom Spooner's number. "Hey, Tom, how's it hangin'?"

"What do you need, Oscar," Tom said. "As if I didn't know."

"They outside of Brown's place in Harlem. Don't know how bad they are yet but sounds like we might be takin' two of 'em to the hospital. I'll meet you there."

******

The deputy was out of his patrol car with his gun drawn as soon as the car skidded to a stop in front of the bar, lights flashing. Before the wailing siren had time to wind down to a whine, Oscar Lloyd was barking orders at the crowd of bystanders milling around the front door.

"Everybody move back inside the buildin' and stay there!" he shouted.

A man holding a bloody knife sat on an orange crate in front of the barred window, gasping for breath, and a woman lay splayed on her back in front of him.

"Throw down that knife and put your chin on the ground," Oscar called to the seated man, who bent over and clutched his chest with one hand.

"Do it!" yelled Oscar, looking down at the Jamaican through the sights of his .38 Colt.

Pierre St. Clair looked up at the gun, then down at his bloodied hands. He let the knife slip to the ground, but didn't move.

"Anmwe!" Pierre said, reverting to the Creole of his childhood. "Nou bezwen yon dokte, touswit! Souple! Souple!"

His cries for help and a doctor went unheeded by the deputy, who waved his gun in the direction of the crowd to speed their departure, then stepped up and kicked Pierre in the middle of his back, sending him face down onto the gravel.

Oscar pulled his handcuffs from his waist with his left hand, knelt in the middle of Pierre's back and snapped the cuffs around his wrists.

Pierre moaned.

"Non, non," he cried. "That other man there, he try to kill me and the gal, there. Eske ou ka ede nou, spouple?"

"Yeah, well, whatever the hell it is you're saying, I'm telling you right now your ass is under arrest."

Tom Spooner's long black hearse pulled up alongside the patrol car, and Spooner got out and pulled a stretcher from the rear door. He spread an old, stained tarpaulin over the red-carpeted interior of the hearse, and another over the clean sheet on the stretcher.

"Who's first?" Spooner said, then took a Lucky Strike from his shirt pocket, packed it on the side of his stainless steel lighter, and lit it.

Before Oscar could answer, Sheriff Petrie arrived in the unmarked green 1950 Ford of which he was uncommonly proud, even though it did, in fact, belong to the taxpayers of Hendry County.

"I'll take one of those, if you got one to spare, Tom," Petrie said, avoiding the walk back to the car to fetch his cigar. "Passed Travis Boyd down the street yonder holding his guts in his hands, Oscar. I'd appreciate it if you'd go see to him."

"Aw, Sheriff, we ain't even looked at this gal yet, and you know I'm goin' to puke if I have to go…"

"It's all right, Oscar," Petrie said, patiently. "Go and check on him and puke if you need to. That the one that cut him?"

"This here's the one," Oscar said, jerking up on the cuffs around Pierre's wrists and hauling him to his feet.

"He cut?"

"Not so's you'd notice," Oscar said, "but I can't understand a fuckin' word he says."

Pushing his prisoner ahead of him, he opened the back door of his patrol car and shoved him inside.

"Watch your head, asshole," he said, after he'd already slammed Pierre's temple against the doorframe.

Sheriff Petrie and Tom Spooner squatted on opposite sides of Callie Washington, and Spooner spoke to her, gently tapping one side of her face and then the other. When she started to moan he broke a vial of aromatic ammonia and waved it back and forth beneath her nose.

One eye opened wide—the other was already swollen shut—and she began to scream.

The sheriff backhanded her across the face and ordered her to shut up.

"Now that I got your attention, gal, tell me what happened here," he said.

"We was minding our own business, Sheriff," Callie said, spitting blood. "We wasn't bothering nobody when Travis came up and started picking a fight with this Jamaican guy I was talkin' to—just talkin', mind you—and then he started beatin' on me, and then him and the Jamaican got into it and all I saw was blood, Sheriff. Lord God almighty, all I saw was blood."

Callie's top lip had begun to swell from the sheriff's encouragement, and the star in her tooth twinkled in the neon glow of the sign above the bar.

******

"No rush on pickin' up Travis," Oscar said to the sheriff over the two-way radio.

"Is he dead?" the sheriff asked.

Oscar wiped his mouth with the back of his hand, then put two fingers on Travis Boyd's juggler.

"He ain't breathin', and there's no pulse. His bowels is strung from here to yonder, so I'd say he's dead alright. I'm gonna take this Jamaican on to the jail. He admits as how he cut the other guy, but claims the knife ain't his. Leastwise, I think that's what he's a jabberin' about."

"Good enough," the sheriff said. "Tom is takin' that gal Callie over to Doc Moore, but it don't look like she's hurt that bad. I'll call and tell him to pick up that other nigger on his way back. His brother and mother are on their way there now to stay with him, cryin' and prayin' along with half of Harlem, not that it's gonna do ol' Travis any good now. I gotta get outta here, 'cause that howlin' is drivin' me crazy. I got a list of witnesses, though, and I'll talk to them in the morning."

"Jesus H. Christ!" Oscar said, before he threw the mike on the floor. "You fuckin' Jewmaican! Hold your head out the fuckin' window if you gonna pu… Ah, Jesus H. Christ, now look at my back seat!"

It was hard for Pierre to look at anything while Oscar pummeled him with a slapstick.

CHAPTER NINE

Stormy Weather

Saturday, 9 p.m.

The card game hadn't started in Sloan's back room, so Eric sat down at the bar and ordered a double shot of Jack Daniel's from Audra Sloan.

"My eyes are up here, Eric," Audra said, as Eric stared at her breasts.

"Yeah, but that's a real pretty blouse you're wearin' there, sweetheart," Eric said, smiling. "What color is that anyway, titty pink?"

Audra took the dishcloth from the bar and snapped him on the shoulder.

"Ow, Audra," Eric said. "You're as good with a dishcloth as a cowhand is with a whip."

"Yeah? That's because we both have to keep the bulls in their place."

By the time the poker game got rolling, Eric had downed two more doubles with a beer back, and Albert Sloan replaced his wife behind the bar.

"Hit me again, Albert," Eric said, slamming his shot glass on the bar and digging in his pocket for money. His eyes were glassy, and there was dried blood in the corner of his mouth.

"Looks to me like somebody already did a pretty good job of that, Eric, and I'm not serving you any more liquor tonight."

"This ain't the only goddamned bar in town, Albert."

"So go find another."

64

The two stared silently at each other, then Eric pushed back from the bar and headed for the back room.

"The card games are full tonight, Eric," Albert said. "How about I get Audra to fix you a sandwich?"

"How about you kiss my ass, Albert?" Eric said, then turned and swaggered out the front door.

******

Eric drove down Main Street to the Clewiston Inn, entered the bar, and ordered a double.

"A double what?" the bow-tied barkeep said, haughtily.

Eric glared at Timothy Drake, a tall pale man with manicured nails and a ridiculous toupee.

"Anything that's 80 proof," he said.

Drake poured him a Dewar's and said, "That will be two dollars and fifty cents, sir."

Eric whistled, and put a five-dollar bill on the bar.

Through the wide French doors that led to the elegantly appointed dining room Eric could see a party of Clewiston's elite engaged in celebration of a sort that required men to wear tuxedos and gave women an opportunity to show off their fancy gowns and fine jewelry.

A string quartet played from a platform at one side of the room and was ignored by the milling revelers.

"Tough gig," Eric said to the barkeep, "trying to do justice to Vivaldi's Violin Concerto in the middle of a bunch of circus clowns."

Timothy Drake stared at Eric in amazement.

"Close your mouth, Drake," Eric said. "You look like a retard."

Eric picked up his change and entered the dining room.

The partygoers parted as he advanced toward the musicians, where he dropped a dollar into a tip cup attached to a music stand.

"Nice job, fellas," he said to the quartet, then turned on his heel and left, nodding as he walked by some of his occasional poker partners.

"What the fuck you biddies staring at?" he said as he passed a group of white-gloved women.

"Well, I never..."

"Yeah," Eric said. "That's what I figured."

When he spotted Tyler Jones and his wife nearby, he grinned.

"I know. It's an old Jack Benny joke, but it's still funny," Eric said. "And how are you, Mrs. Jones? You're looking particularly lovely this evening."

Amanda Jones smiled weakly and patted her upswept hair, its ink-black ends betrayed by a faint border of gray at the scalp.

"Why, I'm just fine, and thank you," she said. "Have we been introduced?"

"I rather doubt that, Mrs. Jones," Eric said. "But your husband here is a close personal friend of my sister."

Eric laughed as he walked away, listening to the hushed conversation in his wake.

He was still laughing as he walked out the door and got into his truck.

******

At the Canebrake Cocktail Lounge and Package Store in Clewiston, Eric bought a half-pint of Jack Daniel's Whiskey, then drove toward Moore Haven to Sandy's Bottle Club and Dance Hall. He sat at a table in the corner watching couples shuffle around the dance floor to Cowboy Copas' "Tennessee Waltz."

A blonde at the bar sized him up and walked over. She wore deep red lipstick that had crept down into creases at the corners of her mouth, and her eyelids were tinted the same bright turquoise as her dress.

"You looking for company, big guy?" she asked, smiling. The crimson lines did not curl with the rest of her mouth, but stayed where they were, parentheses of excess.

Eric looked up from his whiskey, his gaze drifting from the woman's face to her chipped pink nails to her overrun pumps.

"Not from you, skank," he said, and the blonde walked away in a huff, her satin slip and nylon stockings swishing.

Eric unscrewed the cap from the Jack Daniel's bottle and poured two fingers of whiskey into a glass as a record dropped onto the turntable. He swirled the drink in the ice as Hank Williams sang "I'm So Lonesome I Could Cry."

He drank the whiskey and stood, picked up the bottle and walked out, leaving the Coca-Cola mixer on the table.

It was raining so hard Eric had trouble keeping his truck inside the eastbound lane of U.S. 27 on his way back toward town. He would have found it less difficult if he had turned on his windshield wipers or been a little less drunk and drove a little more slowly than 80 miles an hour.

******

Saturday 11 p.m.

Rena bolted upright in bed and listened.

Frank slept, snoring lightly, beside her. Vicki was asleep on her youth bed an arm's reach away.

She heard nothing but the familiar chirring of crickets and frogs and the rickety hum of the oscillating fan, but her heart pounded against her thin cotton gown, which clung damply to her body.

What had wakened her? She remembered bits and pieces of a dream—pleasant, erotic, at first. She swam at a spring where the crystalline water was cool, and long, whiskered catfish drifted serenely beneath her. She turned on her back to look at the glistening silver tines of water that fell from the bank to curtain the mouth of a large, dark cave, and then suddenly she was being drawn there, pushed and shoved into the maw by those slick dark catfish…

Rena sat on the side of the bed and looked at the luminous green hands of the clock. Would this night ever end?

Eric had come home earlier in the evening and found the note Maureen left for him, saying she wanted a divorce.

> *Let me go, Eric. I can't do this anymore.*
>
> *There's a part of you inside me that will be with me forever, but it isn't love. You killed that like you kill everything that gets close to you.*
>
> *I have to think of myself now—and of the boys. I won't try to keep you from seeing them if you are sober. If you are drinking, stay away from us.*
>
> *If you ever lay a hand on me again, my father will kill you.*
>
> *He told me that, and I believe him.*
>
> *Maureen*

Eric picked up a chair and broke it against the table. He used the splintered back to rake dishes from cabinets. He threw pots and pans at the windows, ripped clothes from drawers and hurled boxes of pictures and toys against the walls.

Rena wanted Frank to go to the pay phone outside the store and call the sheriff, but he refused.

"What a man does with his own property in his own house ain't none of our business," he said. "If the son-of-a-bitch wants to break up his furniture, he's got a right. He bought it."

Rena was relieved that Frank's earlier machismo had seemed to cool in the white-hot light of Eric's rage. Still, she looked at him with veiled contempt.

"He didn't buy the radio," Rena said, remembering the image of Maureen and her broken radio sprawled across her back yard.

It was a long time before she was able to sleep.

Now, as she lay listening to the night, the sky lit up with a flash of lightning. Almost simultaneously, the eyelet curtains blew in over the foot of the bed and she heard a few, then more, then a steady drum of raindrops on the tin roof.

Here it comes again, she thought.

With the clap of thunder that followed, Vicki stirred in her sleep.

Easing out of bed, Rena checked the windows, even though the roof had ample overhang to allow them to remain open. She walked to the kitchen and stood in the welcome coolness of a damp breeze that blew across the back porch and through the screen door. She lifted the hem of her gown above her knees and it billowed behind her like a parachute. Then, over the clamor of the rain, she heard deep, racking sounds of anguish from next door that made hair prickle the back of her neck.

The sobs faded behind the steady rumble of thunder from a spectacular electrical storm in the western sky, where lightning flickered on and off like a child playing with a light switch. Or like battles between ships at sea, she thought, remembering the stories Frank told of World War II.

One mighty bolt lit up the yard, and Rena saw her rag rug still hanging, forgotten again, on the clothesline.

"Dammit!" she said, and counted quietly, "one-thousand-one, one-thousand-two, one-thousand…" The clap of thunder was so loud it rattled the casement windows, and the wind whisked rain across the porch. A light mist filtered through the screen, and it felt cool and refreshing.

With the next flash of lightning, Rena saw Eric Magruder standing on her bottom step, his form undulating behind the sheet of water that poured from the roof. He was shirtless and barefoot, the top button of his jeans undone, showing a thin line of dark hair that ran down from his navel. His hairless chest was branded with an angry red triangle.

"You look like an angel," he said, softly. "I never saw anything more beautiful in my life."

Rena gasped and blushed, then reached behind the door for her housecoat.

"What are you doing here, Eric?" she whispered through the screen. "Have you lost your mind? If Frank wakes up and sees you here he'll probably shoot you."

"Who'd care?" Eric asked. "Not Maureen or the boys. Not Vicki. How about you, Rena?"

Rena looked at Eric for a long time before she answered. She was both repulsed and fascinated by his ability to feel sorry for himself after what he'd done. He was like a child, expecting instant forgiveness after a tantrum.

"You don't make it easy," she said, finally.

"I never meant to hurt anybody, I swear to God I didn't. I was just drunk, Rena. I never meant to hurt anything."

"I know," Rena said. "You never do. Just go home and get dried off before you catch your death of cold or get hit by lightning out there."

Eric shrugged and tossed his head to one side, slinging water from his thick black hair. She could see only the outline of his bare shoulders as he backed down the steps and into the yard.

"I'm sorry, Rena," he said. "Tell her for me."

"Whatcha doing, Mama?" Vicki said sleepily, shuffling up behind her mother.

Rena jumped with surprise, then answered, "Just checking to see if it was raining in, baby. What you doing up?"

"I gotta pee-pee."

"Okay, but you're gonna get wet out there," Rena warned, as she unlatched the screen door and held it open for her daughter. Vicki hesitated, looking at the rain gusting across the porch.

"Well, if I don't go pee I'm gonna get wet in here," Vicki said, giggling as she scooted by her mother.

It was good to hear her laugh, Rena thought, as she looked out toward the rain-shrouded figure in the back yard.

"Mama?" Vicki said in what was supposed to be a stage whisper.

"Shhh, Vicki, I'm right here."

"I didn't really mean what I said about Eric. You know? About wishing something bad would happen to him. You know why, Mama?"

"Why, baby?"

"'Cause I been thinking about it, and I don't think Eric is really mean hisself, do you? I think it's the whiskey that makes him do mean things. Like, it kinda poisons him, and makes him crazy, you know? 'Cause when he ain't drinkin', he's just as nice as can be, ain't he Mama?"

"Yes, baby, he is," Rena said to the man in the dark.

"Remember how Eric tried to teach me how to play his guitar, only my hands wasn't quite big enough? He told me I might not have it yet, but to keep on truckin' 'cause I was gonna be a star one day, remember? And he showed me how to cast a fly rod, so I wouldn't have to put a worm on a hook. He never laughed at me like Daddy did for not wantin' to hurt the worm."

Eric clasped his hands behind his head and rocked back and forth in silent anguish.

Rena recalled the Vitalis-and-Old Spice scent of Eric when they danced to "Blue Moon" at the harvest dance last year in Sugarland Hall. She remembered how he blew on the back of her neck when they dried dishes after playing cards, while Maureen and Frank waited on the front porch for them to bring back coffee and cake. How he laughed at her when she shivered.

"Vicki, hurry up and get through in there, now, so we can get back to bed."

"Did you ever look at Eric's eyes, Mama? They're real, real light blue, like Sally Wilson's Siamese cat's."

Like blue ice, Rena thought as she looked at Eric, then blushed and tightened the sash on her robe.

"And they look real sad, don't they? Even when he's smiling. What you reckon makes Eric so sad?"

"Vicki, I said hurry up! And be quiet, before you wake your Daddy."

"You know what, though? Eric is funny, don't you think? He's all the time making me laugh, saying silly stuff. Like when he got the end of his little finger cut off, he said now he wouldn't have to worry about gettin' boogers under his fingernail."

The din on the roof had quieted to a steady downpour, and Rena heard the toilet flush as Vicki opened the bathroom door.

"You know what else, Mama? One time, Eric told me I was the prettiest girl in Hendry County, except for my mama."

"I know, baby."

"I just don't get it Mama. Why do people drink whiskey anyway, when it makes 'em do bad things?"

"I wish I knew."

Just then, Eric stepped into the narrow stream of light that cut through the rain from the crack between the roof and the shower wall. His face was contorted with grief and some latent torment that stirred pity in Rena.

"I guess some people drink to remember the good times," she said, "and some drink to forget the bad."

Eric crossed his arms over his chest and turned his face to the weeping sky. Rena's heart ached for the broken man who just hours earlier, she had loathed and feared.

Vicki turned and pulled the light cord.

"Well, I'm gonna say a prayer that Eric won't drink no more," she said.

"You do that, baby," Rena said, latching the screen door behind the child and looking out at the man in the dark.

"Cause there ain't no peace you can pour from a bottle."

CHAPTER TEN

Main Street Commotion

Sunday, 1 a.m.

Just as Albert Sloan reached up and slid the deadbolt home on the front door of the pool hall, Eric Magruder's truck rolled to a stop out front.

"Hold on, Albert," Eric yelled through the rain from his open window.

As he stepped out the door, his foot slipped from the running board and he fell back against the cab with a thud. Albert heard him swear as he slammed the door, which bounced back and hit him on the shoulder. He slammed the door again, and then kicked it. He was barefoot and soaking wet. As he staggered toward the door, Eric struggled to put on a shirt, but the sleeve caught on his wristwatch. He ripped the expandable band from his arm, threw the watch on the pavement, and stomped it under his heel. In time, the face of the Bulova joined the mosaic of Pabst Blue Ribbon, Schlitz and Miller High Life bottle caps imbedded in the surface of the tarmac outside the bar.

"Bottle's dry here, Albert," he said, wiggling an empty half-pint of whiskey in the bar owner's face. "Need me another shot or two before you close up."

Albert stepped back from the glass door and said, "The bar's already closed for the night, Eric."

"Then open it again, Albert," Eric said evenly.

"I can't sell liquor on Sunday, Eric," the bartender said, taking another step backward. "You know that, and besides, I already told you I think you've had enough tonight. Why don't you just go on home now and sleep it off?"

Eric looked at him through the thick glass and grinned.

"Open this fuckin' door, Sloan, or I'll open it for you," he said.

Behind Eric, a gust of wind swept a sheet of rain across the front seat of his pickup, and Albert saw the double-barreled shotgun in its carrier behind the seat. Eric followed his gaze, then turned back, the grin gone.

"That might do it, Albert," he said. "Or maybe the truck."

Albert reached up and unlocked the bolt, then walked back behind the bar. He sat three shot glasses in a row on the bar, filled them, then slipped the Jack Daniel's bottle back in its slot between the Seagram's 7 and the Chivas Regal. He leaned back against the mirrored whiskey case.

"Looks like a pretty bad burn you got there," he said.

"Yep. You don't want to piss off your wife when she's got a hot iron in her hand," Eric said, looking down at his branded chest.

"Maureen did that?"

"Yep. Didn't think she had it in her. Surprised the hell out of me, and it hurts like a son-of-a-bitch."

Eric drank the first shot, then poured the other two into the empty bottle. His hands were steady. He stood up and took three dollar bills from his pants pocket and slapped the money down on the lacquered bar.

"Much obliged, Albert," he said, as he walked out the front door.

"Up yours," Albert muttered as he slammed the deadbolt home again.

Upstairs from the bar, Audra Sloan turned over in bed and pulled on the lamp cord as her husband limped up the stairs and into their bedroom.

"Closed up kinda late tonight, didn't ya, honey?" she said sleepily. "You look tired."

"Yeah, it was a busy one," he said.

Albert sat heavily on the side of the bed and crossed his left foot over his right knee. He undid his shoelace, slipped the shoe off and let it drop to the floor. He worked the sock down over his ankle, then carefully eased it off and looked at the blackened nail on his big toe.

"That toe still bothering you, honey? Why don't you go let Doc Watts take a look at it? The damn thing's been making you miserable for two weeks now."

Albert knew the doctor would want to remove the nail he'd injured when he dropped a beer keg on it. The thought of that made him shudder. Moving closer to the lamp, he put his heel on the edge of the bed, bent over and began to work on the thickened toenail with the sharp point of a nail scissors. He carefully drilled a small hole in its surface to relieve the pressure of the blood-engorged tissue beneath. The unexpected squeal of tires and the high-pitched whine of a racing engine made him jump just as the room went dark. The sharp tip of the scissors slipped deep beneath the throbbing nail bed.

"Damnit!" Albert said. Ignoring the pain and the dark ooze of blood from the nail, he hopped to the window just in time to see Eric Magruder's truck go by toward Main Street at high speed, in reverse. A section of light pole dragged from a chain attached to the truck's reinforced front bumper.

"What in the world?" Audra said, padding up behind her husband to peer out the window, her arms crossed modestly over her naked breasts.

"Looks like Eric backed into a light pole and snapped it off. Back of his truck's all smashed. Pissed him off, I guess. He's pulling the damn thing down the street, the crazy son-of-a-bitch."

"Where's the sheriff, you suppose?" Audra said, running her fingers lightly across the back of her husband's neck, down his back and into his back pocket.

Albert looked back at his wife, standing out of view from the window, but bathed in the light of the moon. She had gone to bed without removing her makeup, and there was a dark smudge of Maybelline under each eye. But she had let down her hair and brushed it, so that it fell in long auburn curls around her shoulders.

"At home, making love to his wife, if he's got any sense, just like I'm fixing to do."

"I better *not* ever catch you making love to the sheriff's wife," Audra said, smiling back at him as she walked towards the bed, her shapely backside jiggling provocatively.

"Cute," Albert said. "You know what I meant."

When she reached the bed, Audra turned and fell across it on her back with her feet on the floor and one arm crooked under her head.

"Well," she said, "come and get it, big boy."

Albert limped back to the bed and stood over her as he undressed. Audra hooked her pink-pearl toes in the gaping flap of his boxer shorts and slid her foot down, slowly.

Albert stepped out of the shorts and ran his huge hands over his wife's milky white belly and slid them under her hips, lifting her toward him as he leaned forward and buried his face in the warm, pungent darkness between her thighs.

He soon forgot all about the pain in his big toe and the disorderly conduct of Eric Magruder.

******

Sunday, 1:30 a.m.

Clyde Petrie felt like his head had just touched the pillow when the phone rang. His wife handed him the receiver without speaking.

"Yeah?" he growled into the mouthpiece.

"Uh, Sheriff? It's Oscar. Sorry to wake you up, but we got us a dead nigger down here at the jail."

"Aw, shit, Oscar," Petrie said. "What the hell did you do?"

"I ain't touched him since I got to the jail with him, Sheriff, honest. I just made a bed check and that Jamaican was dead as a wedge."

"You sure you didn't mess with him?"

"No sir. No sir, I ain't touched him since we got here. I swear."

"All right, Oscar. I'll be right there."

"What is it Clyde?" Opal Petrie asked as she hung up the phone.

"Oscar says that nigger we locked up earlier this evenin' died on us. Damnit, we looked that boy over good, and he wasn't even beat up that bad. Course it's hard to tell with them Jamaicans. Black as muck, and you can't understand a fuckin' word they say."

"There ain't no call for that kind of language, Clyde," Opal said, huffily.

Petrie swung his legs over the side of the bed and cupped his head in his hands. "That nigger was jabbering a mile a minute and all we could make out was, "Doktoor, doktoor," the sheriff said. "But he wasn't cut or bleedin' or nothin'. That ol' boy he knifed sure bled, though. God almighty! Beat anything I ever seen. He cut that boy from asshole to appetite. When we got to him, the son-of-a-bitch was walking down Sugar Lane stringing his guts behind him. That nigger was dead and he didn't have sense enough to lay down."

Clyde pulled his pants from the bedpost, shoved both feet in them at once and stood up. His wife had already turned over and gone back to sleep.

"Shit," he said, looking at his pocket watch. "Why the hell do they always wait 'til the middle of the goddamned night to croak?"

******

Sunday, 2 a.m.

Sheriff Petrie stood in the jail cell looking down at two small puncture wounds in the back of the dead prisoner.

"Well, looks like ol' Travis stuck him with a ice pick, Oscar, but who the hell would of noticed them two little holes?" he said. "We know this boy's name?"

"Let's see," Oscar said, shuffling through the small collection of belongings he'd taken from the Jamaican before he booked him. He moved aside the bone-handled switchblade with the initials T.B., still covered with blood, and picked up a rosary of black beads with a silver crucifix. Beneath the rosary was a folded envelope with a name and address, care of Dr. Abram Moore, along with $33 and change that Pierre had in his pocket. Oscar handed the envelope to the sheriff, and as he did, a blue and white marble rolled to the edge of the desk and fell to the floor.

The sheriff looked at the name, then stooped to pick up the marble.

"What you reckon Pierre St. Clair here was doing with an agate in his pocket, Oscar?"

"Don't reckon it matters much now," Oscar said. "He just saved the state the trouble of tryin' him and fryin' him."

"You ever hear of something called self defense, Oscar?" the sheriff said.

"Well, far as I'm concerned, it's just one less nigger in the world, and his mama's probably got half a dozen more just like him at home," Oscar said.

A sudden commotion on Main Street brought both men to the window of the jail.

"What the hell…?" said Oscar as Eric Magruder's dark green pickup went by in a blur, in reverse. Sparks flew from the metal lamp support on the light pole as it scraped and bounced on the street. A block past the jail, Eric did a U-turn and headed back toward Bond Street. When he reached Martin's Department Store, he slammed on brakes and lurched out of the truck.

The two lawmen watched him drain a flask, then smash it against the front of the Ben Franklin Five & Dime store. Eric staggered to the front of his truck, unhooked the light pole, then walked back and threw the heavy chain into the metal truck bed. The sound echoed down Bond Street, bouncing from the Seminole Jewelry to Royal's Department Store, off the front of Babcock's Furniture and fading away against the First Baptist Church on Ventura Avenue. Dogs barked from blocks away.

Neither the Sheriff of Hendry County nor his deputy moved from the window until Eric climbed back in his truck and sped away.

The sheriff pulled his lighter from his pocket, turned it upside down and tapped it on the heel of his hand. He flipped back the lid and lit the chewed up cigar he clenched between his teeth.

"Get a chain and hook onto that light pole and drag it out of the street, Oscar," the sheriff said. "I'll call the power company. Looks like the other end of town's gone dark."

"Then should I go after Eric?" Oscar asked, hitching up his uniform pants, and adjusting his crotch.

"Depends on how much you like breathing, Oscar," the sheriff said, walking toward the door of his office. "Personally, I don't think you got quite enough equipment down there to take on the likes of Eric Magruder."

Petrie grinned as he shifted his cigar to the other side of his mouth.

"Oh, yeah, and call the colored undertaker to come and get that spook out of here when you get back."

CHAPTER ELEVEN

Fishing on Sunday

Sunday, 4 a.m.

On his way to the Clewiston Marina, Cecil Rhodes passed a crew of Florida Power and Light linemen working to restore power to Francisco Street, which was dark from Main Street to Herbert Hoover Dike. Streetlights along Ridge Road were dark as well, and city utility vehicles nosed beside FP&L trucks, where supervisors stood smoking cigarettes and drinking coffee from paper cups.

It was unusual to see city linemen working on a Sunday, but Cecil reckoned some of the voters who lived in Clewiston's toney Lake Ridge area had called the mayor to complain about their big ceiling fans not working.

After he'd launched his boat and parked his truck, Cecil hand-pumped enough gas to fill a spare five-gallon tank by the yellow light of a kerosene lamp at O'Neal's Bait & Tackle. He slid two one-dollar bills through the PAY HERE slot on the station's front door and didn't fret over the 65 cents change owed to him. He figured there were plenty of folks who cheated Riley O'Neal out of what was rightly owed him, then he asked the Lord's pardon for that unkind thought.

Cecil looked forward all week long to his weekend fishing trips on Lake Okeechobee. His job at the sugar mill kept him cooped up Tuesday through Saturday in a hot, noisy, windowless hall where giant vats of cane juice boiled and bubbled. The process filled the plant and surrounding areas with a sickly sweet odor that permeated his clothes, his hair—the very pores of his skin, it seemed.

Cecil loved getting an early start across the open water in the predawn coolness, with no ceiling but the stars and no foreman but the moon. He would be over Nubbin Slough long before the sun slipped through the clouds and let loose the day.

If the morning lay still, Cecil liked to start with a fly rod, hoping to entice a record copper-nosed bluegill or a largemouth bass to leap for one of his hand-tied chartreuse poppers. His catches so far weren't close to being record—a nine pound, six ounce bass, and a one-and-a quarter pound bluegill—but it was a still a thrill for a transplant from the hill country of North Georgia to fool one of those feisty fighters.

When the wind picked up, Cecil cast a Spinnerbait or plastic worms among the bulrushes and pencil reeds. Later, he'd move to the sandy, pockmarked King's Bar bluegill beds, and fish the scattered rocky patches and tall cattails with worms and crickets.

He killed his motor before he reached the beds where less conscientious fisherman cut swaths through the spikerush, their propellers braiding the peppergrass behind them.

Lunch was usually hardboiled eggs, Vienna sausage with mustard on saltine crackers, and a Grapette. Cecil wasn't big on variety. After lunch, he might cast a net for shiners to use later in the day. But often, he'd just pull up to the first shady spoil island he came to and take a little siesta under a tree while the sun was high and the fish weren't biting.

Cecil's wife and her Hardshell Baptist friends were scandalized by his regular desecration of the Sabbath, but no amount of nagging had altered his behavior. They eventually gave up their proselytizing, but prayers were said regularly on his behalf at Wednesday night prayer meetings.

For Cecil, the Sunday fishing trip was an act of communion as reverential as any church ritual. When he dropped anchor at Blindman's Cove, Grassy Island, or one of his secret catfish holes, he was in his place of worship.

There, choirs of whistling ducks, laughing gulls, snail kites and ospreys sang songs of praise, while turtledoves cooed and whippoorwills and quail called roll from the millet fields along the banks of the lake.

At the end of the day, Cecil took his catch to some nearby spoil island. He cleaned enough fish for supper and packed the rest in his ice chest. When he got hungry, he fried fish and hushpuppies in a cast-iron pot over a wood fire. If he had no fish, he made do with pork and beans, or bacon and tomato sandwiches. He could no longer count on his wife to make him biscuits, but he preferred the soft white Wonder bread, anyway, and so did the catfish. Dessert was always the same—a pint of buttermilk and a chocolate Moon Pie.

After dinner, Cecil would sit and watch the sunset gold-plate the water. While the day fled across the lake until all that remained was its pale reflection in the moon, he'd spread his bedroll beneath the pines and watch as the night broke out in stars and fireflies. The bullfrogs serenaded him with their two-note aria, accompanied by the resonant basso of alligators and a symphony of crickets, peepers and tree frogs.

No cathedral, no choir of human voices could bring a man closer to God than that, he thought.

Occasionally, Cecil spent the night in a lean-to he built on Kreamer Island—particularly if the air was still and the mosquitoes were bad. But if the night was cool and breezy, he sometimes pitched a tent on Ritta Island just north of Lake Harbor. He preferred Kreamer, because it was smaller and uninhabited.

Squatters had claimed opposite ends of the two-mile-long Ritta Island. Silas Turner, once a thriving West Palm Beach taxidermist, built a cabin on Ritta's northern tip. Turner had earned a statewide reputation mounting sailfish and blue marlin for deep-sea fishermen at one time, but he traded money for peace and solitude. He now lived frugally on his investments, supplementing his income by mounting bass and bluegills, or an occasional buck's head, for the locals.

Mary Catherine Fischer, a fine arts Vassar graduate turned nature photographer, lived in a fish camp built by her father on the south end of Ritta Island. "Cat" Fischer's father had left her a good deal of money when he died, and she'd managed a tidy alimony settlement from her second husband, a Wall Street broker who had run off with a younger woman.

Fischer had retreated to the quiet of the fish camp to begin working on a book of native Florida flora and fauna. She was a handsome, athletic woman in her mid-forties who kept her dark hair cropped short, and she had earned the reputation of being able to drink any man around under the table. The town gossips had proclaimed her "queer," since she had no children and frequently had female houseguests but never entertained men. She also was an excellent marksman with bow or firearm, and therefore was widely respected, if begrudgingly, by local men.

The smaller of the three cabins that comprised Fischer's camp was reserved for guests. Willy and Clara Williams, and their five-year-old daughter, Millicent, occupied the other. Clara, a native of Jamaica and half-sister to Pierre St. Clair, was Fischer's housekeeper; Willy maintained her boats and handled upkeep of the camp and its gas-powered generator, in exchange for free housing and a small salary. He also worked a weekend night shift as a dishwasher at Tina's Bar-B-Q in Lake Harbor, and was allowed free use of one of Fisher's small motorboats to travel back and forth between the island and the mainland.

Cat Fischer had become attached to little Millie, who frequently accompanied her on boat trips to Belle Glade or Clewiston for groceries and other supplies.

They were good, clean, Christian Negroes, Fischer had told Turner when she hired the couple. But their presence on the island was a bone of contention between the two neighbors. They seldom spoke to each other after that, but there was little need; they were separated by a half-mile-long thicket of Australian pine and sabal palm, and a small grove of native and exotic fruit trees—white guava, mango, papaya, persimmon, lychee nut, and several kinds of citrus—that Fischer's father had planted years before.

Turner lived without benefit of running water or electricity. He had a 250-gallon drum covered with screen and mounted on a 15-foot tower to catch rainwater for drinking and cooking, and he had built himself an outhouse. There was seldom a need to haul water from the mainland.

Fischer's generator ran a water pump that sucked water from the lake, ran it through a purifier and into a covered drum that fed the house. She had an indoor toilet and lights that ran off the generator as well, but she typed by the light of a kerosene lantern, finding the noise of the generator a distraction.

Cecil shied away from either end of Ritta and camped in the middle of the out-flung side of the crescent-shaped island.

******

Sunday, 4:30 a.m.

On this trip, Cecil's preparations were interrupted by the sound of squealing tires and grinding metal as Eric Magruder's truck skidded into the marina. The truck's tailgate bore the imprint of collision, and sparks flew from its dragging exhaust pipe.

Cecil noticed these things in passing, without alarm or curiosity, as one might register a flattened armadillo on the roadside. When a homicide investigator asked him about it later, he would say, "It weren't none of my business."

Cecil nodded at Eric, spat a stream of amber tobacco juice into the black waters of the lake and went back to the task of readying his boat.

By the time Rhodes coaxed his Mercury outboard to a sputtering start, Eric had passed out in the front seat of his truck. He didn't hear the old man putt-putt through the hyacinth-choked boat slip, pass the lock house, exit the channel and start his journey over the wide expanse of Lake Okeechobee.

When he reached the marker he was looking for, Cecil steered his boat toward the east, cut the motor, sipped a Thermos of coffee, and watched the sun rise. It bobbed up from the sodden grip of the lake like a ball of butter dropped in a hot toddy, puddling briefly around the edges. Then it lifted free, dripping brilliance and lining the lake's purple collar of clouds in silver as it hid the stars behind the yellow light of day.

When he yanked the crank again, only God could hear Cecil's thin voice above the noise of the chugging outboard:

"Shall we gather at the river,/Where bright angel feet have trod?/ With its crystal tide forever,/Flowing by the throne of God."[2]

CHAPTER TWELVE

Breakfast with Granny

Sunday, 6 a.m.

Vicki stayed in bed as long as she could, then slipped quietly out from under the sheet and into the kitchen. It was her parents' one day to sleep late, and she was not supposed to make any noise.

I don't know how anybody could sleep through that racket, she thought, listening to the raucous celebration of frogs and cicadas. From the back porch, she could see that half the yard was covered in rainwater. She strained to look around the corner of the house, holding to the stair rail and leaning out to avoid having to wade. Some of the dirt had washed away from the mound of Boots' grave, but it was still above water.

"Lord, please don't let Boots be wet," she prayed. "He don't like the water."

Vicki eased the screen door open and went back into the kitchen. From the ironing basket by the cupboard, she took a clean pair of shorts and a T-shirt and got dressed. Then she sat down at the table and wrote her mother a note on the back of an envelope with a blue crayon:

Dear Mama,

I am going down to Granny's house. I will be back in time to get ready for Sunday School. If Granny is making biskits I will eat breakfast with her. Then I will come home.

Love and XXXXs,
Vicki

She dotted her i's with little blue hearts, and propped the note next to a loaf of bread on the table.

******

Leona Talloway's daily schedule was easy to calculate. If the sun was up, so was she. By the time Vicki had slipped out the door and hopped on her bicycle, Leona's chickens had been fed, their eggs gathered, and her house was fragrant with the scent of buckwheat biscuits and fried bacon. A pot of black-eyed peas simmered on the stove for dinner, and Leona was in her rocking chair on the front porch, sipping her second cup of coffee with her quilting box at her side.

Vicki pedaled with abandon down the marl road to her grandmother's house in Hall's Court. She did not deliberately run through the potholes that pitted the road, but she did not avoid them either.

At the edge of the marsh, she stopped and stood spraddle-legged to watch a great blue heron stitch the hem of the ditch with his long beak. He balanced on one leg and held the other high as he searched for frogs and minnows and skinks, stepping forward slowly, so as not to alarm his prey.

A small breeze muttered down the flooded ditch and wedged ripples against the bank.

"Heyah!" Vicki shouted, and the big bird lifted on cumbersome wings, flapping awkwardly overhead in a labored, pointless flight. He landed gracefully a few yards behind the bothersome child, and resumed his compulsory ballet.

The bank of the ditch, quilted in yellow coreopsis and blue-eyed grass, sank into a marshy field of pickerelweed and bog buttons. Cattails stuck their velvety brown heads above pillows of fog, and an anhinga posed on the crooked knee of a cypress tree.

The air washed clean and cool against Vicki's face as she rounded the corner in front of the church. It was reassuring to see her grandmother's familiar shape on the front porch, which pitched and yawed with the settling of the rich black humus beneath its foundation. Around its perimeter, old coffee tins, rusted-out buckets and thunder jugs held cascades of caladiums in white, jade, and scarlet, as well as Leona's prized new Pink Beauty, its ruby veins bleeding into lime-green ruffled edges. On the steps were pots of purple petunias, pungent buttery marigolds and multi-colored lantana. The walkway of pine straw and oak leaves leading to the front steps was lined on either side with tiger-striped daylilies and pink-eyed periwinkles, which had taken a beating in the thunderstorms of the previous two nights.

Leona shifted her chair to favor the long-shadowed light of early morning as she worked on one of her sought-after hand-stitched quilts. She wore a stainless steel thimble, its inside lined with leather and flattened a bit to fit on her crooked middle finger. A bar of Ivory soap on the porch rail was porcupined with needles trailing lengths of pale pink thread. Her hands were not as nimble as they once were, the flesh sunken between the ropey sinews from wrist to gnarled knuckles, but her stitches remained no less even and admirable.

For this quilt, she'd made a Rose of Sharon pattern, alternating swatches of dark fuchsia and rose-bud printed cotton around a center of old rose satin on a creamy background. The satin came from the drapes of some Clewiston resident who had donated them to the Salvation Army Thrift Shop. The rest of the material came from feed or flour sacks, and scraps saved for her by the Christian Women's Union of South Clewiston, whose charities would benefit from the sale of the quilt when it was finished.

"Hey, Granny," Vicki called, propping her bike against the live oak that covered one corner of the front yard.

"Well, I'll be," the old woman said, smiling. "Look what blowed in just in time for breakfast. You out kinda early ain't you, sugar? And where are your shoes? You rinse off them muddy feet with that watering can before you go a tracking up my porch. You're likely to get the ground itch running around barefooted, leastwise the hookworms. We'll have to be a painting you with gentian violet and worming you like we did the hound puppies."

Leona chuckled, but Vicki turned solemn as she rinsed her feet then climbed the stairs to give her grandmother a long, hard hug. She loved the scent of her grandmother—the sweet, old, talcum-powdered fragrance of her that was unlike anyone else. Then she sat on the steps and studied the petunias, picking away the spent flowers as she'd been taught, so the plant would bloom again.

"I came to tell you somethin', Granny."

"Well, I'm a listening," Leona said, after a minute passed in silence.

"Boots died, Granny. Eric Magruder throwed him through the screen door and broke his back and he died."

"Well, sugar, I heard about that, and I'm sorry as I can be. We'll just have to see if we can't find you another little kitty, won't we?"

The little girl nodded yes, but didn't speak.

"I got some nice hot biscuits in there just waiting for somebody to eat 'em. You want Granny to go and fix you a plate?"

"I can do it, Granny," Vicki said.

"Oh, well, I forgot. You're about to be nine year old, now, ain't you? And might near all growed up?"

"Yes ma'am," Vicki said, as she headed for the kitchen, its windows still yellow from the back porch light, which flickered inside a carousel of gray-winged moths. Vicki stopped briefly at the windowsill to admire the parade of small ceramic figurines her Uncle Phil brought home to his mother after World War II. On the outside sill, a green anole, intent on attracting a mate, stood genuflecting and flashing his bright red neckerchief toward the figurines.

"They're pretty, ain't they?" Vicki said to the misguided lizard.

She routinely picked up and admired the elephant with its genuine ivory tusks most often, and her grandmother allowed her to do so.

Leona loved all her grandchildren equally, but she had a special attachment to Vicki—perhaps because she had been her grandfather's favorite, or perhaps because she was, inside and out, such a beautiful child. Not a perfect child, she knew, but a tenderhearted, loving one, whose feelings bruised as easily as a peach.

And there was something more: a vivid and wondrous imagination. She talked to animals, of course, Leona did that herself; but Vicki communed with all living things—the sunflowers that shaded the pole beans and tomato plants, lizards and frogs and spiders and birds. She could most nearly convince you of their understanding.

She refused to thread an earthworm on a hook—not out of squeamishness, but because she could not bear its writhing agony. She grieved for the fish she caught, demanding they be killed quickly so they wouldn't suffer. She mourned the passing of every creature left flattened on the road, be it gopher, snake or armadillo.

She believed there was something worth caring about in every living thing—even rattlesnakes and cottonmouths. "Else," she said, "why would God put them here?" She wondered about things continually, including why she was different from others.

Vicki was talking in complete sentences by the time she was 11 months old, and she had vivid memories of things that happened when she was still in diapers. She remembered falling from her high chair when she was 18 months old, and seeing a crab emerge from the sand next to her playpen at the beach. She was not yet two when they took her to Bradenton Beach that summer.

Such things about her had delighted Cleveland so, but Vicki's precociousness was sometimes a cause for concern with Leona.

She worried that Frank put too much pressure on Vicki to excel. She was not allowed to say, "I can't." He told her she could do anything she put her mind to. He explained the principles of a task or a skill— riding a bike, for instance—then expected her to do it right the first time.

Rena fished Vicki out of Experimental Pond the first time Frank dropped her in water over her head and told her to swim. Frank didn't speak to either of them for the rest of the day.

The second time they went to the pond, Vicki dog-paddled to the center and back. She clung to a rosary of hope that began with conviction, rather than prayer. Frank was displeased that she didn't do the overhand crawl he had "taught" her. She was five at the time.

Leona feared that Frank viewed Vicki as an extension of himself, rather than as an individual. And he wanted her complete devotion. She had tried to talk to Rena about this, but Rena shrugged it off.

"He loves his daughter, and he wants her to be the best she can be at everything," she'd say. "What's wrong with that?"

Vicki found the biscuits wrapped in a towel in the bread warmer above the oven, alongside a plate of bacon.

"Who all's a coming to your birthday party?" Leona asked, spearing her needle once more into the lubricating soap.

"Numbundy," Vicki called back, her mouth full of biscuit. She put a second biscuit on a heavy earthen plate along with a long strip of bacon, and spooned a thick curl of home-churned butter from a mason jar in the icebox. Then she covered the plate with cane syrup and carried it back to the front porch.

"What did you say, sugar?"

"I said, can I have just a little bit of coffee, if I put a whole lot of milk in it?"

"Well, I reckon so," Leona said. "But what did you say about your party?"

"I ain't havin' no party, Granny," Vicki said, placing the plate on the porch and returning to the kitchen for the mug of coffee she had already fixed, knowing in advance what her grandmother's answer would be.

"You *ain't* having a party? How come?"

Vicki sopped her biscuit and bacon in the syrup, chewed and swallowed two big bites before answering.

"'Cause nobody would come to it, that's why."

"With all these children round here, you telling me nobody would come to a birthday party?"

"Well, ain't nobody from my class at school would come. I asked, and they said maybe if I was to have it in town at the park or somewheres they might could come. But their mamas won't let 'em come to Hooker's Point. You know why, Granny? They said nobody lived out here but the white trash. They said their mamas was afraid they might get the trench mouth or pin worms or somethin' if they let 'em come to Hooker's Point. Ol' Sissy Baker said you could always tell the white trash 'cause their mamas paint 'em up with gentian violet instead of takin' 'em to the doctor. She said we all got purple mouths and purple hinnies. I popped her on the jaw when she said that, Granny. I told her I didn't want her to come to my party anyhow."

Vicki lowered her head and Leona saw a tear splash into the child's breakfast plate.

"But I really did, Granny," Vicki added softly.

"Oh, Lord," Leona said.

The old woman felt suddenly older as she looked at Vicki's slumped shoulders.

Vicki turned and looked at her grandmother. "Are we white trash, Granny?" she asked.

Leona winced. Her head dropped against the high-backed rocker, and her forehead knitted as she shook her head, no.

"Are you all right, Granny?" the little girl asked, leaping up from the steps to her grandmother's side. She placed her small hand on her grandmother's arm and stroked the loose, weathered skin. She traced the diamond-shaped creases and heavy blue veins that moved beneath her touch, laced her fingers through the twisted joints, then searched her grandmother's face.

"I'm okay, sugar," Leona said, patting her heavy thighs. "Come up here in Granny's lap for a minute."

Vicki climbed to the comfort of her grandmother's lap and put her arms around her neck.

"We ain't no kind of trash, Victoria Bayle. *No* kind, you hear me? We're just poor folks, strugglin' to get by is all. Being poor ain't nothing to be proud of, but there ain't nothing shameful about it neither."

"Then why do they say that, Granny?"

"Some folks is just real mean, sugar. I guess they growed up with their bellies too full and their hearts too measly to hold much more than spite. And a lot of 'em, God help 'em, they pass that meanness on to their young'uns."

Leona lifted her granddaughter's chin and studied her face.

"Seems to me like you a learnin' all this way too soon," she said, pushing down with her toes to set the rocker in motion. The floorboards squawked as the rocker tipped back, and sighed in relief as it moved forward.

"Now then, let me tell you what you are, Vicki. But first, you reach down there in my quilting box and hand me a piece of that rose-colored satin."

Vicki leaned over to look in the box, but her grandmother pulled her back.

"No," she said, "don't look. Just feel in there and get me a piece of satin."

Vicki stirred her hand through the cloth in the box until her fingers touched a silky, smooth swatch, and she lifted it out and handed it to her grandmother.

"You see how easy it was to pick out that fine cloth amongst all that plain cotton and muslin?" Leona said.

"Yes ma'am," Vicki answered.

"Well, that's what you are, child," Leona said, hugging Vicki tight. "You are *human* satin, and all them other kids that hurt your feelings, they know you're special. They know it, even if you ain't got a big house and fancy clothes. They know their daddies can't buy what you got."

Leona wiped tears from Vicki's face and kissed her forehead.

"But don't you go a hating 'em, sugar, 'cause hate can rub up a nap on you and make you coarse. You just keep on a being sweet as you are, and one day all them mean ol' young'uns will be a fighting over which ones'll get asked to your party."

Leona rocked the chair, and the floorboards moaned with the burden. Her heart ached from burdens of its own as she stroked her granddaughter's smooth, tan legs.

"Human satin," she said. "That's what you are, sugar. Human satin."

CHAPTER THIRTEEN

The Whipping

Sunday, 7:15 a.m.

From the pasture behind the house, Esmeralda lowed a long, plaintive plea to have her milk-swollen bag relieved of its burden. Maisie, Cleveland's one-eyed yellow plow horse, whinnied in response. Both the cow and the half-blind horse were fat and lazy, and bickered ceaselessly for Leona's attention or the optimum position in the shade of the lone pine in the pasture.

"You want me to go milk Esmeralda, Granny?" Vicki said. "Grannypoppy showed me how, and I was getting real good at it too, before he…I bet I could do it by myself, Granny, if Maisie'll leave me alone."

"I bet you could, too, sugar, but your Uncle Phil should be here any minute to milk her for me. Good thing he comes every morning, or I'd have to sell her off. My hands pain me too much for milking. Of course, I have to bribe him with buckwheat biscuits and sausage gravy. I expect I'd be a making it anyways, though, 'cause you never know who's likely to show up for breakfast."

Leona hugged her granddaughter again, and kissed her cheek.

"I sure do miss Grannypoppy, don't you, Granny?" Vicki asked.

"I most surely do, sugar," Leona said.

A ruckus erupted in the chicken coup, announcing Bullet's arrival back from his morning patrol of the property. He stopped and sniffed around the arbor, where a lush Georgia scuppernong vine spilled its tough-skinned grapes, sweet and pale and juicy, in head-sized clusters. The arbor bore stranger fruit at slaughter time, when hogs and deer were hung, bled and gutted there. The blood made excellent fertilizer for the grapes.

Maisie stuck her head through the barbed wire fence and tried to reach the scuppernongs, then stamped her foot impatiently to discover, once again, that the grapes were just out of reach. She dropped her head and nuzzled her shadow, cropping the grass there instead.

The horse's neck was scarred in a swath about a foot beneath her throatlatch from the annual temptation of the grapes. When they ripened, Vicki fed her a few on the sly, even though they were supposed to be saved for jelly making.

Her grandfather had warned her that too many grapes would give the horse colic, then looked the other way and trusted her common sense.

Suddenly, Leona stopped rocking and whispered for Vicki to be still.

"Look there, on the daylilies," she whispered.

Vicki heard a loud humming, like bees disturbed in a hive, and then she spotted a tiny, sparkling gem poised above a blossom, supping its nectar before moving to the next.

"That's a ruby-throated hummer, and he don't weigh no more than a penny," Leona said. "Ain't that about the cutest little thing you ever saw?"

"He's pretty, alright," Vicki said. "But how does he set in one spot like that?"

"Well, that sound ain't really humming, you know; that's his wings a beating round in a circle. Grannypoppy borrowed a book once that said hummingbirds can beat their wings two hundred times a minute, and they can fly backwards, too. They can even fly upside down, if need be. The Seminoles claim they have magical powers. Cleve made a contraption to feed 'em sugar-water, but it fell and broke a while back, so now they have to make do with the flowers."

"Well, you sure got a passel of them, Granny, so I expect you're still one of their favorite people."

"You think so, sugar?" Leona said.

"Absolutely. Mine, too."

When Bullet rounded the corner the hummingbird flitted away in a flash. Vicki climbed down from her grandmother's lap, lifted her plate and sat down on the top step. Bullet wagged his tail and drooled, waiting for an invitation.

"You ain't gettin' my breakfast, mister, but you can lick the plate when I'm done," Vicki said.

"No he can't, neither," said Leona. "I don't cotton to having dogs slobber all over my eating dishes."

The shrill sound of a whistle—one long quavering trill, followed by three short ones—brought Vicki to attention.

"Was that Daddy whistling for me, Granny?" Vicki asked.

"Sounded like him to me," Leona answered. "You'd best scoot on home."

"I'll see ya at church, Granny," Vicki called, as she grabbed the remaining biscuit from the plate and stuffed it, dripping syrup, into her mouth. She washed it down with her coffee, set the plate on the floor, then hopped on her bike and pedaled for home.

Bullet stood on the bottom step and sniffed at the syrup-covered plate, then looked up at Leona, his brow wrinkled back and his red-lined eyelids drooping in appeal.

"Oh, Lord sakes, go ahead," Leona said to the dog, as she watched her granddaughter disappear around the corner.

Leona lifted herself from the rocker with the aid of the porch rail and straightened slowly, inching her feet apart one at a time until she was sure of her footing. Her knees were not trustworthy of late, so she worried them as little as possible when she walked, lifting each leg in turn from the hip, taxing her tiny feet with the effort. Her terrycloth slippers, the backs worn flat, swished across the linoleum as she entered her bedroom. She pulled the chenille spread up over the pillow on her side of the bed, and tidied it over Cleveland's side. She had not yet washed his pillowcase nearly six months after he died, because it still held the scent of him.

At her bureau, she unbuttoned her housecoat and sprinkled a generous amount of Mavis Talcum under her damp arms and bosom, then dusted inside her drawers and between her thighs.

She stroked the smiling, sepia-toned picture of her husband that stood on top of the bureau, encased in its handcrafted frame. She and Vicki had made the frame one weekend not long after her husband dropped dead of a massive stroke, draped over the fence he sought to repair.

They lit wooden matches and blew them out, then glued them in rows of varied length over a dimestore frame, and varnished it when the glue dried. Both were pleased with the blonde-and-black end result, but most of all, to have the time together.

"Oh, Cleve," Leona said to the picture, wiping away the fragrant dust she had scattered there. "It's a heartache, Cleve. It surely is."

******

A short distance past the curve, Vicki heard her mother's voice calling, "Vic..tor...ia!" Her Aunt Reba's voice came from another direction and farther away, "Vicki!"

"Here I am!" she yelled as loud as she could, her legs pumping nearly as fast as her heart at the tone of her mother's voice.

About 20 yards ahead of her, she saw her father leap across the ditch from the marsh on the other side and stand facing her. He was holding Slim Padgett's Black Mouth Cur, Tug, on a leash, and his pant legs were wet to the crotch. Vicki's feet froze on the pedals when she saw his face. The bike slowed to a creep and she stopped, straddling the bike, several feet in front of her father.

"What's the matter, Daddy?" she asked. "What you doin' with Tug, and why is everybody callin' me?"

"We thought the dog might follow your trail, and he went straight to that cypress head over there. I had to wade out to bring him back, 'cause he treed a coon and I couldn't call him off. Lucky we both didn't get bit by a moccasin or eaten by alligators."

"Good grief, Daddy. I just went down to…"

"Good grief? Who do you think you're talkin' to?"

His voice was harsh and hard, his mouth drawn in at the corners and creased white with anger. Tug tacked back and forth at the end of his leash, eager to escape. Vicki felt the same need to run.

"How many times have you been told not to leave the yard without telling your Mama where you were going?" her father asked.

Vicki paled and began stammering, "But, Daddy, I…I…just went down to Granny's h…"

She dropped her bike and took a step backward as her father walked toward her. "Daddy, please, listen to me, Daddy, I left a… Daddy, I… left…"

"Don't you take another step," Frank Bayle said, fixing his daughter in place with the fury in his voice. When he reached her, he pinned her arms to her sides and lifted her till her face was even with his and shook her. Her head flopped backward and forward like her old rag doll's when she rode her in the basket of her bicycle down a bumpy road.

"You hear your Mama calling you?" he said, shaking her so hard she couldn't answer. "You know your Mama's been crying and calling you for half an hour, out of her mind with worry over what might have happened to you?"

When he put her down, the imprint of his fingers stayed on the blanched flesh of her arms.

"Get your tail back home this minute," Frank said, and Vicki ran, leaving her bike in the middle of the road. Frank reached down and lifted the bike by the handlebars and flung it into the ditch, then turned and walked swiftly after his daughter, dragging Tug behind on his leash.

"Mommie, Mommie!" Vicki called, using a name she hadn't called her mother in years. She caught sight of Rena standing in the front yard with Rachel Padgett, and her mother's face blanched with anger and relief.

"Where on earth have you been, Victoria Leigh Bayle," her mother said. "We've been lookin' all over this neighborhood for you!"

"But Mama…" Vicki started to explain, "I left a…"

"Don't you 'But Mama' me," her mother interrupted, "I ought to take a switch to your behind. That's what I ought to do."

"Not this time," Frank Bayle said, as he reached the group and grabbed the back of Vicki's shirt. He handed the dog off to Rachel and pushed Vicki ahead of him up the steps and into the house.

"Now, Frank," Rena said, following the pair into the house, "I don't think…"

"You stay out of this, Rena," Frank said. "She's going to learn to mind."

Rena was suddenly afraid as she watched her husband unfasten his belt and strip it from his waist. Frank had always had a nasty temper, but in all her life, he had never struck Vicki.

"Frank, you're not goin' to…"

"Bend over that bed," Frank said to the child whimpering in the corner.

"Daddy, please, just listen to me, Daddy, p..please. I left a n…"

"Bend over that bed or you'll take 'em where they land, girl."

"No, Daddy, please!"

The child's hands went up as the belt came down and it lashed across her palms and wrapped around her arms. Vicki screamed with pain and disbelief as her father jerked her up from the floor and threw her face down across the bed. As soon as she hit the bed, the belt came down across her bottom, and again across her legs, and again and again.

"You gonna leave this yard again without permission?" Frank yelled over the child's screams. "Are you?" he said, each time the belt came down, "Are you?"

"No, please, no!"

"No, what?"

The belt landed across her back on its edge, and tiny beads of blood followed its path from her shoulder to her hip.

"No sir, no sir, no SIR!"

Vicki wasn't sure if it was her mother's screams she heard or her own, but the blows stopped and she clawed her way across the bed and into the corner on the other side. She pulled the bedspread over her head to hide her shame. She had peed in her pants, and the briny urine stung her bottom and her legs where the leather left its mark.

Vicki could hear the sound of flesh hitting flesh and the scuffling of feet on the floor and she heard her father say, "You want some of this?"

and she heard her mother say, "You hit me with that and it'll be the last thing you ever do to me."

She heard her father's heavy footsteps, and she heard the front door slam and then her mother was there, pulling her from the corner onto her lap on the bed and saying, "It's all right, baby. It's all right, now. Daddy didn't mean to hurt you. We was just so scared with all this business with the neighbors and the cats and then you run off like that…"

Vicki pushed her mother's arms away and slid down to her feet, sobbing violently—deep, racking sobs that made her chest heave and robbed her of speech. She tried several times to tell her mother where she'd been, but couldn't make herself understood.

Finally, she turned and limped into the kitchen, rubbing her legs and her arms and then her bottom, trying to rub away the sting and the humiliation. She looked for the loaf of bread on the table, where she had propped the note. It wasn't there. Neither was the toaster or the sugar bowl. Someone had moved the things from the table to the counter top, and there, face down beneath the bread, she saw the envelope.

Rena walked up behind her as she slid the note out, turned it over and handed it to her mother. She heard her mother say, "Oh no, baby. Oh, Daddy's just gonna be sick when he finds out."

"Daddy?" she sobbed. "You worried about how *Daddy's* gonna feel?"

It don't matter now, Vicki thought as she walked out the back door and locked herself in the bathroom. *Nothing will ever be the same again.*

And nothing ever was the same.

✱✱✱✱✱

Sunday, 8 a.m.

Rena sat on the back steps taking furtive drags from a cigarette until she heard Vicki turn off the shower, then she snuffed it out on the side of the step and flicked the butt under the house.

Hurriedly, she washed her hands and rinsed her mouth with Listerine so her daughter wouldn't know that she'd been smoking.

"For God's sake, Rena," Frank would say when he saw her sneaking smokes. "It's not a sin to smoke a cigarette, but if you're going to do it, why be a hypocrite and sneak around?"

"I don't want to set a bad example for Vicki," Rena would answer, guiltily.

"So, quit," he'd say.

"I'm going to, and you ought to, too," she'd say, defensively.

"I ain't quiting," he'd say, and that would end the conversation.

Rena called through the door to ask if Vicki needed a towel.

"Vicki? Did you hear me?" Rena called, listening at the bathroom door. The toilet flushed, but there was no response from her daughter.

"Victoria Leigh, do you hear me talking to you?"

"I already have a towel," her daughter said evenly.

"Do you have your housecoat?"

"Yes."

"Yes, what?"

"Yes ma'am."

"Then come on out of there and get dressed for Sunday school," Rena said.

"I don't want to go to Sunday school."

"What do you mean you don't want to go to Sunday school?" Rena said, with a cheery tone she didn't really feel. "The Baptist Women's Association is giving out awards for the Vacation Bible School's Bible Drill this morning, and I bet one of them is going to have your name on it."

Slowly the door opened and Vicki emerged, her eyes still red from crying and her hair damp on the ends and around her face.

Rena took the towel that hung on a nail next to the basin and started to rub her daughter's wet hair between her hands. Vicki ducked away and into the house.

Rena hung the towel back on the nail, followed her daughter into the front room and sat down on the bare mattress. She'd stripped the damp sheets and spread from the bed while Vicki was in the bathroom and wiped the damp spot on the mattress with pine oil. She turned the knob on the fan so it wouldn't oscillate, and aimed it at the spot. She put the sheets and spread in the washing machine and turned it on. *Maybe I'll have time to put them through the wringer and hang them before church,* she thought, *and any nosy neighbors who object to doing laundry on Sunday can just go jump in the lake.*

Vicki sat against the wall on her bed with her knees tucked under her chin and covered by the little pink seersucker robe she got at Easter to match her mother's. It was already way too short.

"She's going to be tall like the Bayles, thank goodness," Rena often said of her daughter. Rena was barely 5 foot 2, and had always wished she were taller.

"I need to put some Mercurochrome on your back, Vicki, and I want to see your legs," Rena said.

Vicki rocked back and forth, shaking her head no, and clutching her robe around her knees.

"Let me see, I said."

Slowly, without lifting her head, Vicki straightened out one leg and then the other. Rena stared at the angry red welts that crisscrossed her daughter's legs and chewed on the inside of her lip. When she reached to touch her, Vicki drew her legs back under her chin.

"You can wear your new blue pants with that little red, white and blue shirt with the sailboats on it and nobody will see," Rena said softly.

"Wear britches to church?" Vicki asked, incredulously. "Mrs. Spires will have a hissy fit!"

"What you wear to church is none of Connie Spires' business, nor Brother Spires' neither," Rena said, knowing the child was right.

******

"What on earth are you doing wearing pants and long sleeves to church in this heat, child?" Leona asked her granddaughter outside the church after Sunday school.

Vicki looked left and right to make sure no one else was looking before she pulled up one sleeve to show her grandmother a long red stripe on the back of her arm. The skin on one side of the welt had begun to turn blue.

"I got a whipping this morning, Granny, 'cause Daddy said I left without telling Mama where I was going and she got scared and thought I was kidnapped or something and everybody was looking for me. But I left 'em a note, Granny," Vicki whispered, her face buried in Leona's bosom.

Leona lifted Vicki's chin and kissed her forehead.

"They just didn't see the note 'cause they moved the stuff off the table and the note was under the bread so Daddy beat me with his belt and I peed in my britches, Granny."

Vicki blushed with humiliation at the confession, and hid her face again, her arms wrapped as far as they would reach around the old woman's waist.

"Sweet Jesus in Heaven," Leona said. "Your Daddy did that to you? For a coming to my house? Why, I never knowed him to lay a hand on you that wasn't loving from the minute you was borned. What in the world is going on around here? Must be the Devil, hisself, come up among us."

CHAPTER FOURTEEN

Backsliding

Sunday, 9:30 a.m.

Frank grabbed the underside of the driver's door and scooted on his shoulders out from under the Kaiser, sat up and wiped grease from his hands with a filthy rag.

He got in the driver's seat, wiped his hands again on his overalls, and turned the ignition. The car started immediately.

"Well, at least you can still run, now let's see if you can go," Frank said, as he backed out of the driveway.

Slim Padgett sat in a once-aqua metal chair in his front yard, in the picket of phthalo shade from tall pines along the road.

Frank pulled in his driveway and applied the brakes.

"Looks like I got her fixed," he told Slim. "Wanna go for a ride?"

Padgett closed the *True Detective* magazine he was reading and reached down beside the chair for his cup of coffee.

"I'll pass, thank you," he said. "I begged off church this morning 'cause my back is acting up. I go off somewheres with you, I'll be in the doghouse when Rachel gets home."

"You get more pussy-whipped every year, Slim," Frank said.

Slim grinned widely in response.

"Yeah, but it's mighty good pussy."

"There you go," Frank said, then backed around and pulled back into his own driveway.

He'd changed clothes and begun working on the car right after Vicki's whipping, and hadn't spoken to his wife or child since.

The first thing he saw when he entered the kitchen was Vicki's crayoned note. Rena had added a note of her own in pencil:

Frank,

> *Vicki left this for us this morning and we just missed it. We'll probably come home right after Sunday school. I don't think either one of us is up to listening to one of Brother Spires' sermons.*

R~

Frank picked up the envelope and looked at the little blue hearts on Vicki's note and slammed his fist into the wall.

******

Vicki sat between her mother and her grandmother in the fourth pew, waiting for the Bible School award ceremony to begin. The congregation sang "When We All Get to Heaven," but Vicki did not sing along. She stared at her mother's Sunday school booklet, with its verse for the day:

"Thou shalt not avenge, nor bear any grudge against the children of thy people, but thou shalt love thy neighbor as thyself: I am the Lord." *Leviticus 19:18.*

Vicki closed the booklet, leaned her head against her grandmother's breast and closed her eyes. Leona took a wood-paddled Passion of Christ fan from the hymnal holder and fanned her granddaughter, whose forehead was beaded with perspiration.

In the pew in front of them, Cassandra and Nellie Padgett cupped their hands and whispered in each other's ears, then turned to look at Vicki and giggle.

When they faced the front again, Leona turned the fan on edge and whacked each of the girls on top of the head.

"Sorry. Flies," Leona said, when Elton Padgett's sister turned to glare at her.

When she turned her back, Leona popped Nellie even harder on the head, causing her to yelp.

Her aunt reached over and slapped Nellie on the leg and whispered crossly, "Behave yourself."

Rena smiled at her mother and shook her head.

"Let's just go, before one of the deacons asks us to leave," she whispered. "It's hot as hell in here, anyway."

******

Rena waved goodbye to her mother as she stood talking to her twin, Reba Fay Knight, who lived across the street from her, next door to the Padgetts.

The two women easily could be mistaken for each other, but in fact, they were not at all alike. Their images were mirrored, but not their personalities.

Rena May was outgoing, at ease with all kinds of people, fun loving and kind. Reba Fay was prim and distrustful of strangers, and overly critical of her daughter, Penny, a beautiful, olive-skinned sparrow of a child whose trouble at school was exacerbated by her mother's constant disparagement.

Penny hid behind her mother's skirt and tugged at her waist.

"Why don't you run give Granny a hug before she leaves?" Reba said, brightly. "You haven't seen Granny all week."

"I don't want to," Penny whined. "I want to go home and color."

"We're staying for church, and then we'll go home."

"No!"

"Yes, and that's that."

Reba wrested her daughter's hands from her waist and straightened her dress.

"This child is driving me crazy," she said to Rena. "I don't have to worry about *her* ever running off, 'cause I can't get her out from under my feet."

She instantly regretted the comment.

"Vicki didn't run off; that's the sad part," Rena said. "She left a note saying she was going to Mama's house, and we just didn't see it. Frank was working on the car when I left, and I couldn't face telling him. It's gonna kill him when he finds the note."

"Oh my word! Well, I might feel sorry for him if I hadn't heard him beating that child. It's one thing to spank a kid that needs a lesson, but that… Why, I had to go out to my hen house and put my hands over my ears. I could hear those blows on my back porch."

"Yeah, I guess the whole damn street heard."

"Rena May!"

"Oh for heavens sake, Reba. I said damn. Big friggin' deal!"

Reba Fay Knight turned on her heel, took Penny's hand and climbed the wide front steps that led into the church. Pastor Spires and his wife stood on opposite sides of the doorway, shaking hands and wishing the congregants who entered a blessed morning.

From inside, Rena heard Rachel warming up the crowd with a rousing rendition of "I'll Fly Away."

Reed Hooker led the singing from behind a podium next to the piano. Because of his generous tithe and enthusiasm for the job, the congregation overlooked the butcher's slightly off-key baritone.

He led with his fist, like he was pounding out meat along with the glory.

******

Sunday, 10 a.m.

Eric slept fitfully in the oven-hot cab of his truck, caught in an old, familiar dream: Cornered shadows wore strange faces and had many limbs that searched for him in the night and then curled back into the blackness. The dark thing howled and then it exploded.

He woke with a start at the sound of a scream. He wasn't sure if the sound was real or part of his dream, and then he heard it again: a limpkin, whose blood-curdling calls often terrified the Yankee tourists who came to fish the lake and take home trophies to mount on their walls.

He grabbed the steering wheel, pulled himself upright, and gagged. Every part of his body ached, and he hadn't showered or changed clothes since Friday morning. He reached in the glove compartment and took out a bottle of aspirin, poured four of them into his palm, popped them into his mouth, chewed and swallowed. He immediately stepped out of the truck and vomited blood onto the pavement.

Making his way slowly around the pickup, he surveyed the damage. He'd need help to wire the muffler back up, and he doubted it would come from Sarah after the way he behaved Friday night.

He sat on the running board and pulled on his boots, then limped across the boat ramp to Sarah's houseboat, one hand jammed in his pocket, the other clutching his side. She saw him coming through the tiny window over her sink, and met him at the door.

"You look almost as bad as you smell," Sarah said. "Go back and take a shower, and I'll make you some breakfast."

"I'd be grateful for some coffee," Eric said, sheepishly, then walked behind her toward the bathroom, cupping her chin briefly in his hand as he passed.

When he emerged wrapped in a towel and feeling better, Sarah paled at the sight of his chest, purple from armpit to waist on the right side and branded in the middle. She handed him an old pair of jeans and a clean shirt he'd left there, and walked back to the bathroom to retrieve his dirty clothes. A thin film of blood floated in the toilet, and she flushed it before she walked to the back deck of the houseboat and threw the dirty clothes in a hamper.

"Don't put on the shirt until I dress that burn," she said.

"I doubt I could lift my arm enough to get it on, anyway, Sis," Eric said, as he sipped the hot coffee and started on bacon and eggs and toast.

"What's goin' on, Eric," Sarah asked. "What the hell is goin' on with you?"

Tears streamed down Eric's face, but he just looked at her and didn't answer. As far as he knew, Sarah was the only person still breathing who had ever seen him cry.

"I can't help you, Eric, if you don't tell me what's wrong."

"Maureen and the kids left me," he said. "The old man came and got them, and she says she ain't comin' back."

"What did you do this time?"

He told her the whole story—the cats, the fights, everything.

"You know I ain't never been able to abide no cat since Ma died," he said, at last. "She'd probably still be alive if she hadn't gone lookin' for that damn cat."

"So that's the fault of every cat in the world, Eric?" Sarah said.

"Well, they give you ringworms, too," Eric said. "Never could stand the thought of that. Don't you remember how Ma used to paint us with that old purple medicine and all the kids at school would make fun of us?"

"Well, that wasn't the cat's fault, either, was it?" Sarah said.

"You remember what a pretty little thing Ma was, Sarah? Remember how she taught us to do Irish jigs and reels, and how when she laughed it was like birds singing? I like to think about her like that, instead of, like, you know…dead. Just because of one sorry ol' cat.

"I found that son-of-a-bitch a week later. He was half-starved up in a tree and a 'gator had got one of his back feet. I put him out of his misery; held his head under water till the bubbles stopped."

"Well, Ma wouldn't of wanted him to suffer," Sarah said. "And give it time, Eric. Maureen will probably change her mind and come back, eventually."

The lie soured in her mouth.

"She said I was a drunk just like my Pa, Sarah," Eric said. "I went a little crazy then, I guess, her tellin' me I was like Pa. We had some fights and all, Sis, but I ain't never beat her the way Pa beat Ma. I ain't no rapist like he was, neither. Never even hit my boys before.

"I don't know what come over me, to choke her like that."

Tears filled Sarah's eyes, and she wrapped her arms around Eric's neck.

Her brother's torture was beyond her reach. She could not rub it and make it better. She could not kiss it and make it go away.

She could not save him from himself, as he had once saved her from their father.

He searched for peace, cast appeals for absolution that never came, so he boxed his pain and stored it where it festered and never healed. Then every sorrow that rolled from that dark place would knock him down again.

This fall, Sarah feared, would be his worst. This time his anguish lay unsheathed and hazardous.

"Dyer wouldn't let her come home now, even if she wanted to," Eric said, finally. "He got her and my kids away from me, and he ain't gonna let 'em go."

******

While he ate, Sarah stirred honey into some Vaseline to make an ointment for Eric's chest. When he'd finished his breakfast, she cleaned the burn with peroxide, then applied the ointment and covered it with layers of gauze.

"Bet that's not what you usually do with that stuff," Eric said, grinning.

Sarah slapped him lightly on the arm, and he grabbed her in a bear hug, then grimaced and clutched his ribs.

"You really ought to go get X-rayed, Eric," Sarah said. "I think you've probably got some broken ribs."

"I'll be alright," he said. "They don't do nothing for 'em anyway but tape you up. Learned that at Guadalcanal."

She tried to get her brother to take a nap, but he thanked her for breakfast and said he needed to fix his truck.

"You all I got now, Sis," he said. "I still got you, right?"

"You'll always have me, Eric, even when you act like an asshole."

"Well, everybody needs one a them, Sarah," he said, looking down at his ravaged body. "Everybody needs one."

******

Sunday, 11 a.m.

Tiny Tim Tucker and Rascal Ryan pulled into the marina in Tucker's powder-blue Buick just as Eric walked out of Sarah's houseboat.

"Man, am I glad to see you two here this morning," Eric said, limping toward the two men. "I got a problem with my truck, here, as you can see, and I could sure use some help. Think you could give me a hand here, Tucker?"

"We headed over to the locks to do some fishin', Mr. Eric," Tucker said, hoisting himself from the driver's seat. The Buick rocked and leveled as he stood. "You still here when we get back in a hour or two, I'll see about it."

"How about if I go over to Oneal's there and buy you a big mess a catfish right now?" Eric said. "How'd that do ya'll?"

"We fishin' for fun, sir, not for supper."

"Aw, come on, Tiny, what's it gonna take? I'll pay whatever you say. Won't take you long, but I'm kinda busted up, see? I think I got some broken ribs here, and I need to get myself home.

"How about you, Rascal? You can give a guy a little help, can't you?"

While Rascal secured Eric's muffler to the truck's frame with heavy wire, Tiny Tim used the sledgehammer and crow bar he carried in his trunk to bend the back fender clear of the tire. When they finished the work, Eric offered them each two dollars.

The two men looked at each other, picked up their poles and bait buckets, and walked toward the lake, leaving Eric standing with his money in his hand.

"Well, thanks, then," he called after the fishermen. "I appreciate it."

Rascal leaned forward with his thumb against his nostril and sprayed the tarmac with mucus.

"Uh-huh," he said.

******

The bars were closed on Sunday, and he knew Sarah wouldn't give him liquor, so Eric sat in his truck deciding where to go. He watched Tucker and Ryan descend the far side of the dike until the tip of Ryan's red beach umbrella sank out of sight.

At the end of the pier, a congregation of buzzards circled a discarded mudfish that lay bloating in the sun. Eric watched them prance stiff-legged, bobbing and weaving and jockeying for position, until one of them lowered his leathery head and pounced on the stinking fish, tearing at its belly with talons and beak. He spread his wings blackly and hissed at the competition, but his swagger lasted only until it was challenged, and then the square dance began again.

"Allemande left, then do-si-do," Eric yelled from his seat, clapping and stomping out a beat. "Now, half promenade, and star by the right."

Another pair of backsliders loading their boat for a Sunday outing looked at Eric and then at each other. They shook their heads.

Above the glittering water, the ghost of the moon hung chalked against the depthless blue of a halcyon sky, its reflected light wasted on the day.

"I need a drink," Eric declared, and started the truck.

It was nearly noon.

******

Eric parked his truck across from Lincoln Square in Harlem, close to a group of men seated on orange crates, playing dominos on a plywood board. He got out and leaned back against the door, his left arm wrapped around his bandaged ribcage.

"Any of you boys know where a fella could buy a little hootch this time a mornin'?" Eric said. "I ain't particular about the brand, although I'm partial to Mr. Daniel's whiskey."

The men looked up from the board, but no one spoke.

"C'mon boys, I'll make it worth your while if you help me out here."

"Mr. Eric, nobody sells no liquor on a Sunday in Hendry County," said Nobel Washington, a cousin of Callie's. "It's agin the law, Mr. Eric. You knows that."

"Well, I tell you what, Nobel. You just give me the rest of that fifth you got there by your foot, and I'll bring you enough catfish next weekend to throw a fish fry for the whole damn block."

"Mr. Eric, I ain't tryin' to sass you or nothin', but I declare it don't look to me like you oughta be drinkin' nothin' in the shape you're in, nor drivin' neither, sir."

Nobel fixed his attention on the stalk of sugar cane he had peeled, cutting off rings of the sweet pulp and passing them one at a time to his friends to chew.

"You want a chaw of cane, Mr. Eric?" he said.

Eric pulled his cap down lower over his blackened eye, turned and opened the door to his truck and grinned at Nobel.

"Thank you, Nobel, but I think I'll pass," Eric said. "And I don't recall asking for your opinion on my physical condition.

"Matter of fact, I don't know what the fuck you're talkin' about, boy. I may be a little rough around the edges, as you pointed out, but it ain't nothing a little Johnny Walker or Jack Daniels can't fix right up. So what you say you just give me that bottle, like I asked you, nicely, and I'll hook you up next week with all the catfish you want. Sound like a good deal?"

Nobel Washington could see the shotgun hanging across the top of the cab inside Eric's truck, and he looked back at the three men seated around the domino board in front of him. Each, in turn, met his gaze then dropped his eyes to the game board.

Nobel lifted the fifth of Seagram's by its neck and held it out toward the white man.

"That a boy, Nobel," Eric said. "I knew you'd come to the right decision."

CHAPTER FIFTEEN

The Surprise

Sunday, 10:45 a.m.

Frank Bayle sat on his front porch watching for Peyton Talloway's car to pull into his driveway three doors down. When it did, Frank walked back to the kitchen, bent to a cardboard box on the floor, and dropped something into his deep front pocket. He returned to his chair as Rena waved goodbye to her brother and Vicki stood talking to her cousins, P.J. and Elizabeth.

"I'll come back after dinner and we can play in the fort," Vicki said as they walked toward home. Rena took Vicki's hand and stopped.

"You know, Vicki, your daddy loves you more than anything in this world, even me," she said.

"If that's what love feels like, I can do without it," Vicki said.

"Don't give me attitude, Victoria, and you better not give your daddy any, either. Right now, I bet he's trying to figure out how to say he's sorry, but it's really hard for a man to admit he's wrong. Try to remember that when we get home."

When mother and daughter reached the concrete steps that led to the front porch, they heard a whimper.

"Hush now," Frank said, jiggling the squirming thing in his shirt pocket. "You're supposed to be a surprise."

As the screen door opened, Frank grinned at his sullen-faced daughter.

The puppy clawed its way to the top of his pocket until its chin and tiny, pink-padded paws stuck out the top, and it whimpered again.

"A puppy!" Vicki screamed. "Daddy, you got me a puppy?"

Frank lifted the beagle pup from his pocket and handed it to Vicki, who immediately held it to her nose.

"Oh, Mama, smell its nose! It smells just like a puppy!"

"Well, that would make some sense," Frank said, stroking his daughter's hair.

Rena lifted the puppy to her nose, then held it up and looked at its belly.

"It's a little girl, Vicki," she said, looking at Frank. "That means we'll have to be very careful with her when she's older, so she don't go having a mess of puppies every year."

"Oh, I wouldn't care, Mama, I love puppies!"

Vicki set the puppy on the floor, and she immediately piddled on the linoleum.

"Don't worry, Mama, I'll have her housebroke in no time and she won't be no trouble at all, 'cause I'll take real good care of her."

Vicki ran to the back porch to get the mop and Rena picked up the puppy and looked at Frank.

"You need to apologize to her for the whipping."

"She was whipped so she'd learn to mind," Frank said. "If I said I was sorry for that it would all be for nothing, and it would be a lie."

"The one you're lying to is yourself, Frank Bayle," Rena said. "You were mad because I didn't want to stay in bed with you this morning when we woke up and saw Vicki wasn't there. Now that I think about it, you even *said* she probably went down to Mama's when you tried to pull me back.

"Just tell her you made a mistake, Frank. Do you want her to go through life being afraid of you? Being afraid of men, for that matter, after what happened yesterday?"

Rena looked toward the kitchen and lowered her voice even more.

"She's a smart kid, Frank, and she's nobody's patsy, not even yours."

"What'd you say, Mama?" Vicki asked as she wiped up the puddle.

"I said I thought she looked kind of like a Patsy," Rena said, while the puppy licked her nose.

"Hey, I like that name," Vicki said, taking the puppy from her mother in exchange for the mop. "Let's call her Patsy. I think it suits her, don't you Daddy?"

"It's fine, Vicki," Frank said, glaring at his wife. "Why don't you and me and Patsy here go for a little ride?"

"*Now*, Frank?" Rena asked. "I was just going to start dinner."

"Won't be long," Frank said, ushering his daughter out the door.

******

"Where we going, Daddy?" Vicki said, dodging the puppy's tongue as she spoke, but not assiduously.

"Well, I think the Jiffy Mart stays open till noon on Sunday, and we're going to need some dog food.

"Besides, I wanted to talk to you about this morning."

Vicki sat the puppy in her lap and stuck the end of her little finger in its mouth. It sucked her finger, curled up and promptly fell asleep.

"I don't ever intend to have to give you another whipping, Skipper, you hear me?"

Vicki looked at her father's face in profile, his eyes on the road.

"You didn't *have* to give me that one," she said, and immediately regretted it.

His dark eyes flashed in her direction, and she looked down at the puppy.

"You sassing me, girl?" Frank said. "You forgot it already?"

"No sir. I ain't likely to forget that."

After a while she worked up the courage to speak again.

"But I really don't think I did nothing wrong, Daddy. I been going to Granny's house by myself ever since I learned to ride my bicycle, and I left a note."

"Well, as you learned, notes can get lost. It's not the same as asking permission. We clear on that?"

"But ya'll ain't never said I couldn't go to Granny's house that I can remember, Daddy. How was I supposed to know today was any different?"

Frank pulled into the convenience store and stopped the car.

"You know different now?" he said.

Vicki looked at her father and clutched the sleeping puppy to her chest. For all her life, her father had told her she was the light of his life. Her mother told her that. Others told her that.

She saw no light in his eyes now, only brute authority.

"Yes sir," she said. "I know different now."

Frank reached across the seat and goosed his daughter in the ribs. She shied from his touch, and he turned his head away.

"You learned a hard lesson today, Skipper. Don't you ever forget it."

She never would, because he would remind her of the whipping regularly, and with no hint of regret, until he was an old man.

And even then, she would blanch at the memory.

******

By the time Vicki came back through the door carrying Patsy in one hand and a larger, sturdier cardboard box for a dog bed in the other, Rena had snapped a pan of fresh green beans, put on a pot of rice, and cut up a chicken.

She sprinkled the chicken pieces with salt and pepper and dropped them into a lunch bag with flour, shook the bag, then dropped the floured pieces one at a time into bubbling bacon fat.

"I call the liver," Vicki said, and her father gave her a frown and goosed her in the ribs. This time she giggled.

"OK, here's what I'll do," she said. "I'll split the liver with you, but I get both wings. You guys can have the breasts, since you seem to like them so much."

Frank placed one hand beside his open mouth in make-believe shock, and reached over to squeeze Rena's breast with the other.

Vicki laughed and ran out the back door to show her cousins her new puppy.

"Looks like you two have made up," Rena said, smiling and turning her face up for her husband's kiss.

Vicki stopped short at the edge of the yard, and joy drained from her face as she returned to the porch.

"May I go down to Uncle Peyton's house, Mama?" she said evenly.

Frank looked at Rena and sneered.

"Go ahead, Skipper," he said. "But be back here in fifteen minutes."

"Can't you just whistle for me, Daddy?" Vicki said. "I don't have a watch, you know."

"Really? Well, I guess maybe I'll have to give you your other birthday present early, too."

Frank took a small black plastic box from the top of the chifforobe and handed it to Vicki.

"A Timex! Look Mama, it's got hands that glow in the dark," Vicki said. "What time is it right now, so I can set it?"

"It's quarter to one, and don't wind it too tight or you'll break it," Rena said. "It's not waterproof, either, so be careful."

"Ain't there somethin' else you got to say?" Frank said.

"Oh, yeah, thank you, guys. Thank you so much!"

"There you go," Frank said to Rena as he pinched an edge off one of last night's biscuits, then walked to the front porch.

"We got any beer left?" he called to Rena after he sat down.

She brought him a glass of sweet iced tea, without comment.

******

Sunday, 1:45 p.m.

Vicki dried and stacked the dishes Rena washed, then covered the gravy bowl and green beans with aluminum foil. She left the rice in the pot because her father enjoyed pouring milk over the scorched grains in the bottom and scraping it out for a late-night snack.

"If I had some better pots and pans, maybe I wouldn't always scorch the rice," Rena said.

"I like it that way, so what's the use?" Frank said.

Vicki stood in front of the Frigidaire with the door open and studied the arrangement of foodstuffs like a puzzle.

"I don't think I can fit all this in here," she said.

"I'll do it, baby. You take daddy more ice for his tea, then you can take Patsy out for a pee."

"You made a poem, Mama," Vicki said, grinning.

"What are you talking about?"

"You take daddy more ice for his tea, then you can take Patsy out for a pee. It rhymes."

"Lord sakes, the things that go through your mind. If you don't turn out to be a writer, it sure will be a waste of imagination."

Vicki echoed her father's favorite expression: "There you go."

Vicki could count to a hundred and recite her ABCs at age three. She could read Mother Goose books and write in cursive at age five, when her mother enrolled her in first grade by changing the date on her hospital birth certificate. She had been writing stories and poems—sometimes strangely dark ones—since she was six years old. She made straight A's in school, except for math, which she hated, and she sometimes received a "Needs Improvement" on comportment, for failure to stay quietly seated.

Two weeks into fourth grade, the Bayles received a note from Vicki's teacher:

Dear Parents,

I am concerned that the homework assignment Vicki turned in yesterday may have been copied from some outside source, or that she had it written for her by a third party.

She was supposed to write an original poem. (The poem in question is attached.)

Needless to say, both the style and content of this poem are beyond the capabilities of an eight-year-old child.

She denies that she did not write it, so I'd like you to talk to her about it, forthwith. I will withhold her grade until I hear from you. (See attachment.)

Sincerely,
Mrs. Alice Right

ROAD KILL
By Victoria Leigh Bayle

I saw a buzzard on the road
Beside the carrion he craved.
Just yesterday, someone, I bet,
Had watched him soar and pirouette
Above the drifting cumulus
And envied him.
But now he lies there in a heap,
His feathers crushed and talons stiff.
His fearsome beak's a useless tool.
You wonder what his friends will do
When they drop in?
They'll eat him, fool.

Frank Bayle replied promptly:

Dear Teacher,

Vicki wrote the poem in question during a trip last summer after we came upon a hog killed by the roadside.
We had just finished reading J.R.R. Tolkien's "The Hobbit" and Lewis Carroll's "Alice in Wonderland." Her head, therefore, was no doubt filled with fancy.
We keep a small dictionary and a pocket-sized edition of Roget's Thesaurus in the car so that Vicki can look up the spelling or meaning of words with which she is unfamiliar. If she doesn't have a book to read, Vicki will quite often "read" the Thesaurus, "for its music." She says that even the deaf can hear "the melody of words."
A lovely thought, don't you agree?
I think the poem you mention is quite good, even though, technically, she was not yet eight when she wrote it.
Was it the poem itself you disliked, or the fact that she wrote it previously?

*If you would like her to write another, I assure you
she can do so easily. In your presence, if it pleases you. On
any subject you might care to name.
I trust her forthcoming grade will be favorable.*

*Most sincerely,
Mr. Frank Bayle*

When Vicki gave Mrs. Right the note the next day, her teacher made her stay in class at recess.

"You have a lot of books at home, do you, Vicki?"

"No ma'am, I don't have any, except the Bible and the dictionary and a Thesaurus. We gave all my baby books to my little cousin, Beth. And Daddy says why buy books when you can read 'em for free from the liberry? That's what we pay our taxes for."

"The library."

"Yes ma'am, the library. I usually get books from the bookmobile, though, because Miss Tanner at the liberry… I mean, lib*rary* is always making me put stuff back and telling me to pick books from the children's section."

"You don't like those books?"

"Well, yes ma'am, I like 'em OK, but I read most of 'em already."

"You've read all the books in the children's section of the library?"

"Well, not all of them, I guess, but all the ones I liked the look of, like *Black Beauty* and *Heidi* and *Doctor Dolittle* and…"

"Victoria, how many books would you say you've read this year?"

Vicki stopped and thought, and counted on her fingers.

"Mr. Goodenow in the bookmobile, he made me a list of books he thought I might like, so I been working on them…on those books lately. I'd say, maybe fifty?"

"This is September, Victoria. You've read fifty books since January?"

"I'd have to get Mr. Goodenow to look 'em up, Mrs. Right, but I think that's pretty close. I usually get three at a time, and the bookmobile comes ever two weeks. But we went to Bradenton beach for a week this summer and I didn't have a thing to read, 'cause Mama wouldn't let me take my library books to the beach. I just had to read her ol' movie magazines and make do, like she said."

"What are you reading now, if I might ask?"

"Oh, sure. I'm reading *A Tale of Two Cities.*"

"Really?" Mrs. Right asked, adjusting her glasses. "How does that book begin, do you recall?"

"Oh, yes ma'am," Vicki said, smiling. "It was the best of times, it was the worst of times, it was the age of wisdom, it was the age of foolishness... I just love that, don't you, Mrs. Right?"

The teacher turned her back to Vicki and looked at the ghosts of lessons past still visible on the blackboard.

"Do you also write a lot of poems, Vicki?" she asked.

"Yes ma'am. It started as a car game when I was about four, I reckon. My daddy would say one line, and I'd make up the next, like that. It was just to keep me from gettin' bored or carsick. Then, I don't know, I just started writin' them by myself."

"May I read some of these other poems?"

"Well, I don't have any of 'em on me, but I could say some for you."

"You could recite them for me?"

"Yes, ma'am, I guess I could recite one."

"Please."

Vicki stood beside her desk and cleared her throat.

"I ain't very good at recitin' 'cause it makes me nervous," she said, "but I got one about a tree. And I got a lot of poems about birds, because I watch 'em when I ain't...when I haven't got anything to read. Can I... *may* I write one on the blackboard instead of reciting it?"

"Please do, Victoria."

THE PLAY TREE
By Victoria Leigh Bayle

I have a tree that plays with me,
It whispers in my ear,
And bids me climb into its arms,
And tells me not to fear.
The play tree rocks me back and forth,

Up high, where no one sees,
Until at last the game is done,
And then it lets me be.

"You wrote that?" Mrs. Right said, when Vicki replaced the chalk and turned around.

"Yes ma'am," Vicki said. "It ain't…it isn't one of my best poems, but they don't always have to rhyme all the way through, you know."

"Yes, I know that. Did you ever write a poem about a crow?"

"No ma'am, not yet. I don't care much for crows, but I guess they got their place in the world."

"They do indeed, Victoria. Could you write a poem, now, about a crow?"

"May I use the dictionary?"

"Yes, Victoria, you may use the dictionary."

******

Vicki came home from school that day with a note from Mrs. Right:

Dear Mr. Bayle,

I did as you suggested, and asked Vicki to write a poem about a crow. (The new poem is attached for your review.) She received an A for the new poem and the previous one, and I am recommending she be placed in an advanced class for creative writing.

I also suggest that she attend a remedial speech therapy class, however, as she needs to learn to speak proper English, as well as to write it.

Yours truly,
Mrs. Alice Right

ELEGY
By Victoria Leigh Bayle

The dove mourns from an empty nest
Where late her naked chicks
Left bloodstained shells
And took to air.
They had no need for feathers there,
Encased in claw, aloft,
On other wings transported,
Then torn apart.
Nor did they scream, nor draw a breath,
But fed the glistening crows,
Who feasted calling, "Caw, caw,"
With guiltless hearts.
Frank read the note that night and smiled at his daughter.
"There ain't nothin' wrong with the way you talk, Skipper."

CHAPTER SIXTEEN

The Shooting

Sunday, 2 p.m.

By the time Eric skidded to a stop in front of Phillip's Gas Station, he was already drunk. He pulled right, then backed alongside the building next to a high cedar hedge, knocking over the three large trashcans at the back of the alley.

His broken ribs throbbed, but his heart ached more.

Startled by the sound of the metal trashcans being thrown against the side of the building, Phillip Townsend ran from his apartment at the back of the station and stopped dead in his tracks when he saw Eric's truck.

Eric downed the remainder of the whiskey, then tossed the empty bottle out the window, where it hit among the scattered garbage and shattered.

Townsend ducked back behind the station and waited a moment before returning to his home. He locked the door behind him and sat down beside his telephone. When he picked it up, he could hear conversation on the party line.

"Wilma, I'm sorry to interrupt, but I need to place a call," he said into the mouthpiece.

"Well, I'm talking to my sister in town right now, Phillip, but we'll be done in just a couple of minutes."

"Wilma, it's an emergency. I need to call the sheriff."

"Oh, for heaven's sake. Helen, I'll call you back directly."

******

"Well, Mr. Townsend, if I understand you correctly, you want me to call for a deputy on a Sunday because someone spilled your garbage?" the sheriff's dispatcher asked after Townsend explained his situation.

"It's not just that," Townsend said. "Eric Magruder is sitting here on my property drinking whiskey and I want him gone."

"Did you ask him to leave?" the dispatcher said.

"Hell no, I didn't ask him to leave. He's got a shotgun in the cab of his truck and he's drunk, I told you."

"There's no call for cussing, Mr. Townsend, and half the pickup trucks in Hendry County have a shotgun holder in the cab. I'm just trying to figure out whether or not this is a law enforcement problem, since, A) all he's done is spill some garbage, and B) he's parked where customers at your establishment routinely park, in an area that is not posted, and you have not yet even asked him to leave. Does that about sum it up?"

"Listen, you, you better call the deputy sheriff out here right now, or I'm telling you, there's going to be trouble."

"I'm sorry, Mr. Townsend, but Deputy Lloyd is on his way to Goodno. Somebody shot and butchered one of Ralph Raines' heifers last night, and that *is* a matter for law enforcement. I'll tell the deputy about your call, but I don't think he's going to be there any time soon. Maybe Mr. Magruder will just sit there and sleep it off."

"His own driveway ain't a hundred yards away from here, lady. He's waiting for his wife to come get her things. I know that's what he's doing, and I know damn well there's gonna be trouble when that happens."

"He's absolutely right about that, honey," said Wilma Dunn, who was listening in on the party line.

******

Sunday, 2:30 p.m.

Phillip Townsend walked around the far side of his filling station, crossed in front of Eric's truck, and stopped about 10 yards away.

"What's going on, Eric?" he said. "How come you to pull in here and spill my garbage like that when your own house is right over yonder?"

Eric leaned over the steering wheel and moaned.

"I'm sorry about your garbage, Phillip, but I swear to God I ain't in no condition right now to pick it up. I'd also advise you not to give me any lip about it right now, 'cause I ain't in the fuckin' mood, you got that?"

"You better just go on home and sleep it off, Eric, 'cause the law is on the way."

Eric lifted his head and glared at Townsend, who walked swiftly back the way he came. As he turned the corner, he saw Randolph Dyer's truck pass by and pull into the Magruder driveway.

Within the hour, he would place another call to the Hendry County Sheriff's Office. This time, he would have the dispatcher's full attention.

******

Sunday, 3 p.m.

Vicki lay prone, her pillow tucked under her chest, and made the world spin on its refurbished stand at the head of her bed. She laughed as Patsy danced back and forth, snapping at the whirling clouds and oceans and trying to stay the movement of continents with one small white paw.

"No, no, don't you scratch my globe," Vicki said, gently pulling the puppy back to her face where she was rewarded with licks and a nip on the nose. "Ow, now, no biting either! Boots woulda slapped your face if you'd a done that to him, but I bet you'd a learned real quick not to get fresh, wouldn't ya? I bet you and me and Boots woulda had the most fun ever."

"So Mr. Hooker gave you a globe, did he?" Frank said as he sat down beside Vicki.

"Well, somebody he knows was throwing it away because the stand was broke, but he fixed it for me," Vicki said, avoiding eye contact.

Frank pointed to some of the places he'd seen during his stint with the U.S. Navy: the South China Sea and the Coral Sea, the Indian Ocean, the islands of Java and Sumatra and the Philippines.

"It's a big old beautiful world out there, Skipper," he said. "I hope you get to see some of it one day, but not because of a war."

Frank whistled his favorite tune, "Faraway Places," while he sat on the front porch cleaning out his tackle box, and a paper cup on the porch ledge blossomed with rusty hooks and rotted leads. He cut slits into lead sinkers with his pocketknife, the one he always warned Vicki was "sharp as a razor." On top of the neat line of boxed lures, between his prized Dixie Bait Darter and his Bubble Dancer, Frank wedged his .38 revolver, then closed the lid.

"Hey Skipper, come here a minute," he said. "Put this in the chifforobe, and don't drop it."

"I can't reach the top of the chifforobe, Daddy," Vicki said, putting the puppy down and taking the tackle box.

"Just put it in the bottom, by my shoes," Frank said.

"You going fishin', Daddy?" Vicki said.

"I might later on, if it don't rain. Wanta come? You could go out there and dig me some worms."

Vicki looked at her father and knew he was mocking her.

"I'd rather stay here and play with Patsy, thank you."

Frank propped his feet on the porch ledge and began reading the Sunday edition of the *Palm Beach Daily News*. Vicki sat at his feet with the funny papers he offered her, trying to keep the puppy at bay long enough to read *Mary Worth* and *Archie*.

When she heard a door slam next door, Vicki looked out the window, past the Kaiser, and saw Randolph Dyer's truck parked in the driveway of the Magruder house. She picked up the puppy and stood up.

"Hey, Mama? Maureen's come home, but I don't see the boys…"

Rena came from the kitchen and stood just inside the bedroom door with her arms crossed at her waist and her face filled with concern. She motioned for Vicki to come to her, then kneeled and placed one hand on each side of her child's face.

"I want you to take Patsy and go out the back door and down to your Uncle Peyton's house," Rena said in a whisper. "You stay there until I come to get you."

"Why? What's the matter?"

"Go now, Vicki, I think there may be trouble next door."

Vicki dropped the puppy in her cardboard box and did an end run around her mother to stand at her father's side, his right arm encircling her, while the puppy scratched and whimpered for freedom. Her mother protested her disobedience briefly, and then the house grew quiet as the Bayles were transfixed by what they saw.

At the corner gas station sat Eric Magruder's dark green pickup, the afternoon sun glinting on the windshield and thick gray smoke belching from the broken exhaust pipe as the engine revved.

Maureen Magruder hurried down her front steps carrying a cardboard box filled with clothes and dropped it into the bed of her father's truck. Her father followed with a second box, and Maureen started back to help him carry it when she heard Eric gunning his engine. She spun in place and ran back to the truck, yelling for her father to hurry.

"What's goin' on, Daddy?" Vicki whispered, searching her father's face, then following his gaze up the street. Frank's feet remained braced against the rail, but the newspaper slid slowly from his lap and scattered its politics and advertising supplements across the linoleum.

He pushed his wife and daughter back into the doorway.

"Go bring me my tackle box, Skipper," he said, his eyes glued to the green pickup that lurched forward in short bursts. "Go get it, now!"

Vicki started to move, but then she saw Mr. Dyer throw the box he carried into the back of his truck and start back toward the driver's side as Eric's truck began fishtailing toward him, tires squealing.

She saw the old man throw up one arm and run forward, as if he could forestall the speeding truck with some preternatural force of will, like Superman at the picture show, and then Eric's truck swerved and slammed head-on into the side of Dyer's truck where Maureen sat, her arms likewise positioned to avert a blow.

Leona Talloway heard the crash from her front porch nearly a mile away, and she wondered if there had been another accident on State Road 80. A van full of Mexican bean pickers was T-boned by an insurance salesman from South Bay just the day before. Ten people had burned to death in that awful wreck, and two more were in critical condition, both just children.

When she heard the shots that followed the crash, Leona wished fervently that people would not target practice against the dike so close to where people lived.

Especially not on a Sunday.

******

The force of the impact spun Dyer's truck a quarter turn and shoved it against the rear of the blue-gray Kaiser in the Bayles' driveway, rutting its wheels sideways through the muck.

Eric's truck spun out and ended up facing the way it came, the two trucks' rear bumpers locked together like scowling dogs mating. The metallic sound of their coupling echoed to a halt in a shroud of dust, and filled the windows of houses all around with startled neighbors.

Maureen's head left a bloody web on the windshield, and her right shoulder protruded oddly in front, the right elbow askew as well. She slumped semi-conscious toward the driver's seat.

Vicki could hear her mother screaming from the back of the house for her to come, but she could not move or take her eyes from Eric, who sat gripping his steering wheel, which was aberrantly high and bent. Blood ran from a crescentic cut above his right eye, and after a moment, he blinked and wiped his face with his shirttail.

As soon as he moved, Rena began yelling for Frank to leave, pulling at his sleeve and pushing Vicki behind her.

"He's coming after you, Frank," Rena screamed. "We have to get Vicki out of here!"

Both of them shook her off, and then suddenly, she was running for help out the back door and across the fallow field. It was a while before she realized the nearest phone was in the opposite direction, and that somewhere in the field, she had stepped on glass or something sharp and her bare feet were bleeding.

"Vicki!" she screamed and ran back to the house and up the back steps, leaving a trail of bloody footprints.

By the time she reached the bedroom, Rena could see Eric emerging slowly from his truck. He staggered around its crumpled front to the back of the Kaiser and stood looking at Dyer. There was no way for the two men to reach each other except around the front of the car.

Frank sat up straight in his chair and, without taking his eyes from Eric, swept the air behind him for his daughter.

"Vicki," he whispered. "Where's my tackle box?"

Vicki stood at the edge of the door, just out of reach, the open tackle box at her feet.

Randolph Dyer stared at his son-in-law, then opened the driver's side door of his truck and gently leaned his daughter's head back against the seat. He called her name and she moaned in response, and then he stood, placing his hand briefly against his head before reaching beneath the seat.

He pulled out a long-barreled semi-automatic pistol, released the safety, and held the gun at his side.

Rena screamed again when she saw the gun, and civic-minded neighbors who were running toward the wreck stopped in their tracks and retreated.

Vicki fought again to free herself from her mother's grasp and whispered Eric's name. He did not take his eyes from his father-in-law.

"Well, old man," he said, "it looks like we're about to have a showdown."

"No, Eric, we're not," Dyer said, "because I'm going to kill you."

Eric jerked off the cap he wore and motioned to his head.

"Oh yeah? Well, put one right here, Randolph."

Dyer lifted the gun toward Eric and pulled the trigger. There was a hollow-sounding snap, and panic spread like the shadow of a cloud across Dyer's face.

Eric laughed and replaced his cap. He took a step forward, leaning on the side of the Kaiser with one hand wrapped round his chest inside his shirt.

Dyer pulled the trigger again and there was a deafening explosion. Eric grinned, and his shirt brightened about the left shoulder.

"Your aim ain't very good, old man," Eric said, leaving bloody handprints down the side of the Kaiser as he advanced toward the Bayles' front door.

"Well, well, well, look who's here," Eric said. "If it ain't my ol' buddy, Frank. I could cut you in on a little of this action, neighbor."

Vicki screamed Eric's name then, and he looked at her and smiled.

His eyes were locked on Vicki's when the next two bullets hit, one in the chest and another in his right arm. Vicki covered her nose with one hand at the smell of gunpowder. Her eyes stung, but she could not close them or look away.

Eric looked down and blew blood from the wound on his arm, and shrugged his shoulders.

Randolph Dyer had not moved from the spot where he stood when he fired the first shot, but his hand had begun to shake with the weight of the German Mauser he held at arm's length.

Eric ripped open the front of the shirt he wore.

"Put one right here, Randolph," he said, pointing to his bandaged chest, "and let's get this thing over with."

Dyer pulled the trigger again, and Eric stopped and coughed, then took another step forward.

Each step he took met a bullet, until he stopped, leaned back on the front of the Kaiser and held out his hand.

"OK, Randolph, you win," Eric said. "Let's shake on it."

"No, you son-of-a-bitch, I've got one more bullet, and if it takes it, I'll use it."

Eric bent over and put his hands on his knees, but he did not fall.

"No sir," he said, "I don't think that will be necessary."

He turned and staggered toward his truck, bloodying the grass along the way. When he reached for the passenger-side door of his truck he crumpled to the ground.

******

Sheriff Clyde Petrie, who was enjoying a family outing at Fish Eating Creek 35 miles away, would not arrive at the scene of the Magruder shooting until three hours after the fact. An off-duty jailer was sent to fetch him, since he'd left his radio-equipped car parked at the jail.

In an uncommon display of acumen, Deputy Oscar Lloyd meticulously photographed the crime scene before Magruder's body was moved from the position in which he landed, on his side in a cove formed by the three vehicles.

The deputy also took a brief statement from Maureen Magruder before she was transported to the hospital in Belle Glade in the same ambulance Tom Spooner would later use to take Eric's body to the Hendry County Medical Examiner's Office. At the time, with Hendry

General Hospital just under construction, the medical examiner worked from a windowless, refrigerated room in the back of the Clewiston Funeral Chapel and Crematorium.

Along the street as the sheriff approached the wreck, Hooker's Point Road was lined with bevies of agitated people gesturing and recreating the drama for those who were not present earlier.

The sheriff pulled up behind the ambulance, got out, and stopped to light a cigar before he walked up beside his deputy.

"What a mess," Petrie said, looking down at the bullet-riddled body of Eric Magruder. "How many times was he shot?"

"Well me and Tom, we counted nine holes we could see," Lloyd said. "Don't know which is which, you know, entrance or exit.

"The gun I took off Randolph Dyer over there is a Model 1916 German Mauser, holds eight 9-mm rounds, any one of which oughta of knocked the sum-bitch down. There was one round left in the clip."

"I reckon whiskey makes a pretty good anesthetic," the sheriff said. "You talked to Dyer or any of the other witnesses yet?"

"Just the wife, Sheriff, but she was banged up fairly good."

"Alright, then, here's what I need you to do. Go down to the store and call the Palm Beach County Sheriff's office in Belle Glade and ask 'em if they can spare us a couple of guys. We're gonna need some help taking statements on this one.

"Then, you come back here and start with Frank Bayle and his family there, since they likely seen the whole thing. I'm gonna go set on the steps with Randolph and see what he has to say."

The sheriff placed his hat on his knee when he sat down beside Randolph Dyer, a man he'd known and respected all his life.

"Where'd you get the gun, Randolph?" Petrie asked.

"Eric gave it to me years ago, Clyde," Dyer said, dropping his head and shaking it side to side. "He brought it back with him from Germany. Said he took it off a dead Nazi."

"You usually carry it in your truck, do you?"

"No, Clyde. I never had it in my hand before today, not since the day I hung it on the wall at my house."

"How come you to bring it with you today, sir?"

"I figured I might need it, Clyde. Turns out, I did."

******

As Deputy Oscar Lloyd approached the Bayles' front door, Frank turned and picked up the tackle box, set it on the floor beside his chair and pushed it into the corner with his foot. Vicki had taken her whining puppy out the back door, and Rena stood beside her husband, one hand on his shoulder and the other on her chest, as if preparing to say the Pledge of Allegiance. Lloyd carried a lined spiral notebook of the type used by school children in one hand and his county-issued straw hat in the other.

There was no need to knock.

CHAPTER SEVENTEEN

The Investigation

Monday, 8 a.m.

Sheriff Clyde Petrie took a large key ring from a pegboard across from the four-celled jail and unlocked the barred door that confined Randolph Dyer. Dyer sat on the edge of the cot with his head in his hands as he had all through the night, except for brief periods of pacing.

Opal Petrie entered with a tray loaded with biscuits and scrambled eggs, a bowl of fresh fruit and an insulated pitcher of coffee, placed it on a small table next to the cot, and exited without speaking.

"We got a call from the state attorney in Fort Myers, Randolph," the sheriff said as he locked the cell behind his wife. "He says there'll be a grand jury hearing as soon as he can arrange it. You'll have a bail hearing before the circuit judge at 4:30 this afternoon, so we'll have to drive over to LaBelle for that.

"Now, the wife has made you a fine breakfast there. When you're done with it, I'll come back and bring you a razor so you can get cleaned up. I'm sending Oscar over to your house to get you a clean shirt for the hearing.

"Your wife is looking after the grandkids, and I think they're going to let Maureen come home from the hospital today. She had a mild concussion, a broken collarbone and her right arm was broke, but all things considered, she's a lucky gal. Could of been a lot worse.

"Oh, and your lawyer—that Cohen guy from West Palm—he called and said he'd meet with you in LaBelle before the hearing."

"What kind of bail will they ask for, Clyde?" Dyer said.

"I really don't know," Petrie said. "Depends on what the judge decides, based on the evidence presented to him and your criminal history."

Randolph Dyer dropped his hands to his knees and looked at the sheriff.

"I ain't never even got a speeding ticket, Clyde, and you know it."

"Well then, I wouldn't worry too much about it."

"Not worry? How the hell am I supposed to make *any* kind of bail stuck in here? I need to go see about my store and I need to go to the bank."

"And you know I can't just let you out, Randolph, after you shot a man seven times in front of a dozen or so witnesses in broad daylight. Just eat your breakfast now and we'll take it one step at a time."

"We?" Dyer said. "What the hell do you mean, we? I don't see anybody in this jail cell but me."

The breakfast remained untouched except for the coffee until the janitor came to retrieve the tray. Willie Richards carried the tray out the back door, sat down on an orange crate and relished every bite. He didn't mind a bit that the food was cold.

******

Monday, 9 a.m.

Above a large wall-mounted refrigeration unit in the back of Tom Spooner's mortuary was a gold-lettered sign:

HIC LOCUS EST UBI MORS GAUDET SUC CURRERE VITAE

This is the place where death rejoices to help those who live.

The cooler's frosted vent tousled mists that hung a few feet below the ceiling, and the faint sound of organ music leaked in with a fog of warmer air as Spooner entered the room. He wore white overalls, clear rubber boots, a white cloth mask and shower-type hair covering.

Spooner served as the diener for all autopsies performed at his establishment, for which the county paid him a fee, in addition to the rental of the space. It was his job to photograph the body in detail, before and after he undressed and washed the subject, and to otherwise assist Dr. Paul Enderson, the medical examiner, during the autopsy.

Spooner wheeled the sheet-covered body of Eric Magruder from a corner to a spot in the center of the room under a phalanx of bright lights and waited for Enderson to begin, his gloved hands clasped in front of him.

Clothed similarly to Spooner, the medical examiner also wore a black rubber apron and goggles. He nodded at Spooner, then spoke into a microphone that hung from the ceiling, noting the identifying features of the body. A reel-to-reel tape recorder hummed as it captured his comments.

"This is a white, uncircumcised male, six feet tall, 172 pounds, black hair, and, um, blue eyes, who is missing the tip of the little finger on his left hand. He has a tattoo of an eagle with an American flag on his right bicep, and extensive scarring on the front and…yes, front and back of the left thigh. He also has six, no, seven fairly uniform scars, each about four centimeters long, starting just below his rib cage on the right and ending just above the pubic bone on the left," Enderson said, before reaching up to turn off the mike.

"You know if this guy is a veteran?" he asked Spooner. "Those look like shrapnel wounds to me."

"Yeah, he was a highly decorated Marine. Earned a Purple Heart in the Battle of Normandy and the Silver Star at Iwo Jima."

"Made it through all that and then got gunned down like a dog in the street after a domestic dispute?"

"Well, there was a little more to it than that."

Enderson pulled the mike back down and began cataloging Eric's bullet wounds as entry or exit, describing their size, location, and the angle of trajectory of each. He reached up and turned the mike off again.

"Was there more than one shooter?" Enderson asked.

"No, not that I know of," Spooner said.

"Did the shooter have more than one gun?"

"Not that I know of. Why?"

"Well, one of these entry wounds—this one right here, just above the heart—looks different from the others. See how cleanly defined the edges of this wound are, compared with this one here, or this one in the shoulder? And see here, the ovoid shape, beveled at the bottom, suggests a downward trajectory, left to right. Weren't these guys facing each other on the ground?"

"That's what I thought."

"Was the body X-rayed before it was brought here?"

"No sir, there didn't seem to be any need, according to the sheriff. There were over a dozen witnesses who said Randolph Dyer did the shooting, and he confirmed that at the scene."

"Hmm," Enderson said, and rolled the body to the right side. "Well, it appears to be a through-and-through, so in the absence of a bullet, there's no way to know for sure. He could have leaned forward and turned away I guess. Damned if I know how he stayed on his feet to begin with.

"Looks like somebody beat this ol' boy up pretty good before they shot him."

Spooner told the medical examiner about the truck wreck that preceded the shooting, and Enderson nodded.

"That doesn't explain the burn," he said.

Enderson noted for the record a 15.24-centimeter second-degree burn to the right of center on Magruder's chest, just below the level of his nipples.

"Its shape suggests it could have been made by an iron of the type used to press clothing. Blunt trauma to the burn area—probably the result of hitting the steering wheel—ruptured the blister, but I'd say this injury occurred, oh, 24 to 36 hours before death."

He recovered two almost pristine 9-mm bullets from the body, three fragments of slugs and one grossly distorted slug that passed through his right lung and lodged against the fifth thoracic vertebra. He determined that at least three other bullets entered and exited Eric Magruder's body.

The medical examiner also noted two fractured ribs underlying massive bruising on the right side, a hairline fracture beneath a large semi-circular cut above the left eye, and after opening the chest, noted a four-centimeter ulcerated esophageal lesion and mild liver damage, both probably attributable to alcohol abuse.

There was a strong odor of alcohol when stomach contents were examined, and the stomach contained undigested food.

******

Monday, 10 a.m.

When recess came, Vicki's classmates swarmed her like honeybees.

Everyone—particularly the boys—wanted to know the gory details of the shooting the whole town was talking about.

"You didn't actually see that man get shot, did you?" said a breathless Sissy Baker.

Vicki lifted her eyebrows and turned her back on Sissy.

"I most certainly did," she said to a group of boys nearby. "It was very bloody, and it was almost like it wasn't really happening, like something out of a picture show."

The gang of boys surrounded her, armed with questions.

"What kind of gun was it? Did the other guy have a gun too? Were you scared?"

"I'm really not supposed to talk about the details, 'cause I may have to testify at a trial," Vicki said, basking in her newfound importance.

"Get outa town!" said Eddie Goodenow.

Eddie, the bookmobile driver's son, was a grade ahead of Vicki in school and he was the boy all the girls swooned over, particularly Sissy Baker.

"Did you see the guy after he died? Did you see his body?"

Vicki took Eddie's hand and pulled him away from the crowd and over to the monkey bars.

"I'll tell you this, but don't you tell anybody else, OK?" she said, conspiratorially. "The guy that got shot was our next-door neighbor, Eric Magruder."

"Patrick Magruder's father?"

"Yeah, I feel real bad for Patrick and Sean, but the day before he got shot, Eric killed my cat. On purpose. So, I wasn't all that sorry he got hisself shot."

"Wow," Eddie said. "That must have been something. I'd have puked for certain if I had seen all that."

"Well, it did make me a little sick to my stomach. But I didn't really want Eric to die, you know, and I had bad dreams about it last night.

Mama said I didn't have to go to school today if I didn't feel like it, but I didn't want to stay there and have to look at all that blood and them wrecked trucks all day.

"Oh, first Eric tried to kill his wife and Mr. Dyer by running into the side of Mr. Dyer's truck at 90 miles an hour, did you hear about that? It pushed Mr. Dyer's truck up against the back of our car, and now the sheriff says we can't move the, um…the vehicles until after the grand jury decides whether or not to, um, to incite Mr. Dyer for first degree murder.

"I don't know exactly what that means, but that's what the sheriff said."

"Cool," Eddie said. "Will you sit next to me in the cafeteria at lunch?"

"Sure," Vicki said, glancing over her shoulder at Sissy Baker, who looked like her head was about to explode. "But Sissy is gonna have a cow."

******

Monday, 10:30 a.m.

Two investigators from the State Attorney's Office circled the crime scene taking measurements and making notes on legal pads. They photographed the interior and exterior of the two trucks and squatted to take a number of photos of the blood-soaked spot where Eric Magruder died.

Someone had tossed Eric's hat down to mark the spot, but it needed no marking.

Armed with metal detectors, they followed behind four trusties from the Glades State Prison Farm who raked the yards in search of bullets or casings. They found a small nick on the left rear-view mirror of the Kaiser that could have been made by a bullet, and they recovered two slugs lodged in Australian pines across the street from the Bayle house, which they bagged and tagged as evidence. They also bagged Eric's hat.

Just before noon, one of the investigators knocked on Rena Bayle's front door.

"Mrs. Bayle, I'm Todd Smythe and this is Harold Sumner of the State Attorney's Office. May we come in for a minute? We just need to ask you a few questions about what you saw yesterday, and what happened here the day before. We'll try not to take up too much of your time."

Rena was suddenly aware of the strong scent of pine oil in the front room, so she asked the men to come through to the kitchen.

"Would you like some coffee?" she asked, motioning for them to sit at the table.

"That's OK, Mrs. Bayle. We don't want to put you to any trouble, unless you've already got some made."

Rena poured them each a cup of coffee, then poured one for herself. She put three teaspoons next to the sugar bowl, took a quart of milk from the refrigerator and set it on the table before she sat down.

"I've already told the sheriff and Deputy Lloyd everything I know," she said. "I don't know why I have to keep saying the same things over and over."

"Well, in a homicide of this nature, we make every attempt to learn all we can about events leading up to the crime," Smythe said. "We prefer not to have any surprises if the case goes to trial. We're going to need to talk to your daughter, as well."

"Well, she already talked to the deputy, too. What more do you want to know?" Rena said.

"Let's start with Saturday morning, and you just tell us everything that happened up to and including the shooting of Eric Magruder."

Rena sighed, and began at the beginning.

When she had finished, Smythe stood and thanked her for her time. Sumner remained seated, flipping back through his notes, then looked at Rena and said, "One thing more, Mrs. Bayle."

"Please call me Rena. Mrs. Bayle is my mother-in-law."

"Very well, Rena, you neglected to mention the fight your husband had with Eric Magruder Saturday afternoon."

"What fight?" Rena said, her face blanching.

"You weren't aware that your husband fought with Eric at the truck stop on the corner of Main Street and Francisco Street at about 5:30 p.m. or so on Saturday? We have several witnesses who heard your husband threaten to kill Eric if he ever came near his family again."

Rena stood quickly, her hand over her mouth, and ran out the back door and into the bathroom. Sumner rose to leave after a few minutes of listening to the sounds of her vomiting.

"We'll come back later, Mrs. Bayle, when you're feeling better," he said, loudly. "I understand how upsetting this all must be."

Before they exited, Smythe took pictures of a small hole in the front screen door and of the ladder-backed chair that nearly filled the south side of the tiny porch. A tackle box lay on the floor beside the chair, and Sumner looked over his shoulder into the house before squatting to flip its lid back with the end of his pen.

He noted nothing unusual about the box of fishing tackle, and flipped the lid closed again before they left.

******

Monday, 11:30 a.m.

Frank Bayle had just punched his time card when he saw two men approaching the sugar company machine shop wearing snub-nosed revolvers in cross-draw holsters on their belts.

"I get off at four," he said to the man extending a hand in his direction. "You have questions for me, come back then. Right now, I'm on a lunch break."

"That's OK," Smythe said. "You can eat while we talk. It won't bother us."

"Well, it'll bother me," Bayle said. "I only get half an hour."

"You can talk to us here, or you can talk to us down at the jail," Sumner said.

"I got nothing to say I didn't already tell the sheriff."

"Did you tell the sheriff that you had a gun in your lap when Eric Magruder got shot?" Smythe said.

"Why would I tell the sheriff something that's not true, whatever your name is?" Bayle said. "Not that I give a shit what you think."

Frank sat down at a picnic table in the shade of a pair of bow-legged sabal palms that shunned each other for the sun. He popped the key from the top of a can of sardines, inserted it in the tab and carefully rolled back the lid.

Both Sumner and Smythe noticed that he did so with his left hand.

Frank used a saltine cracker to lift one of the tiny fishes out of the can and put the whole thing in his mouth.

Smythe's lip curled at the smell. He hated sardines.

"We have a statement to that effect from your daughter, and Todd Smythe is my name. This is Harold Sumner and we're from the State Attorney's Office."

"Well, you're a liar, Mr. Smith," Bayle said, chewing, as he spoke. "That is not what Vicki said. It so happened that I cleaned out my tackle box yesterday, and that just happens to be where I sometimes keep my gun. Vicki saw it there Sunday morning. That's what she said. Maybe you need to take a remedial reading course."

"There's no gun in the box now, and my name is Smythe, not Smith."

"You two been snooping around my house?" Bayle said, a sardined cracker halting in mid-air on the way to his mouth.

"Not at all. We just went to take a statement from your wife about the shooting, and I noticed the box was open next to the chair on your porch. Your daughter—Vicki, isn't it?—yes, Vicki is not the only one who says you had a gun in that box yesterday. Your neighbor, Rachel Padgett, said she saw a gun there, also."

"Listen, you pricks, you don't talk to my daughter without my permission, you got that?" Bayle said, becoming more agitated.

"We don't need your permission to talk to an eyewitness of a homicide, Mr. Bayle. And judging by her statements, your daughter appears to be an unusually bright and articulate little girl. She might turn out to be the star witness in this case."

"That's it," Bayle said, emptying the can of sardines about an inch in front of Smythe's spit-shined shoes. "This conversation is over."

"Not quite. You see, Frank, the autopsy suggests that a weapon of smaller caliber than the one used by Randolph Dyer might have made at least one, if not more of Eric Magruder's bullet wounds. What kind of handgun did you have in that tackle box, Frank?"

"I *own* a .38 revolver, Mr. Smith, and like I said, this conversation is officially over. Now."

"I just have one more question, Frank," Sumner said. "When was the last time you fired your gun and where is it now?"

"That's two questions, and unless you have a warrant, you can kiss my ass."

Bayle rose and stomped back into the darkened maw of the machine shop, and the two investigators looked at each other.

"This is getting more and more interesting," Smythe said.

CHAPTER EIGHTEEN

Suspicion

Monday, 4 p.m.

By the time the school bus groaned to a stop in front of Hooker's General Store, dread had replaced Vicki's childish braggadocio. She sat, holding on to the seat in front of her, her head propped on the backs of her hands.

"Vicki?" the bus driver called, looking in her big rear-view mirror. "Are you getting off here or down at your grandmother's house?"

"Here," Vicki said, lifting her head and looking down the street toward the clot of cars and trucks in front of her house. "I have to get off here."

The bus driver waited, but the child didn't move.

"Well?"

"I'm comin'," Vicki called, and more softly, "just hold your horses."

She gathered her books and her Wonder Woman lunch pail and made her way down the aisle past the nasty Chaplin boys who always snapped the elastic on her panties or pinched her butt as she passed by—especially when both her hands were full and they thought they could get away with it.

This time, when Waylon Chaplin pulled up her shirt and stuck his hand down the back of her shorts she dropped her books and swung her lunch pail back-handed, catching Waylon off balance and landing a blow on his shoulder that sent him sprawling in the aisle.

"I'll get you for that," he said, over the laughter of the dozen or so students left on the bus.

Vicki walked backwards up the aisle, scooting her books ahead of her with her heel.

"You better keep your hands off me, mister, or I'll tell my Daddy and he'll shoot you," Vicki said.

Suddenly, she was aware of the bus driver and a couple of older students staring at her.

"Waylon's always messin' with me, Mrs. Applegate, and I'm right tired of it."

Vicki changed direction a few yards in front of the bus and walked toward Hooker's store. The core of an apple sailed past her head as the bus pulled away, but Vicki didn't look back at the Chaplin boys, who stuck their heads out the half-lowered filthy windows and hollered. As the bus neared the Holy Ghost Assembly of God Church, Vicki saw it pull into the semi-circular driveway and stop. Soon, the Chaplin boys fell quiet, and the bus pulled back on the road and on to its next stop. Mrs. Applegate kept a wooden paddle beneath her seat with which to remind students that she did not tolerate such rowdiness on her bus.

Vicki sat on the backless bench in front of the store and steeled herself for what she'd see when she got home. Reed Hooker spotted her there, her blonde curls filling one of the Os in the sign on his window, and his cleaver stopped in midair. After a moment, he slammed the blade against a standing rib roast and cleanly felled a steak.

Vicki rose and walked around the far side of the store and cut through her neighbors' back yards to reach her house, where she unloaded her school-day trappings on the edge of the porch. She was about to call out to her mother when she heard voices she didn't recognize coming from the front of the house.

"She should be home any minute now, but I don't want her upset, do you hear?" she heard her mother say.

Vicki eased the screen door open, lifted her jubilant puppy from her cardboard prison, and slipped outside again. She ran behind the clotheslines all the way to her Uncle Peyton's house before she put the puppy down in the grass.

"Go find a pee like a good girl," she said. "And find a poop, too, if you can."

******

Todd Smythe and Harold Sumner stood on the front steps of the Bayle house, talking to Rena through the screen door. Both men noticed that the screen was now ripped from the top of the hole Smythe had photographed earlier to the center brace of the door.

"Mrs. Bayle, when did you last see your husband?" Smythe said.

"He came home just after lunch to get a tool he forgot, but he was only here for a minute or two," Rena said. "Why do you ask?"

"How did he get here, since his car is in the driveway?"

"He rode to work with my brother-in-law. I guess he borrowed his car. I was washing clothes out back, so I didn't really pay much attention."

"Mrs. Bayle, do you know where your husband's handgun is?" Sumner said.

"No, I do not," Rena said, "and please call me Rena."

"You know that he owns a handgun, but you don't know where he keeps it? Even in a house this small and with a young child in the house?"

The comment wasn't meant to be condescending, but Smythe soon realized its impropriety.

"I don't like guns, Mr. Smythe, so I don't pay much attention to them, either. And Vicki was taught as a toddler never to touch her father's guns unless he is with her and she has his permission."

"Please call me Todd, Rena. Your husband has more than one gun?"

"He's a hunter, Todd, as most men are in these parts. He has two shotguns and a rifle hanging right over the door on the wall behind me. He bought the .410 for Vicki to use when he takes her with him to hunt quail or dove, but I doubt she'll ever be a hunter. She can't stand to see anything hurt. But, no, I don't know where the pistol is. That's something you'll have to ask Frank."

"Does he ever keep the handgun in his tackle box that you know of?"

"I've seen it there on occasion," Rena said. "He takes it with him when he goes fishing sometimes—for water moccasins and such."

"Was it in the tackle box yesterday?"

"You'll have to ask my husband that."

"Where is the tackle box now? We noticed it was on the porch earlier."

"You can ask Frank that as well."

"Vicki told Deputy Lloyd that she saw the gun in her father's tackle box yesterday on the porch, just before Eric Magruder was shot."

"She did not! When?" said Rena, her eyes widening with surprise, then narrowing in anger.

"Were you or your husband present the entire time Vicki was being questioned by Deputy Lloyd?"

"Well, no, I went out to talk to Rachel for a minute, and I think Frank went out to speak to Mr. Dyer before they took him away, but the Sheriff wouldn't let him…"

Rena's voice quavered as she realized the men considered Frank a suspect.

"Sir, my husband did not shoot Eric Magruder, if that's what you're implying, and you have no right to plant such an idea in my daughter's mind. She's just a child, and she was very upset by all this violence."

"Ma'am, I haven't even met your daughter yet. I'm just going by what the deputy said. She told the deputy she saw everything; that she was standing right there beside her father the whole time."

"Yes, well, I kept trying to pull her with me out the back door—her father, too—but then, oh, it was just so awful, the whole thing. When I came to myself at one point I was all the way down at my brother's house before I realized that Vicki wasn't with me."

"So, you didn't witness the entire event, then," Smythe said.

"Well, I…no, I guess there was a part of it I didn't see," Rena said. "I wish I hadn't seen what I did, I can tell you that."

Harold Sumner looked at his watch, and then at his partner.

"Is Vicki usually this late getting home from school?" he said. "I just saw the kids across the street walking home from the bus stop."

"I'm sure Vicki will be here any minute. She probably stopped to talk to Mr. Hooker at the store. She does that sometimes."

The sun was a sty in a flatiron sky, and Todd Smythe reached into an inside jacket pocket, took out a carefully pressed handkerchief and wiped his brow.

"Well, I've completely forgot my manners," Rena said. "Would you gentlemen care to come in out of the heat and have some sweet ice tea?"

As soon as she entered the kitchen, Rena saw that Patsy wasn't in her box and Vicki's schoolbooks were on the back porch. She stepped down to the back yard and called her.

Vicki looked up when she heard her name, picked up the puppy and began a slow walk home.

"Hurry up, Vicki," Rena said. "There are some men here who want to talk to you."

"About what?" Vicki said, petulantly, knowing the answer.

"Why didn't you tell me you were home?" Rena said, gaily. "I made some chocolate-chip cookies today. Want a glass of milk and a cookie? It's going to be a while until dinner, but I'm making your favorite—a meatloaf."

"No, thank you. I ain't hungry."

As she entered the back door, Smythe and Sumner stood from where they'd seated themselves at the table, introduced themselves to the child and greeted the puppy attentively.

Vicki was not impressed with their good manners, although she shook their hands politely. Patsy growled and nipped Sumner's finger when he tried to rub her head.

"We need to ask you about what you saw yesterday, Victoria," said Smythe.

"I got homework to do," Vicki said.

"It will only take a few minutes, I promise. And you're not really that eager to do homework, are you? Man, I nearly have to beat… I have to really persuade my son to do his, and sometimes he puts it off until nearly bedtime."

"Well, Mama says the sooner it's done, the sooner it will *be* done."

"Alright then, where were you yesterday when the trouble started next door?"

"What trouble? The wreck or the shootin'?"

"Both."

"Well, I was on the porch with my Daddy for most of it."

"Really? What was your dad doing?"

"He was cleanin' his tackle box, then he was readin' the newspaper."

"Did he say anything to you?"

"Who?"

"Your father."

"He said that Truman had stepped in it again in Korea, and if the price of gas kept goin' up, we'd all be ridin' bicycles. And he asked me if I wanted to read the funnies. I like Archie and Mary Worth."

"You didn't get scared and run away when you saw…when you saw what happened?" Sumner said.

"Well, it was right scary, but no, I didn't run away," Vicki said. "I was mad at Eric 'cause he did somethin' mean to me, but I didn't really want him to get hurt."

"What did Eric do, Vicki?"

"He killed my cat on purpose."

"How did that make you feel?"

Vicki gave the two investigators a look that suggested they might be simple-minded.

"It made me sad, and it made me mad."

"I see," Sumner said, rifling through the yellow sheets of his notepad. "And did you subsequently say to Mr. Reed Hooker that you hoped your father would shoot Eric Magruder for hurting your kitten?"

Vicki looked back at Rena, then down at the floor.

"I said I hoped my Daddy killed him, because I hated him," Vicki said. "But I didn't mean that. My heart was just… I couldn't believe… I was real upset. And I never said nothin' about nobody *shootin'* Eric."

"OK, Vicki," Smythe said. "When you first saw Eric get shot, where were you?"

"I already told you where I was."

"On the porch with your father, right? And did you see the gun in Mr. Dyer's hand?"

"Yes, but then Mama was pulling on me and Daddy kept pushin' me back, but I couldn't seem to move. It's fairly hard to figger, and I've thought about it considerable. It was like one of them dreams where you try to run and your feet are stuck. You ever have one of them dreams?"

"Yes, as a matter of fact I have, and that's entirely understandable," Smythe said. "A lot of people react that way to a traumatic situation. Now, let's talk about some specific things you might have seen."

"Some what kind of things?"

"Some details you might have noticed, like if you saw a weapon of any kind in anyone else's hand or somewhere."

Vicki looked back at her mother.

"They mean like the fish gaffe Eric carried…

"Mrs. Bayle. Please let Vicki answer the questions herself. Otherwise, you're putting words in her mouth."

"There weren't no gaffe hangin' on Eric's pants and he didn't have no gun or nothin' else that I saw, and them words are comin' out of my mouth by theirself," Vicki said.

Smythe bit his lip and Sumner smiled and cleared his throat.

"Did you see any other weapons—guns, knives, anything like that—in anyone else's possession?"

"Yes, I did," Vicki said. "My daddy's gun was…"

A car door slammed in the street, and the investigators heard Frank Bayle take the front steps in two strides and slam the screen door behind him as he entered.

"What did I tell you guys today about questioning my daughter without my permission?" Frank said, jerking off his cap and slinging it across the bed. "You got a subpoena or a warrant or something?"

"Why would we need such as that, Frank?" Smythe said. "No one here has been accused of anything; no one's under arrest. We're just investigating a shooting that lead to the death of a citizen. You being a non-com Naval officer, I should think you'd be eager to help us ascertain the facts of the matter."

"You can for a fact get your ass for certain out of my house, mister," Frank said. "And in the Navy, we're called Chief Petty Officers, not non-coms. My reserve duty ended two years ago, not that it's any of your goddamn business."

"Suit yourself, Bayle," Smythe said, scraping the chair against the floor as he stood up. "We'll be back with a search warrant, and I suggest you find that revolver of yours in the meantime."

*****

"Todd, my man, I think perhaps you've been reading too many Raymond Chandler novels," Sumner said, as the two men made their

147

way around the wrecked vehicles in front of the Bayle house toward a black Ford sedan with a Lee County license plate.

A piebald cat that sat licking the bloodied grass beside Eric's truck ran for cover as the men approached. Sumner noticed vultures circling overhead, gliding on some airy carousel, rising and falling and rising again, attracted by the smell of death.

Sumner stopped and walked back toward the Bayle house, where Frank stood looking down at him. His eyes lingered on the tear in the screen for a moment before he spoke.

"You can wash that blood off your car and off the ground if you've a mind to," he said. "We've documented everything in photographs, and there's no point in having half the county driving out here rubbernecking. They're bringing the grand jury to the scene Thursday afternoon. They don't need to see the blood. After that, the county will send wreckers to move the trucks. You'll be free to use your car then."

"Is the county going to fix that dent in my back fender?" Frank said, sarcastically.

Sumner peeled the wrapper from a stick of Beeman's gum as he returned to the car where Smythe waited. He offered a stick to his partner, who accepted.

"Let me ask you this, Harold," Smythe said, as Sumner seated himself in the passenger seat. "Did you by any chance notice the stripes and bruises on that little girl's arms and legs, or how she moved away when her father tried to put his hand on her shoulder? Who do you suppose ripped that screen today? And where's the gun? If Bayle has nothing to hide, why not just give it up?

"Something fishy is going on here and I intend to find out what it is."

"So you're thinking Frank Bayle got in a few shots of his own, in addition to the shots Randolph Dyer fired?" Sumner said.

"You're talking about a 64-year-old man who hadn't fired a gun in 10 years; he just had a man try to kill him and his daughter with a pickup truck. You really think he could hit a menacing moving target with seven shots he fired from a gun he'd never before held in his hand? Doesn't seem unreasonable to me that he might have had a little outside help."

"Well then, why is it that we have, what, nine or ten witnesses who say Dyer was the shooter and not one of them mentioned Frank Bayle?"

"That's easy, Harold. Everyone was watching Dyer and/or Magruder, or they were running for cover. The only ones who didn't move were Frank Bayle and his daughter."

Sumner spit his gum out the window, took a cigarette from behind the sun visor and lit it. From the Bayle house, the two investigators could hear animated conversation, followed by the slamming of a door.

Vicki Bayle came around the corner of the house, trailing her puppy, and stopped in her tracks when she saw the men sitting in the car.

Sumner looked at the child, and then at his partner.

"It's within the realm of possibility, I suppose," he said.

"Damn straight, it is."

CHAPTER NINETEEN

The Missing Gun

Monday, 4:30 p.m.

Aaron Cohen took his client's elbow and rose as Circuit Court Judge Llewellyn Hammond entered the Hendry County courtroom. Both men stood mute until the bailiff ordered all to be seated.

Randolph Dyer laced his hands on the table in front of him and waited for his old friend to speak.

Judge Hammond leafed through a stack of papers on his desk, adjusted his reading glasses, and cleared his throat.

At long last, he looked up at Dyer.

"It's unfortunate that you had to spend the night in jail, Randy, but I trust you were treated well."

"I was treated quite well, Lew, thank you."

Cohen raised a finger and made a move to stand, but Judge Hammond held up his hand and said, "Please remain seated, sir.

"The state prosecutor is asking for $10,000 bail, Randy, due to the…let's see here, due to 'the possibility of premeditation involved in this incident and the violent nature of the crime.'

"That bond seems to me to be a bit excessive, in view of what I know of your personal history and your standing in the community, so

I'm going to release you now on your own recognizance. I trust you're not planning to leave the county or run off to Mexico or somewhere?"

"I expect not, Lew," Dyer said.

"Good. We're calling in the grand jury on Thursday to decide whether you'll be indicted for a crime of any kind in this matter or whether you acted in self-defense. You are not compelled by law to appear or give a statement before the grand jury, since you are the accused. It may be in your best interest to do so in this matter, but that is something you can discuss with your attorney there. If you choose to give a statement, you'll be advised by the State Attorney's Office when you're to appear, as will the other witnesses.

"That sound fair to you?"

"It does, sir, and I thank you again."

The judge tapped his gavel on the polished circle of mahogany on his desk, rose, and walked out of the courtroom.

Aaron Cohen lifted his palms in futile supplication.

*****

Monday, 5 p.m.

"Vicki, take Patsy outside and play for a while," Rena said. "Ya'll need to get out from under my feet so I can make dinner."

"What about my homework?"

"Do as you're told, Skipper," Frank said. "I got some things I need to talk to your mama about, anyway. I need to ask you something, too, so don't go far."

Vicki felt her stomach churn as she turned and called her puppy to follow her.

Patsy was busy chewing on the thick leather shoelace of Frank's steel-toed work shoe and paid her no mind, so Vicki put her thumb and forefinger in her mouth, tightened her lips around them and whistled to get the puppy's attention.

It was a skill Eric Magruder had taught her in one long and patient trial-and-error lesson several months ago. She had never been able to whistle loudly without her fingers, the way her father did.

Frank's look told her she'd made a mistake, and she reached down and picked Patsy up and walked out the back door.

"Guess I stepped in it again," Vicki said to the puppy.

******

Monday, 5:30 p.m.

State Attorney Stephen P. Rydell listened quietly to Todd Smythe's conspiracy theory about the Eric Magruder shooting while shuffling papers on his desk and looking up points of law in a four-inch-thick leather-bound casebook.

"Am I boring you, Steve?" Smythe asked his boss.

"No more than usual, Todd," Rydell said. "It would help if you'd get to the point. What do you want to do?"

"I want a search warrant for Bayle's gun that includes his house, his car, and his jobsite, and I want to go back out there again with the metal detector after the cars are moved to see if we can find any more spent bullets for examination."

"I'll ask Judge Hammond about the search warrant, but I doubt you'll get it. Eric Magruder was a badass, Todd, and Judge Hammond wants this matter cleaned up and done with. Frank Bayle is apparently a bit of a hothead, but he's got a good reputation at the sugar company, and evidently, he's a pretty sharp guy.

"He's working on a design for some kind of automated harvesting machine that might one day eliminate the need for cane cutters. You know how much money that would save the sugar company?

"They've already lawyered him up—Richard Knight, you know him? He's a cousin of Bayle's brother-in-law who works in the sugar company's legal department. I'd bet money you don't get anything out of Frank Bayle, and if he takes the Fifth, he can't be compelled to answer questions before the grand jury."

"Well, that would tell us something now, wouldn't it?"

"Like what?"

"Well, say the grand jury returns a no true bill against Randolph Dyer, saying it was self defense to shoot a drunk, unarmed man seven times. That would let Dyer off the hook but not Bayle, not if we can prove he fired one of the shots that contributed to the death of Eric Magruder.

"I got a feeling about this one Steve. And I want to talk to Bayle's little girl again."

"Come on, Todd, how old is this kid? Eight?"

"OK, she's young, but she was there, she didn't look away, and she saw everything. I'm thinking she saw things she doesn't even know she saw, but there's something in her eyes. She's beginning to think about it.

"I want to talk to her again, and I want to do it out of the presence of her parents."

"Not likely, Todd. I'll talk to Hammond, but that's not likely."

******

Frank leaned forward to unlace his high-top shoes, took them off, waved his sweaty socks in front of him and then carried shoes and socks to the back porch.

"Thank you," Rena said. "Now, what's going on, Frank? Why are these investigators coming here asking all these questions about your gun? They say Vicki told Oscar you had it on the porch yesterday. Did you know that?"

"They're fishing, Rena," he said. "They don't know shit. They're bluffing."

"They know you had a fight with Eric Saturday afternoon," Rena said. "Why didn't you tell me, Frank? Do you know how stupid I felt that they knew that and I didn't?"

"It wasn't much of a fight. I hit him. He hit the pavement. That was about the size of it."

"They said they have witnesses who heard you threaten to kill Eric. Are they bluffing about that?"

"It was just talk, Rena. People say things they don't mean when they're mad."

"You tell me the truth, Frank. I need to know if you had that gun on the porch yesterday afternoon. Vicki said she saw it in your tackle box that morning. Those guys looked at me like I was an idiot when I said I don't know where you keep your gun, not that I blame them."

Frank opened the refrigerator, took out a beer, reached behind his neck and stripped his shirt off over his head without unbuttoning it.

"Tell me where that gun is, Frank. I looked under the mattress and it wasn't there. I looked on top of the chifforobe and found the empty holster; I didn't find the gun."

"Did you ask Vicki?" he said, then left his wife standing openmouthed as he walked out the front door.

When he reached the front steps, Frank turned, took out his pocketknife and cut a section of screen from the door. He pried off the thin quarter-round strip that surrounded the opening. Rena had been after him to fix that rotten screen for weeks, and then yesterday, Vicki drew a tic-tac-toe on the screen with a pencil. She poked several holes where O's would go, in addition to the foot-long gash that served as one of the vertical lines.

Rena had noticed the investigators looking at the stained and rusted screen, which by rights should have been replaced long ago by their landlord, Reed Hooker. She was reluctant to complain, though, because she knew if Hooker replaced their screens he'd have to replace the screens in all his rental houses, in which case their rent might go up.

She reminded herself regularly that pride goeth before a fall.

At least for now, replacing the torn section would help keep the mosquitoes out.

When he finished the job, Frank walked to the oil drum at the edge of the back yard, threw in the screen and the scraps of wood and lit it and other trash in the barrel with a squirt of lighter fluid and a thrown match.

He watched for a minute until black smoke twirled up and raced away in a huff, then walked back to the front of the house. Rena heard him screwing the hose to the bib by the front door, and the squawk of the rusty faucet sent water whooshing through the pipe and clattering against the floor. She walked to the front door and saw the swirls and whorls of the dark brown handprints turn red again when the water hit them, then slide down the side of the car in sheets of gore.

She returned to the kitchen and took a package of ground beef, half a red bell pepper, two ribs of celery and an egg from the refrigerator and placed the items in a row on the countertop.

She chopped the vegetables on a scarred and scoured cutting board with a small oinion, then unwrapped the butcher's paper and dumped veggies and meat into a large blue bowl. She stood staring at the bloody juices that ran in rivulets from the center of the clump of meat, then placed both hands on the edge of the counter, closed her eyes and swallowed hard. She picked up the egg, broke it into the bowl, plunged her hand into the mixture and squeezed.

******

St. Vicki of Arc had just climbed the tower, bean-pod sword in hand, to save the helpless Princess Patsy from the evil King Peyton Junior, when Frank Bayle whistled for his daughter to come home.

Vicki leaned back against the assemblage of cardboard refrigerator and washing machine boxes, its rain-sodden sides sagging and its carefully drawn colored-chalk outlines barely visible, and sighed heavily.

"I gotta go now, P.J.," Vicki said, propping her duct-taped cardboard shield against the wall and fetching her yapping pup from inside an orange crate in a corner of the fort-turned-castle. "Daddy's calling me."

Vicki lifted the rag towel cape from around her neck and hung it on the edge of the boxes.

"Maybe it'll all dry out by tomorrow, if it don't rain," P.J. said. "Come back after school and we'll play again, OK?"

Vicki didn't answer, but walked on toward the silhouette of her father leaning with one bare foot propped against the crucifix that supported the clotheslines in the Bayles' backyard. Cane poles supported the lines' sagging middles and increased their visibility, to help avoid neck injury to careless children who ran across the yard in the waning light of evening. In the distance, a curtain of leaden clouds dragged tendrils of rain across the sky, gaining on the last coral rays of sunset.

"Is supper ready, Daddy?" she said. "It sure smells good, and I'm really hungry, 'cause I didn't..."

"What did you tell Deputy Lloyd and the sheriff, Vicki?"

"What do you mean, Daddy? I just answered their questions about what all I saw yesterday and...and stuff."

"What kind of *stuff*, in particular, did you tell them you saw?"

"You know what I saw, Daddy, you was right there. I saw the same thing you saw, I reckon, and..."

"Did you tell anybody you saw me with a gun?"

"No sir. No sir, I did not say that. Deputy Lloyd asked me if I saw another gun yesterday, and I said I seen one in your…"

"You told him I had a gun on the porch when Eric got shot? You planning on getting me sent to jail for murder, Skipper? What are you and your Mama gonna do if I get sent to jail?"

"Daddy, I swear, I ain't told him you shot Eric nor nobody else. That is not what I said. I remember smelling the gunpowder and how it stung my eyes and stuff, but…all I said was that I seen your gun in the tackle box that mornin'. I just told the truth, Daddy, like you always tell me to."

"Vicki? Frank? Dinner's ready," Rena called from the back porch. "Ya'll come get washed up, now."

"We'll talk about this later," Frank said. "Meanwhile, you keep your mouth shut about yesterday. You don't have to answer any more questions about that from anybody, you got that?"

"Yes sir. I got it."

Vicki picked up Patsy and started for the door.

"Skipper?" Frank said, softly. "What did you do with the gun?"

Vicki looked back over her shoulder at her father. She lifted the puppy to her face and kissed her on the nose, then turned and climbed the steps.

******

"I went ahead and fixed your plate, Vicki, 'cause you still got homework to do, remember?" Rena said.

Vicki lifted her fork and looked at the meatloaf made just the way she liked it with a thick crust of catsup. She replaced her fork and looked at her father.

"I ain't very hungry, all of a sudden," she said, and ran for the bathroom.

Rena rose to follow, but Frank stopped her.

"Let her be, Rena," he said. "Just let her be."

By the time Vicki turned off the shower, dried off and wrapped herself damply in her thin robe, Frank and Rena Bayle had searched the tiny house top to bottom and sat on the back steps, staring at yet another squall flash and shimmer on the horizon.

"I wish to hell it would just go ahead and rain," Rena said, slapping a mosquito that buzzed by her ear. "Maybe at least it would cool things off a bit."

She took a drag off Frank's cigarette, and waved her hand in front of her face as Vicki opened the bathroom door.

Clutched to Vicki's chest, wrapped in a washcloth, was Frank's .38 Smith & Wesson revolver, which she had retrieved from its hiding place behind the toilet tank. She held it out to her father, then walked through the house to her bed, picked up her math workbook, and returned to the kitchen table.

A look of relief passed across Rena's face, and she followed her daughter into the house.

"Do you want me to warm your dinner now, or fix you a meatloaf sandwich?" Rena said.

"No ma'am, but I'll take some milk and cookies."

Frank sat on the steps with the gun in his lap until he finished his cigarette. He walked through the kitchen into the front room and returned with a long, thin metal box and a rolled green felt mat and sat down across from Vicki. He unwrapped the gun, flipped open the cylinder, and looked up at his daughter. His face was an unasked question.

Frank laid the gun on the felt, took solvent, brushes, rods and patches from the cleaning kit, then pulled on the string cord that hung from a roller at the top of the window. The paper blind lowered to reveal Vicki's five-year-old crayoned artwork and to conceal from anyone who might walk by the fact that he was cleaning a handgun at the table where his daughter added and subtracted fractions.

It was nearly 9 p.m. before either of them finished their homework.

Rena did not object when Vicki took the puppy to bed with her. Patsy was asleep, her tiny paws twitching, long before her master stopped stroking her floppy velvet ears and kissing her softly on her head.

******

Frank sat on the back steps and drank another beer while Rena replaced a couple of missing buttons from one of his work shirts.

When she finished, she walked out the back door and sat down beside him.

"What's the matter, Frank?"

"The gun was loaded when I put it in the tackle box. It was empty when she handed it to me a while ago."

"Did you ask her what she did with the bullets?"

"Not yet. I'm not sure I want to know."

CHAPTER TWENTY

Rituals

Tuesday, 8 a.m.

Rena and Rachel stood on the tiny porch and looked in on the ruin that was Maureen Magruder's home. Broken dishes and spilled staples littered the kitchen. The back door hung open from the top hinge, welcoming the field rats, whose tracks etched the scattered flour and sugar on floors and countertops.

The remainder of one of the cornmeal-dusted thieves, head and tail neatly excised, lay on the back steps where Mama Kitty had no doubt lain in wait for it, too timid to enter the dwelling of humans.

Or perhaps there was in her some primal memory of what had happened to her kittens in that particular house.

"Well," Rachel said. "I guess we might as well get busy. This mess ain't gonna clean itself up."

The two women hummed hymns in harmony as they worked with brooms and mops and cleaning rags. They flipped the mattress, one at the head and the other at the foot, and worked in concert to defrost and clean out the refrigerator, which smelled like death.

The electricity had been off in the house for two days, so they threw the spoiled meat into the oil drum and burned it with a new load of trash; Rena carried two catfish fillets that hadn't thawed completely out to Mama Kitty's lair and left them there for her.

As soon as Rena reached a safe distance, the old cat staggered out of hiding and settled, warily, over the feast. Her belly squirmed with a new litter of kittens.

Rena carefully folded the few shirts left hanging on Eric's side of the closet, and boxed them together with his underwear and shoes. She put his personal items—shaving brush, comb, toothbrush and such—into a brown paper lunch bag and left it on the counter.

When the women came across a cigar box full of photographs, they sat on the edge of the bed passing them back and forth, smiling through tears: Eric and Frank grinning and holding strings of bass and crappie; Eric with Sean on his shoulders, Frank with Vicki on his, waist deep in the water at Experimental Pond, playing "Topple the Totem"; the neighbors sitting at a picnic table while Eric played his guitar by a campfire where the kids roasted marshmallows on sticks.

Rena sobbed when Rachel passed her the last photograph: a shirtless, barefoot Eric holding Vicki, her legs wrapped around his waist, her arms and head thrown back in laughter.

"I thought you two came over here to clean," said Reba Fay Knight, as she walked in the front door tying a blue cotton scarf around her pin-curled hair. "I didn't know you just came to sit and bawl. Now, what can I do to help?"

Rachel and Rena looked at each other and answered in unison: "Windows."

******

Tuesday, 11 a.m.

"This was so nice of you to do this," Maureen said, standing in the doorway, her white-plastered arm saluting her neighbors.

"You'd of done the same for any one of us, honey," Rachel said. "Besides, what else could we do?"

"You know I can't stay here, after you've gone to all this trouble to make the place livable," Maureen said.

"Well, we reckoned you might not want to," Rena said, "but the place still had to be cleaned up, and you're sure not in any shape to be scrubbin' floors and washin' windows, now are you?"

Reba Fay gave Maureen half a hug and grunted.

"Those two weren't in any shape to wash windows, either, sweetie," she said, with mock disdain. "They left that for me to do. How you doin' anyways; you holdin' up alright?"

"I'm still numb, I guess, but the funeral is tomorrow at 11. Ya'll will be there, won't you?"

"I'll be there, Maureen," Rena said, "but I don't know if Frank and Vicki will. He says he thinks it would be too hard on Vicki."

Rena wondered if it was Vicki's feelings or his own he worried about, to tell the truth.

"Well, you can tell Frank it's gonna be a closed casket, if that helps," Maureen said. "Tom Spooner did the best he could, but Eric was beat up so bad, that I... Oh, Rena, I'm not blaming that on Frank; I didn't mean to say that, honey. Frank didn't hit him in the face. Him hitting the steering wheel is what messed up his face."

Tears she thought had all dried up now spilled down Maureen's face.

"I know ya'll been through a lot, too, but I'd just hate it if nobody came to the funeral but me and Sarah and the boys," she said.

"Daddy just can't do it—of course—so Sarah's going to drive us. She's been real good helpin' me with the boys, and Mama has too, but she don't think her heart can stand the funeral.

"I can understand that, and I can understand entirely if ya'll don't want Vicki to come. A funeral ain't no place for a kid to be that don't have to be there. Eric sure was crazy about that Vicki, though.

"And I sure hope the rest of ya'll will come. We was such good friends, wasn't we?"

Rena wrapped her arms around Maureen from the side, and kissed her bruise-marbled cheek.

"Remember when Eric was bringing that churn of peach ice cream in from the back yard and Frank come up behind him and dumped all that salted ice down his pants?" Rena said.

The women laughed at the memory.

"Poor Eric, he spent about an hour cranking that handle to make that ice cream and then Frank made him spill near about the whole dag-gummed churn," Maureen said. "He chased Frank halfway round the block, till he realized that rock salt was eatin' him up. I thought Frank was gonna bust a gut laughin' that night."

"Yeah, but Eric got him back a few nights later, remember?" Rena said. "I'd made that chocolate cake for us to eat while we was playing cards over at your house, and he came with me to help carry it back. He put whipped cream on top of Frank's piece, the way he likes it, but first he broke up a couple of Exlax and poked 'em down around inside the cake.

"Frank had the squirts so bad he couldn't even go to work the next morning. He said, 'I thought that cake tasted kind of weird, but I didn't want to hurt your feelings.'

"I was rollin' on the floor laughing."

They recalled sandspur duels and chili pepper eating contests, and a dozen other ways the two men devised to "one up" each other.

Every memory was a jewel.

******

Tuesday, Noon

Dr. Abram Moore hosted a small memorial service for Pierre St. Clair at his home in Harlem. Mary Catherine Fischer drove the Williams family to attend, and insisted that her housekeeper and family sit in the cab of her truck, rather than ride in the back, for the drive there.

She also stayed for the service, the only white person among the handful of mourners in attendance, and paid to have Pierre's body flown back to Jamaica for burial.

The next time she returned to the mainland for a trip to town, the windshield of her truck had been broken, a dead skunk placed inside the cab, and the words "NIGGER LOVER" painted along its sides with white shoe polish.

******

Wednesday, 11 a.m.

A couple of Eric's Okeechobee cousins left their traps and trotlines on their boats and drove to Hooker's Point for Eric's funeral. Albert and Audra Sloan, and a couple of their regular bar customers showed up, as well. Reed Hooker was one of only two of Eric Magruder's male neighbors to attend his funeral at the South Clewiston Baptist Church.

He felt it was his duty as the church's music director, even though there was to be no choir to direct.

He offered to sing his funereal special, "Lead, Kindly Light," but Maureen said she thought it better if Rachel just played the piano.

"I don't think I could stand to hear the words, Reed," she said. "It would just make me too sad."

Still, Reed left the store to Ethel and showed up for the funeral.

It seemed like the decent thing to do, he told his wife.

Peyton Talloway, a deacon, escorted his mother to the funeral, and the Rev. Matthew Spires delivered a mercifully brief eulogy.

"I can't say that I knew Eric Magruder well," Pastor Spires said, from behind the pulpit. "You all know he wasn't a church-going man. From all accounts, he was a troubled, passionate man, bedeviled by drink and burdened with sin.

"Still, it is not for us to judge this man, but to hope, with the assurance of our Savior, that today, he is in paradise.

"It is our fervent prayer that in the last moments of his life, with the agony of his tortured body, like the thieves crucified with Christ he called out, 'Lord, save me,' and that his cry was heard by almighty God, our Father, and his Son, our Redeemer.

"We ask God's blessings upon these here who mourn for Eric Magruder: his wife, his sons, his sister and his friends.

"I caution you to learn from his mistakes, and to grieve lightly. For what is the death of one being in the grand scheme of this world? It is but one breath not drawn, one heartbeat stilled, one tortured soul set free."

At the cemetery, uniformed pallbearers from the Hendry County National Guard bore Eric's casket to its final resting place, and an honor guard fired a 21-gun salute for the decorated war hero.

Maureen clutched the traditionally folded flag to her chest with one arm, and flinched at the sound of each volley.

******

Wednesday, 4 p.m.

"Was Sean and Patrick at their daddy's funeral, Mama?" Vicki said, as soon as she came in from school. "Was they cryin'? Do you think they're mad at me for not goin'?"

"Well, Maureen decided Sean was too young to go, so she left him with his grandma," Rena said. "Patrick was there, but he's so much like his dad, I didn't see him shed a tear. I'm not sure that's a good thing. Sometimes it's best to let it go and get it out. That's kind of what funerals are for, I think."

"I wish Daddy would of let me go. I doubt it woulda made any difference, though. I don't think I'll ever let it go or get it out. I reckon Patrick won't neither."

"Oh, honey, you're not even nine years old, yet," Rena said. "By the time you're grown, you'll have so many good things to remember that this will just be like some bad dream, near forgotten. I promise."

Vicki looked at her as if her mother were the child and she the adult. It occurred to her then that her mother, despite her age, was still an innocent.

Vicki set her schoolbooks on the kitchen table, and rifled through the stack to find a pencil and loose leaf paper. She walked out the back door and sat down on the back steps to make a list of all her happy memories:

1) The night Mama helped me make Cane Syrup Taffy for my third grade class.

2) Being picked the Queen of the Christmas Parade in the third grade.

3) Learning how to play "Fur Elise" with Mr. Hooker and Rachel.

4) Watching Suey have her piglets.

5) Grannypoppy.

Vicki looked at the list and crossed off number one. When she brought the bag full of taffy to school, each one twisted in butter-smeared waxed paper, Mrs. Delmar had refused to give her extra credit or let her hand out the taffy to classmates, even though she brought the recipe written on a 3X5-inch card, just as Sissy Baker had done with her jar of home-made mango chutney and shortbread.

"The difference is, you say you pulled this taffy with your hands," Mrs. Delmar said. "That's not sanitary. One might spread all manner of contagions if one were not extremely conscientious about cleanliness."

"Good grief, Mrs. Delmar," Vicki had said. "We washed our hands, and how else would you pull taffy, except with your hands?"

Vicki had to stand in the corner for five minutes for being impertinent.

She crossed number two from the list because the hem of her yellow taffeta dress had gotten caught on the edge of the float as she jumped down at the end of the parade. She was momentarily suspended about a foot off the ground with her skirt over her head until the seam gave way at the waist. By then, half the people in town had seen her Saturday-monogrammed panties.

She crossed off number three because she didn't have a piano to practice on, and four, because Suey had killed two of her piglets before Grannypoppy could get them away from her.

"It's just the way of nature," he had told Vicki. "She ain't got but 10 teats to feed 'em, so she killed the littlest ones. We could of hand raised 'em if I'd of got to 'em quick enough, but there ain't no use in grieving about it now. We'll just think about what a miracle it is that anything gets borned at all, 'cause it is a wonder, ain't it?"

She stared at number five and crumpled the list in her hand.

"You doin' your homework?" Rena said from the kitchen door.

"No ma'am, but I reckon I better," Vicki said, taking out a clean sheet of paper. "I gotta write two new poems for that class Mrs. Right put me in. It don't seem fair. I mean, I like writing poems, but I don't like this high school teacher, Mr. Platt, and I ain't even met him yet. He writes me these long notes about how I need to learn about iambic pentameter and trochaic tetrameter, and nobody else in my class has to do it. It just takes all the fun out of it, if you ask me. I'd rather write poems by ear, like Rachel plays the piano.

"Then, Mrs. Right says I have to practice my multiplication tables, 'cause the wheels on that side of my brain ain't spinnin' fast enough to keep up with the other side. And, she gets on me all the time for sayin' ain't. It just ain't fair."

"Well life *isn't* always fair, as you should know by now," Rena said.

"I reckon I oughta, but I keep hopin' it'll be different," Vicki said.

After a minute or two, she stood and walked to the other side of the house where she thought she heard a kitten mewing.

She soon returned to the porch, sat down and began writing.

THE CATBIRD
By Victoria Leigh Bayle

The Catbird has outfoxed me once again.
I heard its cry and wondered,
If it really was a kitten, there
Beneath the azure blooms of our plumbago.
I wondered if the little thing
Was wounded or abandoned, and
His mewing wouldn't stop, of course,
Until I went to check.
And there, his tiny head askew,
With yellow eyes of mockery
The wily slate-grey catbird sat in silence.
He darted back and forth among
The shelter of palmetto fronds
Until I walked away.
He twittered then, and mewed at me.
You are so easy to deceive,
The counterfeiting rascal seemed to say.
And knowing what I know of me
How could I ever disagree?
How could I ever disagree
With what the catbird thinks of me?

"Hey Mama? Could you please hand me the dictionary so I can check these words?" Vicki said. "I ain't sure I spelled counterfeit right. I thought it was i before e except after c, but that don't look right. I don't know why they have these dadburned rules anyways, when there are so many exceptions."

The second poem was shorter:

THE HUMMINGBIRD
By Victoria Leigh Bayle

Not every lovely flighted thing makes music.
Some simply please the eye.
They sparkle, gemlike in the sky
And thrill us with their antics.
The hummingbirds are acrobats
With ruby throats and emerald backs.
They do not soar, they hardly sing,
But ah, the hummingbird has wings.
While we are grounded, flightless things
The songless hummingbird has wings.

"Hey Mama, do I have time to go down to the church and play the piano for a while before supper?" Vicki said.

"Did you practice your multiplication tables?" Rena said.

"Can't I do that after supper?"

"Do it now, 'cause Daddy's gonna be home in a minute, and he might want to talk to you."

"Well I don't want to talk to him."

"Victoria!"

"Sorry, Mama. Seems like ever time somebody wants to talk to me they want something else outa me or whatever they want to talk about just gets me in trouble."

Vicki rubbed noses with Patsy, who wagged her tail from her shoulders down.

"Sometimes I think I like dogs better than people, Mama. All they want is for you to love 'em."

"Well, Vicki, honey, I think that's what most people want, too."

CHAPTER TWENTY-ONE

The Hearing

Thursday, 8 a.m.

State Attorney Stephen P. Rydell faced the 15 members of the grand jury—11 men and four women—and thanked them for their service to the people of Hendry County and the State of Florida.

"The decisions you make in this and other cases that come before you have a dramatic effect on the conduct of law, and you are obliged to take your duty most seriously. The assistant state attorney has reviewed with you the handbook you were given explaining the function and autonomy of the grand jury system. I am here to present evidence gathered by law enforcement and investigators, and to question witnesses in the matter before you. I also act as your legal advisor.

"Please do not hesitate to ask if you have any questions regarding these proceedings. You are also entitled to ask questions of any witness who appears before you.

"Are there any questions at this time, before I call the first witness?"

"I got a question," said Clarence Hall, scraping his chair against the feet of the juror behind as he stood. "How long is this going to take? I got business to attend to."

"Sit down, Mr. Hall," Rydell said. "Until this hearing is concluded, this is the business you will attend to.

"The State calls Hendry County Deputy Sheriff Oscar Lloyd."

Deputy Lloyd placed his left hand on the Bible and raised his right, swearing to tell the truth, the whole truth, and nothing but the truth.

He took a chair across from the jurors whose names, by law, were picked at random from voters' lists. Despite a population that included nearly 45 percent minority races, the Hendry County grand jury was all white.

As the deputy sat, carefully lifting his uniform pants by their uncommon creases, he noticed a drop of snuff had splattered on his patent leather boots when he rid himself of his dip before coming into the courtroom.

He took a brown-stained handkerchief from his back pocket and wiped off the top of his boot, then wiped his mouth and smiled yellowly at the panel.

"Deputy Lloyd, when did you arrive at the scene of the Eric Magruder shooting on September 10, and what did you see when you first arrived?" Rydell said.

"Oh, I got the first call within five-ten minutes of the truck crash, but seeing as I was slap near to Goodno at the time, it took me a while to get there. The shootin' was all over by then."

"Deputy, you may refer to your notes from the dispatcher's log, if necessary. What time was it when you arrived at the scene?"

Lloyd took three many-folded sheets of paper from his pocket, pressed them out flat on his lap, then lifted the top sheet to within three inches of his face.

"Says here 3:55 p.m."

"Tell the jury what you saw."

"Well, first thing I seen, besides the wrecked vehicles, you know, was Randolph Dyer a settin' there on the steps of Eric Magruder's house with a damn big gun in his hand."

Lloyd shifted in his chair and looked expectantly at Rydell.

"And?"

"And I took cover and drew my weapon and hollered for him to drop his."

"Yes, well, if you could, Deputy Lloyd, please tell us in your own words what transpired from that point on, and I'll try to interrupt as little as possible, OK?"

"Yes sir. Well, Randolph, he looked fairly shook up, and he laid his gun—was a real nice ol' German Mauser, war gun he said it was—and he laid it down on the steps and I walked over and picked it up and looked at it and put the safety back on and stuck it in my own belt.

"I asked him what happened here and he said he'd killed Eric Magruder for a tryin' to kill him and his daughter, and I asked him where Eric was and he motioned over yonder behind his truck."

"Did you ask him if Eric Magruder was armed?"

"I don't recall that I did, no, because he said the man was dead and I figured he wouldn't be no threat, you know."

The state attorney sighed, then said, "Please continue."

"Well sir, I walked around the front of a Kaiser that the trucks was all smashed up against and I seen Eric a laying there on his side next to his truck in this little patch of grass, with one arm up like this here and his knees tucked up—kindly like a youngun'll do—and I think at that time he might of still been a breathin' some, but he was shot all to hell. I heard him kindly sigh, like he was real tired, and I'm fairly sure that's when he died. Leastwise, he didn't move after that when I kicked his foot, you know. That was about the time Tom Spooner got there with the ambulance. Tom went over and felt his neck for a pulse—didn't have none, he said—and then we went over to Randolph's truck, and Rachel Padgett, she'd come from across the street with some ice in a rag and she was a holdin' it to Maureen's head and talkin' to her, so we had to get Rachel out of the way before we could get Maureen out of the truck."

"And Maureen is…?"

"Eric's wife, Maureen. We had to pull her out the driver's side door because the passenger side where she was a setting when Eric rammed Randolph's truck with his was caved in right smart and froze up."

"And did you question Maureen Magruder about what had happened?"

"Well, I did some, yes sir, but she was knocked kindly senseless from hittin' the windshield there, and it weren't too clear what she was a sayin', you know, kindly mumblin' like. She said something like, 'He killed his daddy and he killed the cats and now he's a tryin' to kill me.'

"We put her on a stretcher, me and Tom did, and she went to screamin' cause that one arm of hers was twisted plumb backwards, like, and I tell you what, the sight of that right there come close to makin' me lose my cookies. Then Tom, he bound her up the best he could and then he had his boy drive her in the ambulance to the hospital in Belle Glade."

"Who else did you see at the scene, deputy?"

"Well, damn near the whole neighborhood was walkin' around gawkin' by then. They all came out, onced the shootin' stopped. Me and Tom, we had to keep shooin' them outta the way so's I could take pictures of the trucks and everything."

"Did you determine if there were any witnesses who might have seen the entire incident?"

"Well, yes sir, after the Sheriff got there he told me to go talk to Frank Bayle and his wife 'cause Frank, see, he was setting on his porch the whole damn time. Said he never even moved when the trucks crashed, 'cause right after that the bullets started flyin', and his girl, Vicki, she was on the porch with him."

"Did you take statements from Frank and Vicki Bayle?"

"I did, yes sir, and from Frank's wife, Rena May, too, but she was right worked up about the whole thing."

"But not Frank and Vicki?"

"No sir. Cool as cucumbers, the both of 'em. That girl there, I think she might of been in shock, though."

"Deputy Lloyd, did you find any weapons on the body of Eric Magruder?"

"No sir, not even a pocketknife. They was a double-barrel shotgun in a carrier back of his truck seat, but he didn't have nothin' on him."

"Thank you, deputy. Unless some member of the jury has a question for you, you are excused. You may, however, be called back at some point to give further testimony."

A moment passed and Deputy Oscar Lloyd rose to leave, already fishing a can of Copenhagen from his shirt pocket.

He sat back down when Norma Jean White, the elected chairperson of the grand jury, stood and addressed him.

"Deputy, did you ask Frank Bayle why he didn't try to aid the victims involved in such a terrible accident?" she said.

"Well, ma'am, it weren't no accident," Lloyd said. "Eric ran into Mr. Dyer's truck dead set on killin' his wife, from all accounts I heard. And Frank, he didn't know but what Eric was gonna come after him next, 'cause he beat the stuffin' outta Eric the day before, down there at the truck stop. Leastwise, that's what he told me."

"Do you know what they fought about?"

"Yes ma'am. Eric Magruder throwed Vicki Bayle's little ol' kitty cat through a screen door and killed it that morning. Threw his own boys' cat and killed it, too, the mean sum-bitch.

"Excuse my language, ma'am, but that kind of stuff just gets my goat."

When Norma Jean sat back down, her hand to her mouth, the deputy rose and left the room. He had his bottom lip stuffed with snuff before the door closed behind him.

******

The statements of Hendry County Sheriff Clyde Petrie and Tom Spooner took up the better part of the next three hours, largely because the sheriff spent an unseemly amount of time with platitudinous oratory, even though the election was still two years away.

During a break, the sheriff stopped the state attorney in the hall and asked him if he had a cigarette.

"Do you ever buy your own nails, Clyde?" said Rydell, taking a pack of Kool filters from his coat pocket and offering it to the sheriff.

"I asked if you had a cigarette, Steve, not some mentholated piece of glasspack my wife won't even smoke."

"Suit yourself, Sheriff. There must be somebody else here you could bum off of."

The sheriff took out a cigarette and grinned, waiting for Rydell to light it for him.

"Good God," he said, as he took the first drag. "Why the hell would anyone smoke these piss-ass things?"

"Speaking of piss-ass things, Clyde, how long has it been since your deputy had his eyes examined? You ever notice how close he has to hold something to read it?"

"Hell, Steve," the sheriff said, "I didn't know the ol' boy *could* read."

A group of jurors at the end of the hall turned to wonder what the state attorney and the sheriff found to laugh about at a time like this.

*****

Thursday, 11 a.m.

Stephen Rydell motioned Rachel Padgett to the witness chair, and watched her walk toward it, her ungirdled buttocks shifting beneath a thin cotton dress of pale green, cinched at the waist with a wide elastic belt that was almost—perhaps once was—white. She crossed her legs as she sat, then uncrossed them and crossed her ankles to the side, demurely.

"Mrs. Padgett, where were you when you heard the trucks collide across the street from your home last Sunday?"

"I was in my back yard, picking the last of my guavas to make marmalade," Rachel said. "They're real sweet."

"Yes, I'm sure they are," Rydell said, smiling solicitously. "And what did you do subsequent to hearing the crash, Rachel? May I call you Rachel?"

"Well, Steve—may I call you Steve? I dropped the guavas I had gathered up in my skirt, and I went running to my front yard to see what happened."

"And what did you do then, *Mrs.* Padgett?"

Rachel Padgett flashed Rydell a smile and the slightest of winks, and crossed her legs again, letting her sandal slide and catch on one toe as she pumped it gently up and down.

Rydell cleared his throat and motioned for Rachel to continue.

"Well, I ran to the truck where Maureen was—there was blood running down from this cut on her head and she was moaning—but I couldn't get the door open, so I started around the front of the truck to the other side and then I noticed Mr. Dyer standin' there with a gun in his hand and I screamed and ran back to my house and I woke my husband up. He usually takes a nap after Sunday dinner, but I don't know how he could have slept through the sound of that truck crash, except that we have a big window fan in that front room and he snores like a freight train. But, anyways, I woke him up and I told him somebody was fixin' to get shot, and where were the kids? And then I ran out the back door lookin' for Buster, my little boy, and my two girls, but then I remembered they all went swimming out at Experimental Pond with the SonShine Baptist youth group, and about then, I heard shots and I ran back in the house and hid behind the Frigidaire."

"How many shots did you hear?"

"I'm not sure. Six or seven or… I don't know. I was screamin' the whole time."

"Did you see anyone other than Randolph Dyer with a gun that day?"

"Well, I went over to Rena's right after church to ask if she had some paraffin to seal my jars with 'cause I just plain forgot to buy it on Saturday. She did have some, and I told her I'd save her a couple of jars of jelly if she'd loan it to me, and she said she'd rather have the marmalade because Frank and Vicki like to eat it after supper with biscuits, and…"

"Mrs. Padgett. Could you please answer the question I asked?"

"What was that, honey? Oh yeah, I saw the grip of Frank's gun in his tackle box that day, 'cause he was cleaning his gear out on the porch. But you know, I'm not real sure about that. It could of been the handle of a fish scaler, for all I know. That's the only other gun I saw that day, if it was a gun, but I know who did the shooting, if that's what you're gettin' at. Randolph Dyer is the one that shot Eric, 'cause I heard him tell Maureen she wouldn't never have to worry about that…is it alright for me to cuss?"

Rydell nodded.

"He told her she wouldn't never have to worry about that son-of-a-bitch hurting her ever again because he'd shot him dead. That was just before they took Maureen away in the ambulance."

******

Thursday, 12:30 p.m.

Fourteen members of the grand jury enjoyed lunches of pulled-pork barbecue sandwiches, fat cottage fries, coleslaw and sweet iced tea from Lazy Jack's Bar-B-Q Shack on U.S. 27 east of Clewiston. Miss Lorena Platt, a 50ish spinster who supported her ailing mother by giving piano lessons, chose to eat a brown-bagged lunch of hard-boiled egg, sliced apple, chunks of cheese and whole-wheat crackers. She asked only for water, no ice, which was brought to her in a large waxed-paper cup by Willie Richards, an employee of the sheriff, who had delivered the lunches.

Miss Platt cracked the eggshell exactly 40 times before she peeled it. If her obsessive compulsion had required six octaves rather than five, several members of the grand jury might have gotten in a whack of their own, particularly Norma Jean White, a sales clerk at the Toggery Shop in Clewiston, and Clarence Hall, the Realtor whose patience had worn thin before the first witness took the stand.

After lunch, the members of the grand jury filed out of the Clewiston branch of the Hendry County courthouse and climbed into a small yellow school bus for the ride to Hooker's Point.

By the time the bus pulled to a stop beside the road in front of her house, Rachel Padgett's kitchen table already was lined with Mason jars waiting for homemade guava marmalade and jelly, a savored task previously interrupted by violence.

Wiping her sticky hands on a dishcloth, Rachel stepped to her front door in time to see Lorena Platt walk briskly back from the wrecked trucks to the bus and mount the steps to return to her seat. She sat close to the window about halfway down the bus, placed a brown paper bag over her nose and mouth and took deep, slow breaths. Rachel watched the bag inflate and deflate several times before the woman stopped, lifted her purse in front of her face, and took a small sip, then a long swig from a flask she kept there—strictly for medicinal purposes.

"I'm fine, I'm fine," she said a few minutes later, when the assistant state attorney offered his hand to help her from the bus. As she stepped down, the lawyer noted about Miss Platt the unmistakable scent of Cognac, with overtones of Chanel #5.

Rachel walked back to her piano and sat down to play the tune Vicki had insisted she learn from Reed Hooker.

The sound of "Fur Elise," played distinctively, drew Lorena Platt's attention to the Padgett house for a moment, before she walked on toward the mayhem.

"I've never heard that played in anything but A minor," Miss Platt said to her escort.

CHAPTER TWENTY-TWO

The Salesman

Thursday, 4 p.m.

Just before the school bus reached the railroad tracks, a wrecker and a flatbed truck passed by, headed toward town. The wrecker dragged a pickup truck crookedly on its back wheels, the truck's crumpled cab hitched high and swinging; the second caved-in pickup rode the flatbed, gaffed in front by a heavy steel hook like some metallic fish, and anchored in the rear by thick canvas straps.

Vicki swiveled in her seat to watch the trucks disappear around the corner, and met the leering face of Waylon Chaplin, who wagged his scummy tongue from side to side inside his foul-smelling mouth, lined top and bottom with grey teeth pitted with cavities.

"Your breath smells like an outhouse, Waylon," Vicki said. "Why don't your mama take you to the dentist?"

"Why don't you come back here and suck my peter?" he said.

"Why don't you eat turds and die, Waylon?" Vicki said. "I told you about that nasty talk. If you don't leave me alone, I'm gonna tell my Daddy and he's gonna whip your butt."

"Oh yeah? You mean like he whipped yours till you pissed your pants?"

"Who told you that?" Vicki said, her eyes searching a dozen pairs of others on the bus, then settling on a grinning Nellie Padgett. "You told him that!"

"Everybody kno-ows, everybody kno-ows," Waylon and his brother chanted in unison.

Soon, the Padgett girls joined in and Vicki turned back to face the front and covered her ears.

By the time the bus arrived at the stop in front of Hooker's Store, the chorus had changed to "Vicki got a whip-ping, and she peed her pan-ties."

Vicki readied to run as soon as she swung down from the top step to the bottom one in front of the open doors, but she was launched by a hand in the middle of her back and fell forward in two awkward giant steps, the jagged pavement leaping up to meet the heels of her hands, the tip of her chin and both knees. The sheath of papers she carried took flight above her head, dervishes whirling in the convection following the Tasty Treat truck that pulled past the bus to the dusty edge of Hooker's Point Road and stopped. Most of the school papers settled across the road behind the bus: a spelling test on which Mrs. Right had marked a large letter A in red ink; the math homework for which she'd received a grade of 89; a water-color painting of a screech owl, mounted on purple construction paper that bore a gold star; her science homework for the evening. The Padgett girls and the Chaplin boys lined up in single wing formation beside the bus, and she could hear Mrs. Applegate calling from her seat, as she reached for the compressed-air door lever.

"You OK there, Vicki?" she said, her voice fading with the whosh of the folding doors. Vicki called out, "I'm OK, Mrs. Applegate," and turned to sit up, shaking her stinging hands and surveying her scraped knees. She glared back at the jeering kids and refused to cry.

Waylon snatched a health and hygiene handout from the side of the bus where it had pasted itself momentarily, then ground it into the gravel beneath his heel.

"I hate you kids," Vicki yelled. "You're mean kids; you're all just mean!"

At the sound of the ice cream truck's calliope, the group of children instantly dispersed toward home to beg money for cones of chocolate-dipped custard with sprinkles on top. Vicki spat on her hands and wiped them on her shorts, blew on her knees, then stood up and picked up her lunch box. As the bus pulled away, she saw a strange man moving toward her across the road, gathering up her scattered papers.

"Here you go, my dear," said the man, proffering her spoilage. He was no taller than Vicki, but wore a neatly trimmed beard and a sweat-stained derby. When he walked, he swayed deeply from side to side on thick-soled shoes canted by wear to the outside, and he leaned heavily on a walking cane for support. His left shoulder blade protruded sharply above a pronounced hump in his spine that pulled his jacket off center.

A large square briefcase with metal corners hung from a leather strap across his shoulder.

"Do you live far, dear? Your chin is bleeding a bit. You should probably go and let your mother clean that up for you."

Vicki took her papers and thanked the man timidly.

"Those kids are bullies," she said.

"Yes, well. I am most familiar with bullies of that type, but please, allow me to introduce myself. My name is Dudley Stuart Phelps, and I am a traveling salesman."

"You are?" Vicki said, straightening the papers and making a conscious effort not to stare. "What do you sell?"

"Oh, lotions and potions and notions and such," the dwarf said, smiling broadly.

Vicki looked up and smiled back, holding out her skinned hand, and said, "I'm Vicki."

Dudley Phelps tipped his hat, then accepted the fingers of her right hand with the stubby fingers of his left, and bowed. Vicki noticed that he wore two large rings on each hand. He had a wide forehead with deep-set eyes of a deeper blue, and long, thick lashes a shade darker than his auburn hair and beard. A flawless smile carved a handsome dimple in one cheek.

"Would you like to see my wares, miss?"

"Um, no sir, I better go on home, like you said, and get cleaned up."

"Of course," Phelps said. "Perhaps I'll come by your house later."

"Well, see ya, and thanks again."

Rena saw her daughter limping toward home through the kitchen window, and by the time Vicki had climbed the front steps, her mother was ready with a roll of gauze and a bottle of peroxide.

"What happened?" she said.

"Waylon happened, that's what happened."

******

Rena frowned and made faces each time her daughter winced as she cleaned bits of dirt and gravel from Vicki's hands and knees and chin. She steeled herself for a fight, then opened a jar of Ichthammol ointment. Tears already ran silently down Vicki's face.

"I know this burns, Vicki, but it will help the cuts get well sooner," she said.

"Why can't you just use the mercurochrome? That doesn't burn."

"Because you have to go and give a statement to the grand jury tomorrow, remember? You don't want to be painted like an Indian, do you?"

"I don't care. I don't want to go, anyways. Daddy said I didn't have to answer no more questions about that, and I don't want to go!"

"Well, Daddy doesn't have any say in the matter and the law does…"

The knock at the door was brief, but firm, and both Vicki and Rena looked through the newly screened door at a man whose eyes barely showed above its center brace.

Dudley Phelps waited patiently without knocking again until Rena left her daughter seated on the kitchen table and walked to the porch.

"Yes?" she said.

"Good afternoon, madam," Phelps said, removing his hat, and holding it against his barreled chest. "I wonder if I might show you some of the unique items I'm offering for sale, today?"

"No thank you, I don't need anything."

Vicki walked up behind her mother and spoke to the man at the door.

"Hey," she said, wiping her face with the back of her hand and smiling.

"Hello, again, my dear."

Rena looked down at her daughter and back to the man and back at her daughter.

"This is the man I told you about, who helped me pick up my papers," Vicki said.

"But you didn't say…you didn't mention…"

"What was that, madam? Did your daughter not mention that I was a traveling salesman?"

"Well, yes, I think now she did, but, at any rate, I don't care to buy anything, thank you."

"I happen to have here a cream developed by a physician in London—the place of my birth, I'm proud to say—that aids in the healing of scrapes and burns and lessens the severity of scarring.

"And, I'm happy to say, it causes no discomfort whatsoever, and it is a completely natural product, formulated with a base of beeswax and containing no petroleum byproducts."

"I said no, thank you."

"It's quite reasonably priced, my lady."

"Let's get some of that stuff, Mama, if it don't burn," Vicki said.

"I'm sorry, sir, but I don't care to buy whatever it is you're peddling and I haven't got time to listen to your sales pitch."

Rena turned and pulled Vicki with her back toward the kitchen.

Vicki watched over her shoulder as Dudley Phelps replaced his hat, shifted his satchel to the other shoulder, and made his way down the steps and across the road, to the Padgett's front door.

By the time her mother had finished swabbing the stinging ointment on her skins and scrapes, the salesman was on his way to the Knight house, trailed by Buster Padgett.

"Hey midget! You a midget! My sister says you oughta be in a carnival! Hey midget, I'm talkin' to you!"

******

"There wasn't no call for you bein' rude to that man, Mama, just because he's different," Vicki said. "He can't help that no more than a crow can help bein' black instead of blue."

The tears that ran down Vicki's cheeks now were not for herself, and Rena looked away and longed for a cigarette.

"You could of bought that stuff he said he had or some little somethin' or another, just to help him out some. Look at him, Mama. Everybody's just tellin' him to get lost, and nobody will even look at what he's tryin' to sell."

"Vicki, I don't have no way of knowing what kind of junk that man is selling, but I know I don't have money to throw away on stuff we don't need. Now, that's enough. Why don't you get this puppy out from under my feet while I cook supper and go down and play with your cousins?"

"Fine," Vicki said. "That's all you ever say, Mama. You and this puppy get outa my way. Go play. Well, that's just fine. I got my own money, you know."

Vicki walked to the front room and retrieved her Seven Dwarves bank from the windowsill over her bed. She stood looking at the circle of slotted dwarves, six of whom accepted different-sized coins: pennies for Grumpy; nickels for Bashful; dimes for Dopey, quarters for Sleepy, half-dollars for Sneezy, and silver dollars for Doc. Happy held the folded dollar bills she sometimes got for Christmas or good report cards.

She left Patsy on the front porch and walked around the house to the cinderblock top of Boots' grave and sat the bank down, then walked to the clothesline and unclipped the rag towel used to clean soot from the line before hanging clothes. She wrapped the rag around the plastic bank and smashed it against the concrete.

Dudley Phelps was making his way down her Uncle Peyton's front steps when she caught up with him.

"I'd like to buy some of that cream you was talkin' about, mister, if it don't cost too much," she said.

"Well, your mother had a change of heart, did she?" Phelps said, his jacket now slung over his shoulder and his armpits half-mooned with sweat.

"No sir, I had some money in my…in my piggy bank, and I ain't even counted it yet, so I'm not sure I got enough."

Vicki dug into the pockets of her shorts and pulled out hands full of coins and folded dollar bills.

"The Surgeon's Balm is only $1.99, miss, so you've quite enough money to buy that and more, should you so desire."

"Can I see what you got?"

"Certainly," Phelps said, seeking first the shelter of shade from a row of Australian pines, and then lifting the lid on his case of samples.

By the time he closed it again, Vicki had ordered the balm, a jasmine-scented hand cream for her grandmother, guaranteed to diminish the appearance of lines and wrinkles, and some lemon-scented shampoo for herself, with oil of citrus to add a lustrous shine to blonde hair. She ordered her mother the pomegranate-scented shampoo designed for brunettes, and for her father, a tin-enclosed Salt of the Sea shaving soap that softens even the toughest of beards for a closer shave.

"These will arrive by post within three weeks," the salesman said, handing her a receipt along with her samples, "and as a bonus, I'm including this lovely stainless steel locket with a genuine blue sapphire heart. Isn't that pretty?"

"Wow. Sapphire is my birthstone, and I'm just about to turn nine."

"Really? Did you know the name sapphire comes from the Persian word 'safir,' meaning beloved of Saturn?"

"Actually, I did, 'cause I read it in a book. I don't have any books of my own, but we get the bookmobile out here and I read a lot."

"Yes. I thought you might."

Dudley Phelps waited until the screen door of Vicki's house slammed behind her before he turned to walk on toward the church. He crossed to the other side of the road as he passed the Chaplin house.

In his front yard, Waylon Chaplin sat in the rumble seat of a Model A Ford that slumped in the weeds for want of wheels. He was armed with a slingshot and held a coffee can half-full of rocks between his legs. He was using them to methodically pelt a mangy dog tied to a nearby tree with a rope. The dog had run round and round the tree until the rope was wound short and he could only hop, one side to the other, to try and escape the torture. He frantically chewed at the rope to try and free himself, and yelped piteously each time he was hit.

"I say there, young man," Phelps yelled from across the road. "Have mercy on that poor animal!"

Waylon turned his attention to the little man and laughed. He stood up loading the leather pocket of his slingshot and launched a rock in Phelps' direction, then loaded it again.

"Run, midget, run!" he called, and Phelps did his best, lifting his case behind his head as a shield.

As he jogged awkwardly down the side of the road, the door-to-door salesman left a trail of free samples and half a dozen necklaces like the one Vicki now proudly showed her mother.

When the salesman was out of reach, Waylon stomped the samples until they voided their fragrant lotions and conditioners onto the road. He threw the necklaces into the tall weeds by the side of the ditch before he returned to torturing the dog.

CHAPTER TWENTY-THREE

The Testimony

Friday, 7:30 a.m.

"What's this?" Vicki said, stooping to pick up a small package leaning against the front step.

"It's for me! It has a card that says, "Happy Birthday, Victoria. Regards, Dudley Stuart Phelps."

"OK, OK, just bring it with you and get in the car," Rena said. "We're supposed to be at the courthouse to meet your father and the lawyer before the hearing starts, and I don't want to be late."

Vicki climbed in the back seat and rolled down the windows before tearing open the brown paper wrapping.

"It's a book, Mama, look," she said, as her mother backed the Kaiser out of the driveway.

"Vicki, get that out of my face, please, so I can see where I'm going."

"*The Little Lame Prince* by Dinah Maria Mulock Craik," Vicki said. "It don't look brand new and the pictures ain't in color, but it looks like a nice little book, Mama, and there's a note."

My Dear Miss Bayle,

This was my favorite book as a child, and to this day, it is among those I most cherish. I do hope you haven't read it yet. It is a classic that I trust you will enjoy rereading for years to come, as I have.

You'll see there is a prefatory note to this edition, written by my great Aunt Elizabeth. There is little I can add to what she wrote, in particular the fact that this book contains "the last truth that is usually taught to children, yet it is the first that life will force upon them. No child will be sadder, and many may be happier, for learning, without knowing it, how to bear suffering if it shall come..."[3]

And, for another piece of wisdom often accredited to Mrs. Craik, my dear, I leave you with this thought:

"Believe only half of what you see and nothing that you hear."

Sincerely,
Mr. Dudley Stuart Phelps

"Well, that sounds cheery, especially from somebody who goes around selling junk to people who buy it just because they feel sorry for him, and who probably won't ever see the stuff they spend their hard-earned money on," Rena said, tilting the rearview mirror and transferring a touch of lipstick from her lips to her cheeks, smoothing the makeshift rouge with her ring finger.

Vicki's stricken face flashed in the mirror as Rena readjusted it to the rear, and she regretted her tone.

"Oh, don't mind me Victoria, I'm just in a foul mood this morning," she said. "Let me see that book. Are you sure this is a children's book?"

"Good grief, Mama. You sound just like Mrs. Tanner at the library."

Rena paged through the book while she was stopped at the railroad tracks, then tossed it into the back seat.

"Well, to each his own, I guess. You want to read a book about a crippled prince, you go right ahead.

"Did you brush your teeth after you ate your cornflakes?"

******

Vicki squirmed in the slippery wood chair and tried to focus on her book.

Attorney Richard Knight and her father whispered in one corner of the small anteroom, and she sat with her mother, unnaturally upright, in the other.

"Mrs. Rena May Bayle, would you follow me please?" said a man who appeared in a green and white uniform, wearing a gun on his hip.

Rena rose clutching her purse and flashed a reassuring smile back at Vicki, then disappeared behind the tall polished oak doors of the courtroom, accompanied by Knight.

The state attorney, having studied her earlier statements, didn't waste time asking Rena about the shooting.

"Mrs. Bayle, what kind of man would you say Eric Magruder was?"

"Well, he was just as nice and friendly as could be if he was sober, but when he drank he was a devil."

"Would you say you had a close relationship with Eric, Mrs. Bayle?"

"Well, I don't like your tone one bit, Mr. Rydell, but me and my husband was good friends with Eric and Maureen, and our kids are friends, too."

"I meant no disrespect, Mrs. Bayle, and I beg your pardon. I only want to know the nature of your friendship; how well you knew him."

"Well, we all played cards together of an evening, and we went to picnics and dances—all the things that neighbors normally do."

"Did you ever see or hear any kind of domestic disputes between the Magruders?"

"Yes, I'm afraid so. Like I said, he was a demon when he was drinking. It made me nervous, all that yellin' and cussin'. I never have been able to abide that kind of behavior, you know, 'cause that's not how I was raised, and Lord knows, I wouldn't stand for no man hittin' me. I told Maureen that, too. To her face."

"Did you ever see Eric hit his children?"

"No, I did not. Eric had a soft spot for children and animals," Rena said, and then looked down at her hands. "Except for cats, obviously. He hated cats, for some reason."

******

Frank Bayle crossed the room and sat down next to his daughter. "Whatcha readin', Skipper?" he said.

Vicki held up the open book so he could see its cover without taking her eyes from the page she was reading. She had already met the Little Lame Prince's godmother, and was whisked away by the "poor little fellow, a helpless cripple, with only head and trunk and no legs to speak of…carried in a footman's arms, or drawn in a chair, or left to play on the grass, often with nobody to mind him, a pretty little boy with a bright, intelligent face and large, melancholy eyes… They rather perplexed people, those childish eyes; they were so exceedingly innocent and yet so penetrating. If anybody did a wrong thing—told a lie, for instance—they would turn round with such a grave, silent surprise…that every naughty person in the palace was rather afraid of Prince Dolor."[4]

Frank attempted no further conversation with his daughter, except to tell her he was going to step outside and smoke a cigarette.

"Victoria Leigh Bayle?"

"Victoria?"

The bailiff crossed the room and stood looking down at the little girl, who sat with her legs stuck through the slatted back of the chair and her book propped against its backrest, which she had not found at all restful. She jumped like she'd been shocked when he touched her shoulder.

"It's time for you to give your statement now," he said to the startled child, who extricated herself from the embrace of the chair and stood, one finger marking the page she'd left off reading. There was no jacket flap on the book with which to mark the page, so Vicki noted its number—easy to remember, she thought, because that's how old Jesus was—and then closed the book.

It offended Vicki when people turned down the corners of a page, as if a book were something worthless, rather than a thing to treasure.

Mr. Goodenow told her she'd make a fine librarian one day, but she told Mr. Goodenow she would rather write the books than loan them.

As the bailiff opened the big door, Vicki squared her shoulders and approached the state attorney with her right hand already in the air.

She held *The Little Lame Prince* under her arm and placed her left hand on the Bible, just as she had rehearsed doing earlier that morning.

"Do you swear to tell the truth, the whole truth, and nothing but the truth?" the tall man asked her.

"If I have to," Vicki said, and took the witness chair.

The state attorney frowned and introduced himself, then said, "The customary answer to that question is yes, or I do."

"Ain't that what you say when you get married?" she said, and several members of the grand jury put their hands to their mouths to conceal a smile.

"Will you tell the members of the grand jury what you saw on the day Eric Magruder was shot in your front yard, Victoria, and do you promise to tell the truth without leaving anything out?"

"Mr. Rydell, I'll do the best I can," Vicki said, seriously. "Ain't nobody can do better than that, my Granny says."

Even the state attorney smiled then.

Vicki's new black patent leather Mary Jane's hung three inches off the floor, and she swung her feet and jiggled her skinned knees nervously as she spoke, which was a considerable distraction to Clarence Hall.

It was the small triangle of white cotton that appeared and disappeared and appeared again between the little girl's smooth, tanned thighs that riveted his attention.

******

"Did you see Randolph Dyer shoot Eric Magruder last Sunday, Victoria?"

"No sir, I did not."

"I beg your pardon?"

"I heard Mr. Dyer tell Eric he was going to kill him, and I saw Eric get shot, but I can't say for sure if Mr. Dyer shot him 'cause from where I was standing, all I could see was Mr. Dyer's head. The bottom half of our porch is wood, you know, and our house sets up kinda high."

"But at one point, before the shooting started, you saw a gun in Randolph Dyer's hand?"

"Yes sir, I did."

"And you could see Eric Magruder?"

"Yes sir. I was lookin' at Eric through the screen door, and where he was standin' I could see all the way to the ground."

"How many times did you see Eric get shot, Vicki?"

"I don't know," Vicki said, softly. "A bunch a times…"

"Vicki, you're going to need to speak up so the jury can hear you."

Vicki's eyes pooled with tears, and she cleared her throat.

"I don't know how many times he got shot; lots of times," she said evenly. "There was a whole lot of noise and things were happenin' real fast—even though, when I think back on it, it seems like it took a long time, sort of."

"That's not an unusual observation in these kinds of situations, Victoria," Rydell said. "Please tell us what you remember."

"Well, I remember hearin' people screamin'—Mama and some other people—and I remember hearin' Eric yellin' at Mr. Dyer to go ahead and shoot him, and I remember seein' smoke and smellin' gunpowder…"

"Vicki, how would you recognize the smell of gunpowder?" Rydell said, leaning closer to the child's chair.

"It's easy to smell gunpowder, even over garbage. See, me and my Daddy, we go out to the dump sometimes to target practice. That's where he taught me how to shoot."

"When was this?"

"Oh, I don't know. A year or so ago, I reckon."

"How old are you, Vicki?"

"I'm eight now, but I'll be nine next week."

"And would you say you are a good marksman?"

"My Daddy says I'm a natural."

"OK. Let's get back to last Sunday. Which way was Eric facing when you saw him get shot?"

"Well, the first time he was standin' sideways to me, but then he started walkin' around our car toward our house and I yelled his name and he was lookin' right at me the next time he got shot."

"Did Eric say anything to you when you yelled at him?"

"No, he just smiled at me," Vicki said, a sense of wonder in her voice.

"What happened then?"

Vicki looked down at the book in her lap, ran her hand over the gray linen face of it, and looked up at Rydell.

"He yanked open his shirt and told Mr. Dyer to get it over with, and he got shot three or four times in a row real fast, and there was lots of blood…"

"What was your father doing all this time?"

"He was settin' on the porch."

"And your mother?"

"She was pullin' on me and yellin', runnin' back and to out the back door most of the time."

"And your father just sat there, doing nothing?"

"He was cleaning his tackle box out there that mornin', gettin' ready to go fishin', then we was reading the paper. I wasn't watchin' him, though, I was watchin' Eric."

"You hated Eric, didn't you, Vicki?"

Vicki looked down at her lap, then back at the state attorney, tears dotting her starched white blouse.

"No sir. I loved him."

"You loved him?"

"Yes sir. I didn't know it until you just now asked me, but I reckon I loved him."

Rydell turned and walked to a table where his assistant sat with Harold Sumner and Todd Smythe, rifled through some papers, spoke briefly with the investigators, then walked back to face the child, holding a sheet of notes.

"On the day before Eric Magruder was shot, Vicki, can you tell the jury here what happened to your cat?"

"He died."

"How did it die?"

"He. He was a little gray kitty I named Boots because he had four white feet, and somebody throwed him through a screen door and killed him."

"And do you know who that was, the person who killed your kitten?"

"I know who people say did it, but I didn't see it happen."

The state attorney referred to the sheet of paper in his hand and then said, "Eric Magruder threw your kitten through a closed screen door and it died later that day, probably of a broken back, according to the testimony of your mother. How did that make you feel, Vicki?"

Vicki looked up at Rydell in disbelief, then placed the book she was holding to her chest back in her lap, leaned forward and held her hands heavenward.

"Why do you people keep askin' me that? It made me feel awful. How would it make you feel if somebody killed somethin' that you loved?"

"Of course. That would make anyone feel awful. But, did you not tell a friend of yours that day, a Mr. Reed Hooker, that you hated Eric Magruder and you hoped your daddy would kill him?"

"I already told them men over there that I was upset when I said that and I didn't really mean it."

"So, you were upset with Eric Magruder that day, and when your father got home from work you described for him what had happened and how you and a colored man, the late Mr. Pierre St. Clair, had buried your kitten in the back yard."

"What do you mean?" Vicki said, knowing as she asked that it was a term used to refer to dead people, like the late President Franklin Delano Roosevelt. "Why did you say the late Mr. St. Clair?"

"Well, Vicki, I understand that Pierre St. Clair died later that same evening in a bar fight in Harlem, but that's of no consequence to this hearing. Now..."

"What do you mean, it's of no conis…of no…are you sayin' it don't matter? Pierre was my friend. He was nice to me. Pierre is dead, too?"

Tears drained unfettered from Vicki's eyes and nose, and Stephen Rydall reached in his front pocket and withdrew his monogrammed handkerchief and offered it to her.

"I'm sorry, Victoria," he said, glaring at Richard Knight. "I assumed someone would have told you this already."

Richard Knight stood and put his hand on the back of Vicki's chair and addressed the members of the grand jury.

"Obviously, this child is too upset to give further testimony at this time," he said. "I suggest we dismiss her entirely and rely on the many accounts of this incident available from competent adult witnesses."

Rydall faced the jurors and asked if they agreed.

"By all means," said Miss Platt. "I think this child has been through enough."

******

Vicki ran to the arms of her mother, who stood with Frank and others in a pall of cigarette smoke just outside the courtroom.

"What happened?" Rena asked Knight, who passed through the door behind Vicki, smiling.

"She's a little upset because she just found out that Jamaican guy who buried her cat and gave her that old globe is dead."

"I thought you said Reed gave her that globe," Frank said.

"Who told her?" Rena said, lifting Vicki into her arms, and swinging side to side with her, as she had when Vicki was a toddler.

"It came out in the questioning, but don't worry," Knight said. "Vicki did splendidly, and I doubt they'll call her back again.

"Oh, and here, the sheriff gave me this and said Vicki might want it back. Reed Hooker said she gave it to St. Clair, and they found it in his pocket."

Vicki lifted her head from her mother's shoulder and looked at the blue and white marble in Knight's hand.

"Put me down, Mama," she said.

Vicki took the agate from Knight and looked up at her mother.

"Pierre gave me the whole world, Mama, and all I gave him was this ol' marble."

She dropped the marble in the small ruffled pocket of her blouse, and covered it with her hand.

******

"Rydell says the medical examiner is going to be available after lunch, Frank," Knight said. "I was hoping those bean pickers would keep him tied up longer, but at any rate, if he's delayed, they may call Maureen

Magruder next. You might as well take your wife and daughter home and then come back. They may not even get to you today."

"What the hell? You mean I might have to miss another day of work, Dick? Are they going to dock me for that?"

"They'll probably take it off your vacation time."

"Son-of-a-bitch! I figured as much. Like I have any control over what these state pricks do. Son-of-a-bitch!"

"Don't get all worked up, now. Just take Rena and Vicki home and come on back. There's an outside chance you won't have to appear at all."

"Are you serious?"

"By the time Maureen finishes telling them how Eric strangled her and then tried to kill her and her father with the truck, I suspect Dyer himself won't need to appear, although he seems set on it."

"And Vicki didn't say anything about me having a gun on the porch?"

"Rydell never asked the question, Frank. She answered the questions he asked, and he never asked the goddamned question.

"You should have seen the jurors' faces, Frank. She was something else."

CHAPTER TWENTY-FOUR

Ammunition

Friday, noon

The black sedan with Lee County plates pulled directly across Frank Bayle's scraped and scarred driveway, blocking his exit. Todd Smythe and Harold Sumner walked side-by-side to the idling Kaiser and stood looking down at the driver.

"We need to talk to you for a minute, Frank," Smythe said.

Frank took a Camel from the pack in his pocket, lit it, and blew the smoke out the window.

Smythe didn't back away.

"You know," Frank said, "my lawyer seems to think that's a bad idea, guys. Personally, I don't think he likes you much, Todd, but that's just my impression. Now, if you'll move your frigging car, I really need to get back to the hearing. Ya'll have a nice day, ya hear?"

"You needn't hurry, Frank," Smythe said. "There's a recess until 2 p.m., so the medical examiner can pull his thumb out of his ass and get to court."

"Well now, I would think that's something you might be able to help him with, Mr. Smythe, something you seem suited for, you know, like browbeating little girls."

"You find your gun yet, Frank?" Smythe said, slapping a sheath of papers on the window frame. "You going to produce it for us this time, or are you going to make us go looking for it?"

Frank snatched the search warrant from Smythe's hand and tapped it on the steering wheel.

"Right this way, gentlemen," he said, turning off the ignition and opening the car door hard against Smythe's shin.

"Oh, excuse me, Todd. Was that your leg?"

******

With gloved hands, Harold Sumner laid the tooled leather holster on a white cloth he placed on the kitchen table. He looked at Smythe, who uncapped an ink pen, flipped over the vinyl flap of a small notebook he removed from his back pocket and took notes.

"Left-handed holster," Sumner said, then unsnapped the safety strap and lifted the gun out carefully.

"Smith & Wesson Victory Model Revolver, .38 caliber six-shot with a four-inch barrel, fixed sight, parkerized finish and Altamont service wood grips. It's your standard, military-issue sidearm."

Smythe lifted the camera hanging from his neck and took a picture of the gun, ejected the now opaque and darkened bulb from the flash unit onto the table and inserted a new, crystalline blue bulb. He quickly pocketed the spent bulb when he saw its heat had made a mark on the oilcloth.

"Sorry," he said.

"Don't worry about it," Rena said, opening the refrigerator and taking out a tray of ice cubes. Frank leaned against the sink and polished off a spiced ham sandwich while Rena fixed a glass of iced tea and handed it to him.

"Would you guys like some sweet ice tea?" she asked.

"She's the perfect little hostess," Frank said, and lit another cigarette.

"I think we're good here, ma'am, but thank you."

Sumner thumbed the catch and pushed the cylinder out with his middle finger, pointed the gun at his face and put his cotton-white thumb behind the barrel.

"The gun is not loaded, and appears to be recently cleaned."

Frank smiled at the investigators.

"Have to keep 'em oiled in this climate, fellas," he said. "Humidity's a bitch, and I appreciate you not getting your sweaty fingerprints all over it."

"Where do you keep your ammo, Frank?"

"Well, right now, all I got is shotgun shells and rifle bullets, but it's all right there in the bottom of the chifforobe. You're welcome to take a look. I need to get me some wadcutters, though, so me and Vicki can go plinking. There ain't a boy her age around here could outshoot Skipper, I'll tell you that."

"Most children Vicki's age don't shoot guns, Mr. Bayle," Sumner said.

"Oh yeah? What part of the South are you from, New York City?"

******

Sumner and Smythe sat in their car in Frank's driveway and fumed.

They had now searched the house, the car and the machine shop. They and others had raked the Bayles' and surrounding yards, and swept the area with a metal detector.

They found empty snuff cans, toy wheels, some rusty roofing nails, a pair of broken eyeglasses and some loose change. In the tall grass across a ditch some distance away, they made the puzzling discovery of several silver-toned lockets with blue glass stones on chains turned green, each one attached to a rain-sodden card that said: "A free gift, to thank you for your purchase."

"We could drive the gun down to Miami for a ballistics check, Harold," Smythe said. "We could at least do that."

"For what, Todd? We have no bullets other than the ones from Magruder's body and two we dug out of those pine trees, and they all came from Dyer's gun. We have no casings other than those from Dyer's gun. We don't have a damn thing to connect that .38 or that man to this shooting except some gut feeling you have, fueled in part by a little girl you can't get out of your head and a photograph of a hole in a screen, which could have been made by a pencil or a goddamned bow and arrow, for all we know.

"Give it up, Todd. In a day or two, the jury is going to return a no true bill against Randolph Dyer. They're going to call it a justifiable homicide, and that's that."

"We'll see," Smythe said. "Do you know anything about forensic pathology, Harold? You know the difference, say, between an entrance wound made by a round-nosed bullet and a wadcutter?"

Sumner looked at Smythe and grinned.

"A wadcutter makes a hole like a paper punch, my friend. Usually clean as a whistle."

Smythe made a U-turn and spun out as he headed back to town.

******

"Where's Vicki?" Frank said, as he stood watching the black sedan disappear.

"She's down playing with Beth," Rena said. "They're probably out in the fort. I was just getting ready to call her to come eat lunch."

Frank stepped out the front door and whistled.

In a couple of minutes, Vicki rounded the corner at an easy trot, with Patsy running full speed to try and keep up with her.

"She can run fast to be so little, can't she Daddy? And, man, is she smart! She already knows how to shake hands. Watch this."

Vicki knelt in front of the panting puppy, held out her hand, and said, "Shake."

The puppy instantly pawed at her hand.

"She's left-handed, Daddy, just like you. Every time you tell her to shake, she lifts her left foot. Don't matter where you put your hand, watch."

"Vicki, I need to talk to you about the bullets," Frank said.

Vicki stood and looked up at her father, shielding her eyes and squinting.

"What bullets?"

"The bullets that were in the gun, where are they?"

Vicki walked to the front steps and sat down.

"Ain't nobody ever gonna find 'em."

"Vicki, why did you hide the gun, and what did you do with the bullets?"

"I was afraid you might get in trouble."

"Why did you think that, unless you thought I did something wrong?"

"It was my fault, 'cause I said I wanted you to kill Eric for what he did to Boots, and then…and then somebody did kill him."

"Mr. Dyer shot Eric, Vicki, but if you don't tell me where those bullets are, somebody might find them and decide that I shot him too."

"There was one empty round in the cylinder, Daddy."

"Vicki, I sometimes keep an empty round in the chamber as a safety measure. You *know* that."

Vicki looked at her father, then reached down and picked up her puppy.

"Yes sir, I know that. You put an empty round in the chamber to the *right* of the barrel. It wasn't on the right side, Daddy, it was on the left."

Vicki recognized fear in her father's eyes.

"Don't worry, Daddy. I took care of it. Ain't nobody got no proof of nothin'. Ain't nobody gonna get none, long as I keep my mouth shut, like you said."

Frank sat down on the steps and put his head in his hands as his daughter stood and walked in the house.

"What we having for lunch, Mama?"

******

Friday, 2:30 p.m.

Stephen Rydell saw that Dr. Paul Enderson's highly scientific ruminations about the kinetic energy and ballistic coefficient of bullets and their effect on human tissue had two effects on members of the jury: some were starting to nod off, and others were turning pale.

When he began posting diagrams and autopsy photographs of Eric Magruder's body, all gave him their full attention, but the pale ones began to turn slightly green.

"I need to be excused," Lorena Platt said, as she made her way past a line of jurors, a lace-trimmed hanky over her mouth and her purse clutched to her chest.

Rydell suggested a fifteen-minute break, to the annoyance of Dr. Enderson, who had a number of other chests to bifurcate.

In the bathroom down the hall, Norma Jean White splashed water on her face and accepted a hand towel from a young black woman seated in a chair at the end of the room.

Miss Platt occupied one of the three toilet stalls.

"Have you been cleaning the mirror?" Norma said to the maid as she blotted her face and dried her hands. "It smells like alcohol in here."

******

"Dr. Enderson, were you able to determine how many times Eric Magruder was shot, and which of his wounds might have caused his death?"

"He was shot seven times, in my opinion, but the body had 12 bullet wounds," Enderson said, pointing to a black and white diagram of the human body. "These three wounds are exit wounds caused either by a bullet which passed cleanly through the body or by projectiles which fragmented upon hitting bone. One bullet passed through the left bicep and lodged in a rib, causing these three wounds.

"But Eric Magruder died of exsanguination, after a bullet entered the left side of his chest, pierced the abdominal aorta, here, just below the heart, passed through the right kidney and exited here."

"Eric bled to death?"

"He bled to death. Had he been transported to a hospital in time, there's an outside chance he might have survived six of the seven gunshot wounds, but he would not have made it to the hospital after that one."

"Did you determine if more than one weapon caused the wounds on Eric Magruder's body?"

"That's impossible to know. All the bullets I examined, those recovered from the body and those recovered at the scene, came from the 9mm Mauser introduced into evidence by the sheriff. The rifling marks left on the bullets by the lans and grooves of the gun barrel prove this conclusively.

"That's not to say some of the bullets that passed through Eric Magruder's body and were not recovered could not have come from another gun.

"In the absence of a bullet, it is, for all intents and purposes, impossible to tell the difference between a wound made by, say, a .357 magnum, a .38 or a 9mm bullet since they have essentially the same .357-inch diameter.

"The shape of the bullet, its trajectory, the distance from which it was fired, those kinds of things tell the story. As they say, every bullet keeps a diary of where it has been and what it has done.

"No bullet, no diary."

******

Sumner and Smythe sat at a table perpendicular to the jury and shook their heads.

"We might as well pack our bags and head on back to Fort Myers," Sumner whispered to his partner.

Smythe spread the crime scene photographs across the table in front of him, carefully positioning those showing the body of Eric Magruder so that they could not be seen from the jury box.

He picked up the photo of the hole in the screen and studied it closely, then shoved the rest of the pictures into a folder, stood and motioned for Sumner to follow him out of the courtroom.

The two investigators passed by Frank Bayle and his lawyer in the anteroom as they walked out the front door.

"I got it all wrong, Harold," Smythe said, handing Sumner the photograph.

"You'll pardon me if I'm not blown away by that revelation, Todd, since I've been telling you that for two days now."

"Look at the picture, you schmuck," Smythe said. "The wire protrudes out, not in, and that darkened area around the hole has to be gunpowder residue. It has to be. Look at it. Doesn't that look like the tattooing around a gunshot wound from five, six feet to you?"

"Yes it does, Todd, but that hole in the screen could have been made years ago, for all we know. And guess what? We don't have that section of screen and we didn't test it for gunpowder."

"True, but listen. Frank was sitting on the left side of the porch, and he's left-handed. That hole is in the screen door to his right, directly in line with the rest of the doors in that shotgun shack. That's why they call them that; it's a clear shot through the house from one end to the other.

"If Frank Bayle remained seated the entire time the shots were fired, as everybody we talked to said he did, there's no way he could have fired a gun through the screen door unless he held it out like this in midair, with his right hand, and fired without aiming. That would have been a little obvious, don't you think?"

"I think you just proved that Randolph Dyer killed Eric Magruder."

Smythe took the photo back and looked at his partner.

"Not necessarily, Harold. You remember how Deputy Lloyd said he thought Vicki might have been in shock? How she said she remembered the smell of gunpowder? What if she fired the gun her Daddy sent her to get? I want to go over Magruder's truck again. It was directly behind Eric in line with that screen door.

"And, I want to talk to Vicki Bayle again."

"Oh, for God's sakes, Todd, are you completely nuts?"

CHAPTER TWENTY-FIVE

Doubt

Friday, 4 p.m.

Maureen Magruder was sworn in next, her right arm encased in a plaster cast and propped in front of her at a 90-degree angle by a metal brace that circled her waist. She lowered herself painstakingly into the witness chair.

Nothing she said was new to Smythe. He'd heard her story, and dozens like it during his 15 years as an investigator for the State Attorney's Office.

"My husband was basically a good man, but he had a problem with alcohol," she told the state attorney.

"Had he hit you before?"

"He didn't hit me, and he didn't hit the boys. We fought a lot about his drinkin', but he never hit me. He'd push me up against the wall or pin my head down on the bed, like to smother me, but he never hit me. He was just very, um, possessive of me, you know, like, if I even talked to anybody else. He broke a chair over this guy's head once just for whistlin' at me."

"What kind of relationship did your husband have with your next-door neighbor, Frank Bayle?"

"Oh, they was good friends. They was always competin' with one another, you know, each one tryin' to outdo the other one—bag the biggest buck or catch the biggest fish, win at arm wrestlin', that kind of thing. But they was good friends, and alike in some ways, too—real jealous, you know. And they both thought the sun rose and set on that Vicki. We have two boys, you know, and Eric loved 'em somethin' fierce, but he thought little girls were real special. Or leastwise, he thought Vicki was."

"And how did Eric feel about Frank's wife, Rena May Bayle?"

"Oh, well, he was real fond of her, too, because, you know, Rena May is pretty, for one thing, and Eric, he did love pretty women. I know he cheated on me durin' the week sometimes when he was stayin' in Okeechobee. I know he did that, but we had some good times when he came home for the weekend."

"Are you implying there was more than friendship between Rena May Bayle and your husband?"

"Oh, Lord sakes, no!" Maureen said. "We was all good friends, like I said. Frank was one of the only guys Eric didn't mind me dancin' with. Of course, that meant he got to dance with Rena, and them two, they could really cut a rug on the dance floor. Frank and me, we don't have much rhythm. Eric always said between the two of us, me and Frank, we had four left feet."

"Did you get the impression that Frank might have been jealous of Eric and Rena?"

Maureen's eyes searched the wall, as if the answer might be written there somewhere.

"I think Frank is more jealous of Vicki than of Rena," she said, finally. "He sets the bar pretty high for Vicki, you know. He's always tellin' her she can do anything she sets her mind to, and she pretty near can. And Vicki just idolizes her daddy. Then Eric comes along and he pays Vicki a lot of attention, and they got to be real good buddies. I don't think Frank liked that much. He wanted to be the one Vicki looked up to, and nobody else."

"I see. You said that Eric never hit you, but you fought when he was drinking. How did you fight?"

Maureen searched the wall again for answers, then dropped her head and spoke softly.

"Well, I was usually the one who hit him," she said. "He'd come home drunk and I'd know he'd been out partyin' who knows where with who knows who, or he'd lost all his money in some poker game when I needed it to feed my kids, and it would make me mad and I'd yell at him and slap his face."

"And he didn't hit you back?"

"No sir, he'd usually start breakin' things, or hittin' the wall. He told me I could go anytime I wanted to, and not to let the door hit me in the butt—well, he didn't say butt, if you know what I mean. But he warned me never to try and take his kids away from him or he'd kill me.

"He always said he was sorry when he sobered up, though."

"Had you left him before?"

"Yes sir. Twiced."

"But you came back willingly?"

"Yes sir. I figured my boys needed a daddy."

"When your father brought you back home to pick up your things the day your husband died, did you know he had a gun with him?"

"No sir."

"Had you ever heard your father threaten to kill your husband?"

"Yes sir, the time before this, when Eric came and got me."

"What did he say?"

"He told Eric if he ever laid a hand on me again, he'd kill him."

"And what was Eric's response?"

"He laughed."

"Did you ever hear your husband threaten to kill your father?"

"Yes sir. Eric told my father if he ever tried to take me and his kids away from him again, he'd kill him."

"Your husband threatened to kill your father."

"Yes sir. He told me later that he killed his own father, so it wouldn't be no problem for him to kill mine."

"And did you believe him when he told you that?"

"Well, he was drunk at the time, but yes sir, I believed him."

"And you still loved him?"

"Well, like everybody says, Eric was a different person when he wasn't drinkin', and he always said he was gonna quit. I didn't really think he *could* quit, but I was always hopin' he would."

Smythe never ceased to wonder how a woman could stay with a man who abused her.

It was easier to understand such behavior in children, who, in his experience, often would go to extraordinary lengths to protect their abusers and to avoid being separated from them.

Children were like dogs in that regard, Smythe thought, but a grown woman? He just didn't get it.

As Maureen's testimony droned on, often monosyllabic and acquiescent in the background, Smythe reminded himself not to be so judgmental. His job was to find facts, not to assign blame.

******

Randolph Dyer took the oath looking weary, and the state attorney apologized for the lateness of the hour.

"We'll make this as brief as possible, Mr. Dyer," he said. "I know how difficult it must be for you to talk about."

"Well, I appreciate that, sir," Dyer said.

"Did you plan to kill Eric Magruder on September 10th when you brought your daughter home to pick up her belongings?"

"No sir. I just brought the gun to try and protect myself and Maureen from him, if he came at us."

"And did you have reason, sir, to think that was a possibility?"

"Yes sir, I did. He'd threatened to kill me if I took his family away from him. But you see, I never did that. He did that his own self. He's the one drove them off, not me. I just got stuck in the middle, where, as God is my witness, I never hoped to be.

"Still, when your own flesh and blood is threatened, when another man tries to destroy something precious in your sight, you got a God-given right to protect it, don't you?"

"That will be for the grand jury to decide, Mr. Dyer. Usually, for a claim of self-defense resulting in a death to be considered a justifiable homicide, there is an obligation to retreat if it is possible to do so. Why did you continue to fire your weapon multiple times after you saw Eric had been wounded?"

"Well, it had been a long time since I fired a gun and nothing happened that first time I pulled the trigger. I kind of panicked then and just kept pulling the trigger. I can't believe I even hit him, as scared as I was."

"But you did see Eric react to gunshots, you saw blood, and you knew he'd been hit."

"I did. But he kept on coming at me and I didn't know but what he had a gun or a knife in his pocket. He was a lot younger and stronger than me."

"Yes. But then, Eric indicated that you'd won, did he not, and offer to shake your hand?"

"Well, I didn't trust him anymore than I'd trust a rattlesnake. He could of killed me with his bare hands. I could see it in his eyes."

******

Friday, 6 p.m.

"Forget it, Smythe," the state attorney said. "You are not going to go back and talk to Vicki Bayle. This case is over, or it will be just as soon as that jury hands me their ruling, and I'd bet money that'll be on Monday. They're going to call it a justifiable homicide, and you can bet on that, as well."

"Well you know what, Stephen?" Smythe said. "That's probably because you didn't call Frank Bayle to testify. You didn't put him up there and make him squirm, because you and Judge Hammond want this case to be over and done with, and you don't give a shit who really killed Eric Magruder."

"Watch yourself, Todd," said Stephen Rydell.

"You can go over that truck with a magnifying glass if you want to, but you stay away from the Bayle house."

******

Saturday, 8 a.m.

On the way to Scott's Salvage Yard on U.S. 27 west of Clewiston, Harold Sumner sifted through the pile of crime scene photos and pulled out all the ones that showed Eric Magruder's truck and Frank Bayle's front porch.

He replaced the others and arranged the remaining photographs across his lap.

Three were of particular interest: a close-up view of the flattened front right tire of Eric's truck; a view taken through the Bayles' screen door toward the passenger side of Eric's truck, and a shot taken from in front of the truck, that showed the Bayles' house and car, as well as the front and side of the Magruder house where Randolph Dyer stood the day Eric Magruder was shot.

"OK, we dug two bullets, or fragments of bullets, out of pine trees that the medical examiner determined contained traces of blood from Magruder. Obviously those were through-and-throughs, and with the other bullets found in the body at autopsy, that accounts for possibly six of the seven gunshots. I personally went over that truck top to bottom and didn't find any bullet holes, but do you think it's possible a bullet could have flattened that front tire?

"A bullet fired from inside the Bayle house here could have passed through Magruder from left to right and, since the house is elevated, the trajectory would have put it directly in line with that tire."

"Holy shit, Todd. We didn't check the goddamned tire."

Todd Smythe glared at Sumner until he nearly ran off the edge of the road, but said nothing. By the time they reached the junkyard sign, he'd chewed and spit out two sticks of Beeman's gum and was going for a third.

"Howdy do," said Maxwell Scott as the two strangers approached the propped up plywood front of his workshop. He had to shout to be heard over the roar of an industrial-sized fan in the center of the hubcap-festooned back wall. "What can I do you gents for?"

Smythe made the necessary introductions and asked if they could take another look at Magruder's truck. Two lean Doberman Pinschers, one on either side behind a chain-link fence, barked furiously until Scott shouted, "Quiet!"

The guard dogs immediately sat on their haunches and quit barking. They did not stop snarling.

"Those dogs won't bite, will they?" Sumner said, nervously.

"Not as long as I'm here," Scott said. "Leastwise, not unless I tell 'em to. They'll getcha if you come 'round here after dark, though. They sure enough will."

The two investigators walked down an ally between cliffs of ruined vehicles stacked nose to tail, three or four layers high on either side, to an open lot where newly retrieved vehicles were spread out to be stripped for anything salvageable.

"This is a damn well-organized outfit," Sumner said, noting that the cars and trucks were arranged by make: Chevrolets and Fords were most numerous, but Dodges and Pontiacs occupied respective corners, and a couple of Buicks and Cadillacs crouched in the center, their hoods and trunk lids missing.

Smythe walked directly to Magruder's dark green pickup, ran his fingers through his hair, then stood shaking his head with his hands on his hips. He turned and walked back towards Scott's workshop without speaking to his partner.

Sumner looked at the wheel-less truck and lit a cigarette, disregarding a large, red-lettered sign in the middle of the yard that said, DANGER! NO SMOKING!

"You already stripped the tires off those trucks," Smythe said, loudly. "You didn't save any of them?"

Scott walked to the back of his shop and shut off the fan.

"That one hanging on the wall right there came off the right rear of that green pickup, and it's brand new," he said. "The rest of 'em weren't worth saving. One of the front ones had a hole blowed in the bottom of it, and the other two was retreads that was coming loose."

"Can you show me where you put the tire with the hole in it?"

"You kiddin', right?"

"Do I look like I'm kidding?"

"Well sir, follow me."

Scott led Smythe past Magruder's truck to the back of the lot.

Behind the rusting skeletons of vehicles, a railroad spur held a chain of four open railroad cars. A dragline sat alongside, weaving back and forth, lifting and transferring bucket loads of old tires from a 30-foot mound into the cars waiting to transport them to a shredding and recycling plant in Connecticut.

"There you go," he said. "Have at it."

Saturday, 1 p.m.

"I want you guys to stay together, now, and no runnin' up and down the aisles, or I'll hear about it from Mrs. Duncan, you can be sure of that," Rena said to the carload of cousins she ferried to the Dixie Crystal Theatre.

Ava Duncan's 400-pound frame filled the theater's tiny ticket booth and taxed the high metal stool that jammed her stocking-clad knees against the bottom of the counter. Mounds of flesh rolled from the top and bottom of the whale-boned corset she wore drawn so tight by her husband Lawrence that it was a mystery how she managed to breathe or speak.

Often, she didn't need to speak to ticket-takers, concession workers or children who displeased her in any way; one of her wilting, dark-eyed looks could make all but the boldest of them retreat.

Despite her morbid obesity, Ava Duncan was always impeccably groomed and coiffed. She was quite vain about her milky white hands, as smooth as a baby's bottom. They remained that way because Ava never did any type of manual labor more strenuous than tearing a theater ticket from its roll and making change, both of which put her graceful, manicured hands on display. Her husband or her maid also laced the expensive, low-heeled orthopedic shoes she wore, which were specially ordered for her from a West Palm Beach podiatrist.

Ava's doctors warned her that her diabetes, exacerbated by a sedentary lifestyle, might eventually cause her to lose her feet due to lack of circulation. Their warnings did not stop her from downing several large bags of M&Ms each evening, along with huge quantities of buttered popcorn.

She endured thirst because the energy required for bathroom visits left her exhausted. The resulting dehydration elevated her blood sugar levels even more, so that she often swooned against the ticket booth door, making it impossible for Lawrence to open the door without dumping his beloved on the floor. At such times, Lawrence Duncan had to either summon help or administer a dose of insulin to the back of one of Ava's lovely hands through the opening in the glass outside the ticket booth.

Still, most everyone in town loved Ava Duncan, whose Georgia upbringing and early Southern-peach beauty had taught her the quickest way to anyone's heart: flattery and undivided attention. She was generous with both.

Rena bought matinee tickets for P.J. and Beth Talloway, Penny Knight and Vicki, and made small talk with Ava while she waited for her change.

"I read this is supposed to be one of Jimmy Stewart's best picture shows," Rena said.

"Well, I personally think Jeff Chandler does a better job than Stewart," Ava said. "Even though he does play an Indian, that pagan Cochise."

"Broken Arrow," one of the first major Westerns to side with the Indians, was later nominated for three Academy Awards.

A dozen Seminoles from Immokalee were among the first in line to buy tickets for its opening at the Dixie Crystal, and Ava Duncan reminded the English-speaking man who purchased their tickets that the slightly discounted price—a nickel less per ticket—was for balcony seats only. It was a gentler way of telling the traditionally clothed Indians that the downstairs auditorium seats were for whites only. No reminder was necessary for the bathrooms; a sign above the door read "Whites Only." There were no toilets for people of color who attended shows at the Dixie Crystal Theatre, which meant they seldom did.

Ava Duncan screened every film shown at the theater before it was placed on the bill. If she didn't like the film, it didn't play. "Broken Arrow" was a close call for Ava because, despite its acclaim, she objected to the film's egalitarian message. One of its characters actually condemned racism and claimed that the Bible "says nothing about pigmentation of the skin."

Vicki couldn't wait to quote that line to her mother, and made an impassioned plea for her parents to go with her to see the movie again.

If her parents were with her, she knew she wouldn't have to risk the advances of Lavonne Dawson, even though Lavonne's tastes now ran to boys rather than girls, and he was too big to sit up front with the little kids.

Lavonne now favored the back row of the theater's smoking section, where Lawrence Duncan rarely trained his red-tubed flashlight.

CHAPTER TWENTY-SIX

The Jury

Monday, 9 a.m.

Norma Jean White interrupted the state attorney to remind him that she was the forewoman, not the foreman of the Hendry County grand jury now in session.

"Foreperson will do, if you prefer," she said, haughtily.

"Pardon me, Miss White," said Stephen Rydell. "You called for me because you had some question regarding the law?"

"Yes, well, we have the power to call witnesses other than those presented to us by you at this hearing, right?" she said.

"If you have questions concerning the evidence, or reason to believe there is other testimony you need to hear in order to reach a conclusion in this matter, you have that power, yes."

"What if the party involved is a witness from whom we have not heard?"

"I take it some of you still have doubts?"

"I don't believe we are required to reveal our discussions to you, Mr. Rydell."

"True enough, and again, I beg your pardon."

"We'd like to hear from Frank Bayle."

Clarence Hall's face looked like he'd been standing over a hot stove, and he could no longer hold his tongue.

"Eleven of us already know there's not a shadow of a doubt that this was a justifiable homicide," Hall said. "Just because every biddy in town is clucking down at the Toggery Shop, there isn't a reason in the world to drag this thing out any longer—except that it gives her and the other women on this jury some inflated sense of their own importance."

"Sit down, Mr. Hall," Rydell said, sternly. "You have just violated your oath of secrecy for these grand jury proceedings, and that, I assure you, is not a trivial matter; you could be charged with contempt.

"Miss White has every right—as do any of you—to call any witness she sees fit. I trust you will be able to carry out your duties until the conclusion of this case, Mr. Hall, at which time we'll discuss your breach of ethics here today."

Clarence Hall glanced furtively around the room and realized the gravity of his error.

"I apologize to you, sir, and to the members of the jury," he said. "I find this whole matter extremely stressful."

"It's no less so for the rest of us, Mr. Hall," the forewoman said. "Remember, I work on commission, so I'm losing money being here the same as you are."

"I said I was sorry, Miss White," Hall said, running his finger around his dampened collar.

"Do you think I could get some ice water?"

Monday, 9:30 a.m.

"You're going to get us both fired, Todd," Sumner said, as he walked back down the hall from Mrs. Alice Right's fourth grade classroom at Clewiston Elementary School.

"Rydell said to stay away from the Bayle house; he didn't say anything about talking to Vicki's teacher," Smythe said. "Good Lord, Harold, did you read the stuff that kid wrote? The teacher typed them out to show the 10th grade American Lit teacher, for Christsakes.

"Trees that play with her, and baby doves in crows' claws? That's not stuff your typical eight-year-old writes, Harold. You do know what a metaphor is, right?"

Vicki Bayle entered the hall from the playground with a group of other children shortly after the bell rang. When she looked up and saw the two investigators, she cut and ran in the opposite direction, down a flight of stairs to the big double doors marked Emergency Exit Only. By the time Sumner and Smythe had skipped down the stairs in pursuit she had realized her mistake; if she opened the door, the fire alarm would sound and she would be in even more trouble.

She was trapped, like the Little Lame Prince in Hopeless Tower, with no godmother to give her a magic cape on which she might escape.

She turned to face the investigators, then slid slowly to the floor in the corner and put her forehead on knees.

"Are you takin' me to jail?" she said.

"No, Vicki, of course not," Smythe said, squatting in front of the child. "No one is going to take you to jail. Why would you think that?"

"Because I did something wrong?"

"Regardless of what you did wrong, Vicki, or what you might think you did wrong, we do not put children in jail."

"Not even bad ones?"

"Why don't you tell me what you did, and then we'll talk about what's going to happen next."

"Well, I hid my Daddy's gun from him for a while, for one thing, 'cause I thought it might get him in trouble if you was to see it."

"Were there bullets in the gun when you hid it, Vicki?"

"Why do you want to know that?"

"Well, sometimes, we can compare a bullet that we take from a body, say, with another one from a gun, and prove that one gun or another was not used in a particular shooting."

"But sometimes you can prove that it was, right?"

"Sometimes, yes. But first we need a bullet and the casing it was fired from. What did you do with the bullets, Vicki?"

"I ain't tellin' you that, so you can just stop asking me. The lawyer said nobody has to say nothin' that might incrimulate theirselves, ain't that right?"

"You can't be forced to incriminate yourself, that's true."

"Then I take the Fifth."

"You do what?"

"I stand on the Fifth Amendment."

Smythe stood and held out his hand to Vicki.

"You're going to be late for class," he said.

As she disappeared up the stairs, his partner burst out laughing.

"This is not funny," Smythe said.

But he smiled in spite of himself.

******

Monday, 10:30 a.m.

Frank Bayle turned off his acetylene torch and pushed up his welder's helmet when Todd Smythe tapped him on the shoulder.

"You're up, Frank," Smythe said. "The grand jury has some questions for you."

Bayle looked at Smythe for a moment, then dropped the shield back over his face with his gloved thumb and opened the valve on the torch again. With a flint striker, he lit the blowtorch and adjusted the flow of oxygen until the flame turned from orange to blue and stopped smoking.

But he did not return to the cutting of sheet metal; he stood with the flame hissing toward the investigator until Smythe stepped back, turned and walked to the shop foreman's office.

When Smythe returned with Frank Bayle's boss, the welder was against the wall on a pay phone talking to his lawyer.

******

Back in their car, the radio squawked. Smythe snatched it from its holder and said, "Yeah?"

"The state attorney wants you to call him immediately," the anonymous voice said.

He clicked the button on the side of the mouthpiece twice and hung it back on the dashboard without answering.

"They're gonna walk, partner," Smythe said. "Just like the glistening crows, with guiltless hearts."

"Who are you talking about, Randolph Dyer and Frank Bayle, or Frank and Vicki?"

Smythe looked at him while he unwrapped a piece of gum, then started the car.

"Whatever that little girl knows, Harold, she's going to carry it with her for the rest of her life."

******

Monday, 11:45 a.m.

"He's not going to testify unless the court compels him to," Smythe informed the state attorney.

"It's a waste of time," Rydell said. "You brought me no compelling evidence, no evidence at all, as a matter of fact, that Frank Bayle did anything more than sit on his porch and watch a man get gunned down in his front yard. Under the circumstances, he would have had to put his own life in jeopardy to intervene. The law does not require heroic intervention in such a case."

"I know the law, Steve. And I know in my gut it's not being served here. Something happened on that porch that Bayle hasn't told us. I talked to Vicki Bayle again today, and guess what? After the shooting, she hid her father's gun, and she refuses to answer questions about whether or not it was loaded."

"You talked to the child after I told you to leave her alone, Todd?"

"I didn't go to the Bayle house, I went to the school. You didn't say anything about doing that. But we really don't need her, Steve. We can get the truth from Frank. I know he can't be forced to incriminate himself, but in lieu of that he could be held in contempt if he refused to answer the grand jury's questions."

"Are you attempting to explain the law to me, Todd?" Rydell said.

"Oh, for pete's sake, Steve! You've gone out of your way to avoid calling Frank Bayle to testify. Why is that? Is it all that sugar company money backing him? Why can't you just do your job?"

"Todd?"

"Yeah."

"You're fired."

After consulting with Circuit Court Judge Llewellyn Hammond, the state attorney issued a summons for Frank Bayle to appear before the grand jury on Tuesday, September 19, at 8 a.m.

Harold Sumner delivered the summons alone.

Chapter Twenty-Seven

The Decision

Tuesday, 8:30 a.m.

The state attorney got right to the point after placing Frank Bayle under oath.

"Mr. Bayle, the members of the grand jury would like me to ask if you shot Eric Magruder on the afternoon of September 10th of this year," Rydell said.

"No, I did not," Bayle said.

"Do you know who killed Eric Magruder?"

"I believe Randolph Dyer did, but I can't say for certain."

"You watched Eric get shot seven times, but you're not certain that's what killed him?"

"I'm not a doctor, sir," Frank said. "He could have died as a result of other injuries—hitting the steering wheel, for instance. How would I know? Eric had been on a downhill slide for a long time. A very long time. I think it all just finally caught up with him."

"Yes, well, seven 9mm bullets do catch up with you in a hurry, that's irrefutable. However, you, yourself, caught up with Eric Magruder in a rather one-sided confrontation the day before he died, did you not?"

"Why are you asking me questions you already know the answer to?"

"Try again, Frank."

"Yes. The answer, as you already know, is yes. I kicked the shit out of the son of a bitch down at the truck stop after I found out he killed my daughter's cat."

"That's better, Frank, but we can do without the profanity. Did you also threaten to kill Eric that day?"

"I was mad. People say things they don't mean when they're mad."

"Yes, and sometimes they say things they mean but wouldn't ordinarily say, you know, in the heat of the moment, when their guard is down. Now, Frank, the jurors would like to know if you had a gun with you on your front porch on September 10th?"

"I did. I had my .38 revolver in my tackle box that Sunday morning; I was gettin' ready to go fishing."

"Do you usually take a handgun with you when you go fishing?"

"Depends on where I'm going. I don't like snakes."

"Did you have the tackle box with you on the porch when Eric Magruder was shot?"

"I did not have it then, no."

"Did someone else have it?"

"When I saw Eric walking toward my house after the wreck, I thought maybe he was coming after me, because of the fight the day before. I told Vicki to bring me the tackle box, but then, when I saw Randolph standing next door with a gun, I told her to run, to go with her Mama."

"And did Vicki go with her mother?"

"No. She took a step back and stood just inside the door."

"Did she have the tackle box with the gun in it?"

"I think so, but I can't say for sure. I was watching Eric."

"Did Vicki think Eric was coming for you?"

"I have no way of knowing what Vicki was thinking at that moment."

"Did she take the gun out of the tackle box?"

"I don't know. I was watching Eric."

"That's very convenient. Vicki said the same thing. Tell me this, Frank, is Vicki a good shot?"

"Yes, she is."

"Do you think your daughter would have shot Eric Magruder to protect you?"

"How do you expect me to answer that question?"

"Truthfully, sir."

"I don't know."

"Did you see a weapon of any kind in Eric Magruder's hand?"

"No, but he usually carried a switchblade in his pocket."

"How do you know this?"

"We were friends and neighbors for three years."

"Did Vicki know he carried a knife?"

"Yes. He taught her how to throw a knife, actually, with his switchblade. She was pretty good at it. Made it stick nearly every time."

"Were you jealous of the relationship between Eric Magruder and your daughter?"

"Don't be ridiculous. I didn't like her spending time alone with him, though."

"Why, Frank? Did you think his behavior toward Vicki was in any way inappropriate?"

"Not really. I just didn't like it."

"Did you ever tell Vicki that you didn't like her spending time with Eric?"

"No."

"Were you jealous of the relationship between Eric Magruder and your wife?"

"My wife and Eric were friends, just like we all were."

"Did your wife share your concerns about Eric?"

"Not if he was sober."

"How about when he was drinking?"

"Rena didn't want anything to do with Eric when he was drinking. She doesn't even want me to keep a beer in the fridge."

"OK. Had you ever had a conversation with Eric about his father-in-law?"

"Yes. He said the ol' man hated him."

"Did you ever hear Eric threaten Mr. Dyer in any way?"

"Not directly, no. But he told me if Randolph ever tried to take his wife and kids away from him, he'd kill him."

"Did you believe him?"

Frank looked at the floor and rubbed his thumb across the callus beneath his ring finger.

"Not until he tried to."

******

Tuesday, 3 p.m.

"Steve, I'd like you to reconsider what you said earlier," Todd Smythe said. "I know I was out of line, and I apologize. This is my life we're talking about, my career. Surely you're not going to trash it over one stupid remark."

"I wasn't the one who trashed it, Todd," the state attorney said. "You've been bucking me since this Magruder thing started, and I'm just fed up with your bullshit theories."

"OK, OK, you made your point," Smythe said. "What do you want me to do, get down on my knees?"

The state attorney smiled smugly and began rifling through papers on his desk.

"I didn't know you leaned in that direction, Todd, but I'm just not into it, you know?"

A knock on the door gave Smythe time to regain control of his temper.

"The grand jury has reached a decision," said a secretary, handing Rydell a sheet of paper.

The state attorney scanned the sheet, and then stood and walked out of his office.

"Steve?" Smythe said. "What do you say, Steve?"

******

Todd Smythe walked to the window and lit a cigarette, then turned and made his way down the stairs to the front of the building.

Near the front steps of the courthouse, reporters from the Clewiston News, the Caloosa Belle, the Fort Myers Herald-Tribune and other newspapers stood chatting and smoking in the shade of a live oak. Three photographers with cameras and camera bags slouched on a bench nearby, looking bored. They all jumped into action when Stephen Rydell appeared on the steps.

"The grand jury has handed up a no true bill in the matter of the shooting death of Eric Magruder," Rydell said. "No charges are filed against Randolph Dyer. The grand jury has determined that this was a justifiable homicide."

"Was the vote unanimous?" a reporter asked.

"Grand jury deliberations are secret, but a minimum of 12 members must agree on a presentment, a true bill or a no true bill."

"Can you explain what that means?"

"That means that at least 12 members of the grand jury determined that Mr. Dyer shot his son-in-law because he feared for his life and/or that of his daughter, and that his actions were justifiable under the law."

The state attorney took a Kool from his pocket, cupped his hands around it and was about to light it when he saw a camera aimed in his direction. He palmed the cigarette and stood erect and smiling until the flashbulb flared in his face.

"What it means is that this matter is concluded, and no charges will be filed in the shooting death of Eric Magruder."

Todd Smythe stood at the edge of the crowd and unwrapped a stick of gum.

"What that means," Smythe said, "is that we'll probably never know who really killed Eric Magruder."

A reporter from the Palm Beach Post looked up at Smythe, then left the pack of media and followed the former investigator down the sidewalk.

"Hey, Todd," he said. "Got another stick of gum?"

EPILOGUE

Todd Smythe was accepted into the University of Florida College of Law in Gainesville in the spring of 1951, after State Attorney Stephen Rydell allowed him to resign his position as investigator. He later became a well-known Lee County prosecutor with convictions on several high-profile cases, including the retrial of convicted Hendry County ax murderer Curtis Lavonne Dawson in 1957. During the original trial in 1955, jurors were allowed to hear a witness testify that he heard Dawson's father say to his son, "You killed him, didn't you?"

That jury deliberated only two hours and 15 minutes before convicting Dawson, who at the time of his arrest, was driving the victim's truck with the murder weapon inside, which a Florida Supreme Court Judge deemed as circumstantial evidence.

In 1960, Smythe ousted Rydell and was elected State Attorney for the 20th Judicial Circuit, which includes Hendry County.

Victoria Leigh Bayle enjoyed a modestly successful career as a journalist, a career she took on as a novice in her late 30s, working her way through the ranks of a small Florida newspaper and ending her career 22 years later as an editor.

While her debut novel was fiction, its flavor was crystallized from memory as pure as the refined sugar her hometown produces. She carried the story in her heart for nearly 50 years, and when it was published, it caused some controversy among those Hendry County residents who thought they recognized in characters or events a similarity to reality.

None was ever proved.

Vicki was 44 years old before she told her mother about Lavonne Dawson. It was during a family reunion, while aunts and uncles and cousins milled about picnic tables covered in white cloths and Southern delicacies in Bethany, Florida.

There, beneath the moss-bearded ancient oaks, someone mentioned reading that Dawson was up for parole. He had served 30 years of a life sentence in Raiford State Prison for chopping off a man's head with an ax at the base of Herbert Hoover Dike in Clewiston. He was 19 at the time of the crime, and he claimed the 53-year-old man he killed was trying to sexually assault him.

"Lavonne used to hold Vicki in his lap at the picture show," Rena said to a group of family members. "Can you believe that?"

"You better watch out, Skipper," her Uncle Peyton said. "If that creep gets out of prison, he might come looking for you."

Everyone laughed but Vicki.

"Mama, can I talk to you for a minute?" Vicki said, pulling her mother away from the cheerful gathering.

"Why didn't you tell me?" Rena said, her face stricken, when Vicki had finished.

"There's a lot I haven't told you, Mama, but now is not the time."

The time never came for Vicki to tell her mother more; Rena May Bayle died a few weeks later of a massive coronary. Although Vicki had never seen her mother smoke a cigarette, doctors said smoking contributed to her heart disease.

A dozen years later, the Dixie Crystal Theatre in Clewiston was added to the National Register of Historical Places.

Vicki's father died later that same year of congestive heart failure caused primarily by smoking and alcohol abuse.

One of Vicki's last conversations with him in the nursing home addressed his sneaking smokes in the bathroom.

"Who the hell do you think you are, telling me what I can and cannot do?" he said angrily from his bed, an oxygen tube clamped at the end of his nose. "Have you forgot that whipping I gave you…?"

"No, Daddy," Vicki said, taking his withered hand in her own. "I haven't forgotten anything."

******

ACKNOWLEDGEMENTS

I never would have written this book without the unfailing support of my husband, Mark Weinberg, who for more than 40 years has been my best friend and most honest critic. His editing skills and patient guidance greatly improved *A Homicide in Hooker's Point*.

I also give credit to the late Bob Enns, former editor of the *News Tribune*, who gave me my first opportunity to earn a living doing what I've always loved to do—write. Bob was my beloved mentor and journalism teacher, even though we locked horns many times during the 20 years I worked for him, neither of us ever gave up on the other.

I hope I've made you proud, Bob.

Others who taught and encouraged me, mostly by example, were Tina Benson and Bill Maxwell, both former coworkers and cherished friends. Tina's hand-written note, pinned to my bulletin board, lifted me through self-doubt and procrastination on many occasions, and a photo of her with arms linked around Bob and Mark, hangs on the wall not far from my computer. It warms me each time I look at it. We've lost touch, Tina, but I hold you in my heart.

There are others—too many to name—to whom I am grateful.

But most of all, I am grateful to my daughter, Lori D. Emerson, who read the early drafts, made suggestions and appreciated the time and sacrifice that was necessary to write this novel. Her praise meant more to me than a Pulitzer. She said, "I'm proud of you, Mom."